"Are you... another premonition?"

Alex asked.

"I don't know," Sarah admitted. She couldn't keep her eyes off the tight expanse of shoulders beneath his shirt, the solid forearms exposed by rolled-up sleeves. She looked up to find his eyes in the shadows. Then he approached and held out a hand.

For a moment, she couldn't move. He stood over her, blocking out almost all the light, so that he seemed more a vision than a man, a prescience. A promise.

She didn't remember taking hold of his hand. Suddenly she was warmer than she'd been in a long time. Sweetened with a life she'd never realized she'd been missing.

When he pulled her into his arms, she slid up against him. When he gasped with the sparks of their contact, she smiled.

They stood very still, her hand still in his, her head back so she could look up into his eyes. She felt his arm slide around her back, felt him draw her close, and saw the surprise in his eyes as he bent to kiss her.

She shivered, knowing they would be lovers. Soon. Inevitably. He had just made that decision, and its force struck her like a physical blow.

Dear Reader,

I hope you've noticed our new look and that you like it as much as we do. At last, Silhouette Intimate Moments, the most mainstream line in category romance, has a look as exciting as the stories themselves. And what stories we have for you this month!

Start off with the Award of Excellence title, Linda Howard's *Duncan's Bride*. This story of a gruff rancher who advertises for a wife puts a few unexpected spins on a traditional plot. Reese Duncan wants a woman who will cook and clean and bear his children. Madelyn Patterson is willing to do all that, but she wants something in return: love. Heather Graham Pozzessere's *Wedding Bell Blues* reunites Brendan O'Herlihy with his ex-wife, Kaitlin. As best man and maid of honor for a series of weddings, they are forced to confront each other—and the feelings that have never gone away. With *Lightning Strikes*, Kathleen Korbel brings her irrepressible humor and passion to a tale of a woman who sees the future and a man who won't have a future unless he listens closely and spends it with her! Finally, Mary Anne Wilson offers *Brady's Law*. Watch as a case of mistaken identity and a tiny baby named Rocky bring together two people who never should have met but can't seem to say goodbye once they've said hello.

In months to come, watch for Emilie Richards to provide a sequel to her "sisters" stories, Lee Magner to follow *Sutter's Wife* with *The Dragon's Lair*, and favorites like Marilyn Pappano and Paula Detmer Riggs to offer new books—and all of it will be happening only in Silhouette Intimate Moments. Join us for the excitement.

Leslie J. Wainger
Senior Editor and Editorial Coordinator

KATHLEEN KORBEL

Lightning Strikes

SILHOUETTE·INTIMATE·MOMENTS®

Published by Silhouette Books New York

America's Publisher of Contemporary Romance

SILHOUETTE BOOKS
300 East 42nd St., New York, N.Y. 10017

ISBN: 0-373-07351-8

First Silhouette Books printing September 1990

All the characters in this book are fictitious. Any
resemblance to actual persons, living or dead, is
purely coincidental.

Printed in the U.S.A.

Books by Kathleen Korbel

Silhouette Desire

Playing the Game #286
A Prince of a Guy #389
The Princess and the Pea #455
Hotshot #582

Silhouette Intimate Moments

A Stranger's Smile #163
Worth Any Risk #191
Edge of the World #222
Perchance to Dream #276
The Ice Cream Man #309
Lightning Strikes #351

Silhouette Books

Silhouette Summer Sizzlers 1989
"The Road to Mandalay"

KATHLEEN KORBEL,

the *Romantic Times* Best New Category Author of 1987, has finally hung up her nurse's cap to work for herself. Living in St. Louis with her husband and two children, she writes full-time, only allowing travel and salving an insatiable curiosity in the name of research to interfere. She still admits to owing her success to her husband, who is her best friend and most devoted supporter.

To Dad
(who loves me best)
the man who taught me
that CPAs make great heroes

Chapter 1

At first he tried not to listen. After all, it was only a three-floor elevator ride.

"Oh, no," she was saying behind him, her voice as breathy as a breeze. "Not now. I don't have time to fall in love."

Alex couldn't figure out who she was talking to. He hadn't really paid attention to the other people who'd stepped from the cool stucco-and-tile lobby of the Sunset Building into the elevator. He hadn't noticed who'd gotten off on the second floor. His attention had been on the heat he'd left out on the Phoenix streets and the job that he was headed toward.

A favor for a friend was the only thing that would get him out of Colorado during the height of the hiking season. An independent look at the finances of Sunset Designs to settle the vague unease felt by its director. Alex hadn't been looking forward to the job. He hadn't been looking forward to two weeks in the heat or another round of hotel living.

And now, even before he got started, like an ill omen, he was momentarily stuck in an elevator with a woman who was setting up to confess all her innermost yearnings within inches of his left ear. A woman who sounded uncannily like his ex-wife.

"I don't want to marry him. He's not even my type."

Alex wished the other person would answer. He wished the light would flash for the third floor. He wasn't comfortable with this kind of thing. It was the aristocratic Southern accent, the kind that had once drifted from plantation house porches, that made the admission so disturbing, so personal.

This had to be the slowest elevator in the Western hemisphere.

"Oh, my God." Her voice sounded suddenly distressed.

Alex reacted instinctively. He turned around.

She was alone. Worse, she was looking directly at him. Even worse than that, she was blond. Blond and petite and vulnerable looking, with curls in sweet disarray and eyes the size of China-blue saucers. Alex noticed all that in the same instant he realized that she was going to reach out to touch him.

"Turn down the case," she pleaded, those devastating eyes treating him like an accident victim as she took hold of his arm.

It took a minute for the words to register. Alex was too distracted by her looks—the very looks that always got him into trouble. Blond and sweet and fragile and as dumb as a brick.

"Case?" he finally echoed a bit stupidly. Who had she been talking to back there? And who was it who wasn't her type?

Eagerly she nodded, her loose flaxen curls dancing on her shoulders. "Tell your captain that you can't do it. Tell him you'll take the next murder or robbery or whatever it is you investigate. If you do this one, you'll be hurt."

"Murder?" Alex demanded, the words finally sinking in. "Lady, what are you talking about?"

Pulling her hand away from him to brush at her hair, she bobbed her head again, her expression intent. "It's a little hard to explain," she said. "I know you police don't give much credence to things like this—"

"Police?" he said, trying to pull his gaze away from her petite hands only to find it firmly snared by all that China blue. "What makes you think I'm a policeman?" Alex noticed the bracelets that jangled on her arm, the voluminous teal silk trousers and paisley blouse.

"The case you're about to work on," she said, doing her best with that sweet honeysuckle accent to impress him with the gravity of the matter. "I know that it's going to be dangerous. Please don't take it."

Alex sighed and shook his head. "I appreciate the warning. I really do. But I think you have the wrong guy. I'm a CPA. And the only danger I'm going to be in is if I don't get up to the company who hired me to check their books."

She blinked a bit owlishly. "Oh. Then it doesn't make any sense, does it?"

"No," he admitted, doing his best to step by her. "It doesn't."

Her hand shot out again. Her face folded into sincerity. "Please, believe me. I'm not making this up."

Who could? he wanted to say. Instead he smiled. "Thank you. I appreciate the concern. Now, I have to be going."

And Alex Thorne, who had been an expert at disengaging himself from some pretty intense holds, peeled her fingers from his arm and turned for the door.

Not surprisingly, Sunset Designs took up most of the Sunset Building. A small company that had been founded no more than four years ago by two college roommates, it provided graphic designs for industries as diverse as linens to corporate logos. Alex had slept on Sunset Design sheets and flown on an airline with a Sunset-created logo.

In researching the company before his trip, he'd discovered it to be well managed, imaginative and aggressive in an oddly polite way. Most of its promotion had been accomplished by word of mouth. Customers glowed about genius, innovation and unparalleled creativity. Detractors were still trying to come up with a good reason to complain. The company's profit margin was good. It manufactured some of its products in Phoenix and others in a plant in Virginia, and it was turning over business in the comfortable seven-figure range each year.

And, much to the chagrin of the competition, its sights were as limitless as they were diverse. No one knew quite what market Sunset Design would choose to tap into next. This, in a company whose president, cofounder and inspirational leader still personally approved every job applicant.

"Oh, my God. You're Alex Thorne!"

Alex had just stepped through the glass door into the Sunset Design offices. He was still trying to get over a purple-green-and-blue color scheme that shouldn't possibly have worked as well as it did. Suddenly, a tall, bright-eyed receptionist was standing before him, smiling with every tooth in her head.

Instinctively Alex smiled back. "I'm here to meet Ms. Delaney," he said, a little surprised at the openmouthed shock on the secretary's face. He still elicited this kind of reception on occasion in the Denver area, although most of his recognition came at bars with big-screen televisions.

She was still shaking her brunette head, not sure whether to hold out a hand or straighten her hair. "I can't tell you how many Sundays I spent watching you." She glowed with sincere delight. "God, you were the best. Not to mention being possessor of the nicest set of buns in a huddle in either league. I could spot you from the cheap seats at the ten-yard line."

That seemed to quell her indecision. Giving her head another shake, she held out a well-manicured hand. "I knew

Sarah was expecting a Mr. Thorne. I didn't know it was you."

"It's nice to meet you," Alex greeted her, long since comfortable with letting the rest slide. It had been three years since he'd last suited up and one year since the beer-commercial offers had stopped coming in. He was just as happy that way. Giving up football had been the hardest thing he'd ever done. And, in the long run, the most intelligent. Every time he had to ride up in elevators with talkative lunatics instead of being able to take the stairs, he remembered why.

"Kim," she offered, belatedly letting go. "I'm the receptionist. I'll let Randolph know you're here."

Randolph was the executive secretary, a serious, studious young man who seemed to harbor no fond memories of Alex and Sundays, which was just as well. Alex was ready to get to work.

"Let's see if we can raise her," Randolph was saying as he walked on around to the double doors at the end of the hallway, his attitude resembling a librarian headed for the rare-book section. "She's been asking about you for two days."

Alex couldn't help but wonder how Randolph anticipated raising his president. By radio? Ouija board? Well, Ellis had said that this would be an interesting job. So far, Alex couldn't say he was disappointed.

Then Randolph opened the door onto the president of Sunset Designs, and Alex understood what the secretary—and Ellis—had meant. The woman who rose to her feet behind the cluttered cherrywood desk was the same woman who had accosted him on the elevator. The blonde with the warnings and the sky-blue eyes.

Alex felt the groan escape before he could do anything about it.

Sarah couldn't believe it. She'd just made it into her office, the nausea still chasing her from the incident on the elevator. Randolph hadn't even brought in her tea yet. And suddenly she was hit with it again.

"You," she whispered, stunned, shaken, falling.

"Sarah?" Randolph asked, stepping in to intercede.

Sarah waved him off, knowing that Randolph understood. He wouldn't cosset if she didn't need it. Slowly Sarah steadied herself, wishing the dread would recede, an evil tide slipping away to leave her with sense and sunlight.

But he was here like a reprieve. A second chance to make matters right. To prevent him from making mistakes that could cost his life. All she had to do was convince him. All she ever had to do.

She couldn't believe that she hadn't anticipated this on the elevator. Oh, well, that was how it usually went.

"Are you Mr. Thorne?" she asked with a smile, making it around her desk to meet him.

"Alex Thorne," he answered, taking her hand as if expecting to find a joy buzzer nestled inside. "Ellis told me all about Sunset Design."

He didn't tell me about you, he was thinking. Sarah could see his thoughts on his face and couldn't hide her smile. She knew people like Alex Thorne, and they didn't accommodate themselves easily to the Sarah Delaneys of the world. She was going to have to explain everything very carefully. Looking way up at him, she thought she wouldn't mind at all.

"Ellis recommended you highly," Sarah offered, and then motioned to the chairs clustered over by the window. "Why don't we sit? Would you like some coffee or tea?"

"Coffee," Alex acquiesced. "Thanks."

"Coming right up," Randolph said, and swung out the door.

Sarah led Alex past her cluttered desk, video station and overflowing drawing board to where she'd set up an oasis of quiet in the office. A small island isolated by potted plants and focused on a picture window out to the mountains, it was here she conferred with clients, here she brainstormed with staff and here, often, she napped when she forgot to go home.

Shoving a nest of magazines and a peacock-blue afghan onto a third chair, she settled herself into the purple sectional sofa and curled her feet up beneath her. She'd forgotten to put her shoes back on when Alex had entered the room. She imagined they were still somewhere under her desk with the stuffed pig.

He was so big. Alex, that is. The pig was only big enough to rest her feet on.

Sarah couldn't get over it. She was five foot five in socks and only came up to his collarbone. He had shoulders that almost shut out the sunlight and arms that could probably crumple furniture. And yet his hands hadn't been all that big. They'd been gentle and warm, a friend's hands.

He had tawny looks, with sun-bleached hair and eyes the color of toffee. His face was squared and solid and lined with laughter. It was a face Sarah instinctively liked. A face that gentled his strong, athletic body, eyes that betrayed the intelligence that had brought him here.

She saw openness and logic and a certain hesitancy for the off-kilter world he'd stepped into in her building. A mathematician's personality. A left-brain mind-set. Orderly, logical, fiercely loyal.

Sarah liked him. She thought he was probably one of the ten best-looking men she'd ever sat close to. Still she wasn't sure that was enough to provoke what had happened in the elevator. But then, she'd never had such an instant reaction before. Maybe she'd read it wrong.

No matter, she had other things that needed talking about. The dread, the overwhelming tide of emotion, refused to go away. The sensations so washed her that they swept away her balance and blotted out the sunlight on this bright desert afternoon. These were the things she needed to tell Alex Thorne, and they were the things he wouldn't believe.

"You think I'm crazy," she said baldly.

He seemed a bit disconcerted by her frank appraisal. Sinking into the easy chair with unconscious grace, he settled into comfort without slouching a millimeter. "You ... surprised me, Ms. Delaney."

Sarah couldn't help but laugh. "I surprise everyone," she admitted, taking an absent swipe at her hair. "A lot of times I surprise myself." It was always a shock, that sudden drop in the pit of her stomach, the noises in her head. The borders that shifted in her vision, tilting her world into suspension. She often wondered whether, if she could anticipate them, she could settle herself, curl upon the couch and offset the physical reaction the worst ones brought.

And the one in the elevator had been one of the worst. It had been one without pictures, without smells or sounds. It had been pure emotion, raw possibility and loss.

"Sarah," she said, lifting her head.

"Pardon?"

She saw him start, as if waiting her out, warily watching for surprise moves. Sarah smiled apologetically. "Sarah," she repeated with a small wave of her hand. "My name. I hate being called Ms. Delaney. It makes me sound like an English Lit teacher—or a character in a Tennessee Williams play." Without realizing it, she reached to pull back the afghan, bunching it into her lap. "I've changed my mind."

He looked even more confused. "About your name?"

Again she laughed, a light, airy sound. "No. I'm sorry. About hiring you. I changed my mind. It was probably a rash decision. That's what Randolph says, anyway."

"That's what you've waited two days to tell me?"

The people she knew trusted her. If Sarah told Randolph not to get on the elevator because it would hit bottom, he would take the stairs. If she told Ellis that there was something wrong with the home he wanted to buy, he'd pull his offer. But this man sitting before her didn't know her. He didn't know how to trust her advice yet. And Sarah truly didn't have the ability to think along his logical pathways to

convince him. So, she'd decided that firing him from a po-
tentially dangerous situation was the way to go.

"But why would it be dangerous?" she asked herself
without realizing it. She couldn't seem to pull her gaze from
the path of his golden eyes, caught by the pull of anticipation and danger. Torn by the ambivalence of the dilemma.

"You're talking about this . . . case," he said quietly, his
brows gathered—trying to understand.

"I'm talking about my company," she answered, her own
gaze still lost in her question, her hands worrying at the use-
softened cover. "What could be here that would be dangerous to you?"

"Is that why you don't want me around?" Alex asked.
"Because there's going to be some trouble?" He couldn't
seem to take his eyes from where she was twisting the knit-
ting in her hands.

Sarah noticed peripherally. She was trying to resurrect the
feeling, searching for some kind of clue that would lead her.
Maybe it was merely coincidental. Couldn't Mr. Thorne
simply step out in front of a drunk driver or slip down the
steps at the hotel? Something that wouldn't have happened
if he'd stayed in Denver, but that wouldn't necessarily have
anything to do with her company.

"I . . . I don't know," she finally admitted, still focused
inward, her head tilted as if to better hear or see. There was
no message in the turbulence, though, no guideposts. Only
elemental energy. "I'd just rather not risk it."

Alex Thorne didn't appear very convinced. Leaning forward a little, he rested his elbows on his thighs and folded
his hands. "Why don't you tell me the financial problem
and let me decide?"

Before Sarah could get a chance to formulate an answer
she'd been working on for almost two weeks now, Randolph knocked and entered. Sarah saw that his eyes were on
her. His forehead was creased with worry, but he didn't say
anything. That would be up to her. He'd been through this
often enough that he knew how to take it.

"Connie says she'll be in as soon as she's finished," he told her, skirting the potted figs and schefflera to set down the ladened tray on the table between Sarah and Alex. Briefly his eyes strayed to Sarah's guest, and she could tell he wasn't comfortable.

"Thanks, Randolph," she said with a smile. Randolph hadn't been any happier about outside interference than anyone else at the company. "The new design for Intertell is over on the board somewhere. Could you take it down to production for me, please?"

Randolph took a few moments to unearth it. It wasn't until he had come up with the sheet of paper and carried it out that either Sarah or Alex moved.

"You'll like Connie," Sarah said, reaching to dump two or three teaspoons of sugar into her steaming mug. "She's the sensible half of the partnership. I'm afraid she's not any more fond of this idea than anybody else in the place, though."

"Which idea?" Alex asked, lifting his coffee without embellishment. "Me?"

Sarah grinned. "Do you believe in intuition, Mr. Thorne?"

He was about to take a sip of coffee. Her words stalled his cup halfway to his mouth. "Do you always converse like this?"

Sarah's grin broadened as she once again waved at her hair with her free hand. "If you mean, is it impossible for me to approach a problem head-on, yes. Connie says I think in circles. Ellis says I think in no pattern known to man. It makes sense to me, but explaining the process to anybody else is a bit futile."

"I see." He finally sampled his coffee and grimaced.

Sarah grimaced right back. "Oh, I should have warned you. Randolph's coffee is lethal." She caught a smile from him on that one.

"Which is why you drink tea?"

Sarah nodded with a sheepish grin. "I hired him for his organizational abilities, not his cooking talents."

Another grimace. "Obviously." Alex considered the mug a moment, obviously weighing his health against continued contact with the contents. He kept the cup in hand, but didn't return to it soon. "Why is he so thrilled to see me?"

"That goes back to the question of intuition."

Alex's glance sharpened a little. "His, yours or mine?"

"In this case," she said, holding very still, wanting him to understand, "mine."

Sarah saw him give a little shake of his head, almost as if he'd anticipated this. "Is that what all that on the elevator was about?"

"No," she answered more quietly than she realized. "That was...different. I'm talking your garden-variety feeling that something is more or less than it seems without obvious proof."

Alex nodded, finally ventured another sip and commented without words. "I've been called out a couple of times because a businessperson saw something wrong without realizing it. Is that why I'm here now?"

Sarah tried to hold on to his gaze, to impart comprehension to the honey brown of his eyes. Leaning forward, she balanced her mug on her knee and excluded the rest of the world from her consideration. "Something's wrong with my company, Mr. Thorne. I don't know what. I couldn't find out if I tried. I just don't have that kind of brain. I see the world in shapes and compositions, not in linear progression. What I see is that somehow there's a piece missing, and I can't find it. I'm not even sure which piece it is. I need somebody else to do it for me."

Frustration took hold of Alex. He shook his head and narrowed his eyes. "And nobody else agrees with you?"

Sarah felt the frustration infect her, too. Sighing, she straightened. "Everything looks fine. We've checked ourselves. But something...smells wrong, and I don't know how to search it out. As for the rest of the company, we're kind of a tight unit here. It's almost like a family. I hired everyone myself, and we've fought pretty hard to make it where we are today. To them, you're like an outsider moving into a small town. Of course they're going to be a little resentful.''

"Besides the fact that just by hiring me you're accusing one of them of something illegal.''

Sarah stiffened, hating what he said. Hating the fact that she'd even thought it herself. "I don't know that. I just know that something isn't right, and we need to fix it.''

For the first time, Alex Thorne smiled, and Sarah saw how very rich it could be. There was a wealth of memory in his eyes, both pain and joy, and all of it escaped into his smiles. It didn't negate his size as much as complement it, showing an unexpected depth to the man, an endearing warmth.

"But if nobody's doing anything illegal," he said softly, leaning forward again, "how can it be dangerous?''

"Dangerous?''

Startled, Sarah whipped around. She hadn't even heard Connie come in. Closing the door behind her, Connie bore down on them, the worry in Randolph's eyes magnified tenfold in hers.

"Randolph said you'd had a premonition. Are you all right? Is that what it was about?''

Sarah was on her feet almost as quickly as Alex. First she had to defuse Connie, then deal with Alex. And then deal with herself. She never even noticed that the afghan had fallen into a bright puddle at her feet or that a magazine fluttered after it.

"Premonition?" Alex echoed, eyes on Sarah, cup held as stiff as an alms request. "You have premonitions?''

"So," Connie greeted him, smiling, hand outstretched. "You're Alex Thorne. It's a pleasure to meet you. Ellis had quite a bit to say about you. I'm Connie Mason.''

Sarah envied Connie her easy business manner. Connie was the company's public image: confident, self-assured, meticulously correct. She knew two hundred business associates by name and family history and could quote closing prices in seven countries. Sarah couldn't even find those countries on a map. Come to think of it, she'd be hard pressed to know where to find a map.

Alex shook Connie's hand and returned the greeting, his attention already taken. Sarah wished Connie hadn't spilled the beans so ungracefully. The fact of her "X-ray vision," as Ellis was wont to call it, was something that needed gentle introduction. Especially to someone like Alex, a man who occupied such a solid, unyielding place in the real world.

She could almost read his mind. Premonitions. Next it would be channelers and ancient Egyptian mystics. Usually that kind of attitude didn't bother Sarah. It was the way of the world, especially here in America where everything was built on tangibles. But with Alex, it did make a difference. It had made a difference since she'd looked up and seen his broad back taking up most of the light in the elevator. Since the moment she'd known.

"Are you all right?" Connie repeated, turning worried hazel eyes on Sarah.

"I'm fine," Sarah assured her with an airy wave of her restless hand. "Randolph has dosed me with tea, and Alex is listening to why I'm letting him go."

"Premonitions?" he asked again. "Is that what this is all about? Crystal balls?"

Sarah turned a disparaging smile on him. "You don't have to sound quite so stricken about it."

"You don't know?" Connie demanded of him. "Ellis didn't tell you?"

"All Ellis said was that this would be an interesting job. And that I'd find out when I got here."

Connie laughed. Sarah did not.

"Sarah doesn't just have premonitions," Connie said, weight shifted to one leg, arms crossed in amused challenge. "She has the sight. ESP. She's as fey as a Scottish witch. Has been ever since I've known her. Whatever she says is worth listening to. Now, then, hon," she said, turning her business eyes on Sarah. "What's this about danger?"

Sarah could do no more than shrug in the glare of Connie's immense pragmatism. "I have a . . . feeling that Alex could be hurt if he takes on this job, that's all."

"That's enough," Connie answered, straightening.

"Doesn't the victim have anything to say about it?" Alex demanded, his attention divided between the women.

Both Sarah and Connie turned on him. He was still looking at Sarah as if she were going to disappear into a puff of blue smoke.

"Your warning has been noted," he assured her, and then lowered his coffee cup in a gesture that said they should be getting down to business. "Now, why don't you show me the books?"

Sarah's heart sank. "No," she objected. "You can't."

"I can," Alex retorted. "And I will. Ellis is an investor in this company, and he wanted me here. *I* want me here."

"I don't," Sarah insisted, feeling the weight of guilt. Torn by already wanting him to stay when she knew he shouldn't.

"She's probably right," Connie suggested. "She's been known to be annoyingly accurate in the past."

"I've survived more than the CPA boards in my life," he said quietly. "I'll keep an eye out. Besides, if it's going to be dangerous for me—" Sarah wished his expression showed that he believed it "—it's probably going to be dangerous for the next guy coming in. And I'll guarantee you that he won't be able to handle himself as well as I can."

He seemed as implacable as a mountain, solid angles and strength. In that moment, as Sarah watched him, as his golden gaze warred in silence with her blue one, she believed him. She thought that nothing could bring down this tower of a man. And, unforgivably, she wavered.

"I don't want you to be hurt," she insisted, her voice already surrendering.

He smiled, and she saw those memories again, felt the amassed strength of trials she knew nothing about. Trials that had nothing to do with size and stamina.

"I'll give you a list of referrals," he promised. "They'll tell you how invincible I am."

"Connie," Sarah said, unable to look away from Alex. "Do you want to introduce Alex around?"

Connie let go with a dry laugh. "Kim spread the word half an hour ago. But I'll make it official."

Both Sarah and Alex nodded, each still challenging the other and unsure how to back down, each still curiously caught in the other's gaze.

"Thank you, Alex," Sarah finally said.

Alex gave a shrug of deprecation. "Thank me when I find something."

Sarah couldn't help but smile. "I'm not sure I'll be grateful then."

Alex was headed out the door behind Connie when he turned one last time. "By the way," he said, a hand on the door. "That premonition thing in the elevator."

Sarah stilled. "Yes."

"Who is it you don't want to marry?"

Sarah saw Connie stop and spin, and knew that behind her Randolph did the same. Even so, she couldn't help but grin. She kept her eyes on Alex, anticipating his reaction.

"You."

His reaction was everything she could have hoped for.

Chapter 2

It was enough to give Alex a headache. Not only was he stuck in a city with the mean temperature of a well-done slab of beef, he was trapped with a sweet ditz of a blonde who had premonitions.

Premonitions, for heaven's sakes. He couldn't have just gotten another blond bimbo like his ex-wife, Barbi, whose recommendations began and ended with her wide blue eyes and drop-dead figure. He couldn't have found himself corralled with a legitimate airhead. He had to trip over one who managed to squeeze hocus-pocus in between those cute little ears of hers.

The CPA's manual never covered this one.

"Does she do this all the time?" he finally asked, not exactly sure how to deal with Sarah's last pronouncement—or the delighted grin that had accompanied it.

Connie barely broke stride as she led him down the hallway decorated in Georgia O'Keeffe prints. "Ever since I've known her. And we became roomies in our junior year of high school."

Alex could do no more than shake his head. "Takes some getting used to."

Connie just laughed as he led him down the hall. "Tell me about it. Within fifteen minutes of meeting Sarah for the first time, I'd been given instructions on how to best decorate my half of the room, the names of my proposed suitors for the year and a rather uncomfortable insight into my problem with James Joyce."

"You couldn't understand James Joyce?"

"I *hated* James Joyce. I thought it was because he refused to make sense. Sarah informed me that he made perfect sense, but not to somebody who insisted on thinking logically."

Alex couldn't help a grin as he nodded. "At least that explains my 'D' in Twentieth Century Lit. I'm just having trouble understanding how she gets along in the business world."

Connie shrugged offhandedly. "She doesn't. That's what I'm for. Sarah is like the bright, creative child who has a hundred wonderful ideas every ten minutes."

Alex looked over at the handsome woman who strode through her company like most of the women executives he'd known. Brisk, intelligent, composed. An interesting contrast to the gypsy fortune-teller he'd just left. "And you?"

Connie smiled, and it lit her face with soft whimsy. "I'm the mother who makes her go in one direction at a time."

The two headed on in unspoken agreement. Alex was still trying to piece together the different angles of Sarah he'd gotten so far. "Just how accurate is she with this sight of hers?"

Connie shrugged. "Sarah says nobody scores a hundred percent, but I've turned into a percentage player. I'd rather look foolish than really stupid."

"Does she still supervise your love life?"

Connie shook her head with a wry grin. "Nope. She won't try anymore. Says we're too close. That throws it all off somehow."

"What number prospective husband am I?"

They reached another glass door at the far end of the hall, which Connie held open before answering. "Oh, that. You're the first."

Alex tried his best not to come to a complete halt in the middle of the doorway. Three people looked up inside the modern black-white-and-red office where a mainframe computer whirred and clicked, and a small herd of PCs blinked in syncopation. Connie waited with the door held open, and Alex felt as though he'd just stepped through the looking glass.

Instead of commenting on the feeling of impending doom that was blossoming in his chest as Sarah had predicted, he took a look around at the jarringly spare room that reminded him of nothing so much as Early Hamburger Joint. Found at the end of the purple-and-green hallway, it pulled a person to a standstill. Alex took a minute to look over his shoulder at the lush colors behind.

Connie was already grinning. "Meet the computer staff. They have a very warped sense of decorating."

Alex couldn't help shaking his head. "What does the billing department look like, something out of *Bleak House*?"

"It's all Sarah's fault," Connie admitted brightly. "She encourages the lunatics to take over the asylum." When Alex looked up, she shrugged. "My office looks like a House of Denmark showroom."

He ended up just shaking his head. Suddenly he couldn't wait to get back to the hotel, where all the rooms looked alike. This place was straight out of a Rorschach test.

"Thaddeus," Connie was saying as she stepped into the bright room. "Unpeel yourself and come meet the company."

For the first time since he'd stumbled into this alternate universe, Alex could say he wasn't surprised. The person who came forward was the one he'd expected—an intense-looking young man with a wild thatch of red hair and a mad twinkle in his eye. He looked as if he'd been born with pocket protector in hand. The nineties equivalent of the born accountant. Alex had run to football to survive high school. Thaddeus had obviously escaped into computers.

Thaddeus didn't look terribly enthusiastic to see Alex. Even so, he left his two gaping associates to present himself.

"Thaddeus," Connie said with subtle relish, "this is Alex Thorne. He's going to check on the books for Sarah. Alex, this is our resident genius. Thaddeus is the real brains behind Sunset Designs."

Alex held out a hand that was taken in a slightly damp shake. "All computerized?" he asked.

"Right down to some of the designs," the programmer said with an edge to his voice. His handshake wasn't much, but he had a smile like a pirate's, brash and full of himself. A genius with a special spin on the world. Alex had met a few Thaddeuses in his career and had ended up liking the majority of them.

"Sarah's terrified of him," Connie announced with delight. "She says he's possessed by the spirit of Hal from *2001.*"

"In that case," Alex assured them both, "we shouldn't have any problem at all. You design your own software?"

Thaddeus nodded, the hair that was shorn just shy of his ears flying. "Some. I adapt others. Come back after the tour and I'll explain it all."

The billing department was almost a disappointment. Cherry paneling and celery carpet and white walls. Alex met two key people there, Hector Yglesias, the supervisor, and Jill Bramson, who ran accounts receivable. Jill was a slightly overweight blonde with a bad dye job who chewed pencils, and Hector was a man "on his way up." Energy and hun-

ger radiated from him in equal amounts as he pushed his
wire-rimmed glasses back up his nose and extended a dry,
firm hand.

"I saw you in the Superbowl," he greeted Alex. "The
year you beat Pittsburgh. How do you get to accounting
from there?"

Alex shrugged. "I was in accounting first. Football paid
for college."

Neither of them wanted him here. Alex couldn't miss the
chill that had spread out from the computer section and
followed him through the billing department to the yellow
design floor. Friendly poses and a lot of reserve. A goodly
sprinkling of resentment. Just as Sarah had said, the sense
that he was an interloper.

At least that was something with which Alex was comfortable. He'd investigated more than one company that
really didn't want him there. He'd do this one the same way
and then get the hell back to Denver.

"Where would you like to start?" Connie asked.

"Lunch," Sarah answered from the doorway.

Both of them turned in surprise. There in the hallway, still
in stockinged feet, stood the president and cofounder of
Sunset Designs.

"It's only eleven," Connie reminded her with the sound
of someone who did this regularly.

Sarah grinned. "I know. I didn't eat breakfast, and I'm
finished with the proposal for Endicott. I need a reward."

"What about Bartonberry?"

A shrug. "Safely shoved into the subconscious ooze. I
expect a flash anytime soon."

Connie frowned. "They've been screaming all week."

Sarah gave an expansive shrug, sending her hair bobbing
about her shoulders. "Nothing I can do. Everybody in design is backed up on the new lines and I can't seem to pull
an idea out of thin air. I figured a timely break might help.
Do a little food association," she said to Alex as if he'd understand, her smile as bright.

Still plagued by the feeling that if he turned around quickly enough he'd catch sight of the White Rabbit, Alex smiled back.

Connie instinctively checked her watch. "I have an appointment with Susan over at Dallyripple in half an hour. Sorry, hon."

Sarah turned her attention to Alex. Caught by her bright blue eyes, he had the unsettling feeling that she'd known all along exactly what Connie's plans were. "Alex?"

"Might as well go on." Connie sighed. "She'll drive you nuts until you do."

Alex couldn't help but think that he'd been there less than two hours, and that he had work to do. And damn it if that bright, sweet smile wasn't sapping away all his hard-won common sense. He knew better. *Ellis* had known better when he insisted Alex come down here. Alex had no business getting involved on any level with women with breathy voices and guileless eyes. But here he was passing up a chance to tell her that what he really needed to do right now was dig into her books like she'd wanted him to. Instead he acquiesced with a smile.

"Lunch is fine."

"Great," she sang with impulsive delight. "I'll get my purse."

"Don't forget your shoes," Connie suggested.

Startled, Sarah looked down. "Oh, yeah," she murmured with another grin. "That'd probably be a good idea, wouldn't it?"

Alex was building up for another groan when Connie shook her head. "Don't let her get away from you, will you? She might not find her way back."

It didn't take a fortune-teller to know what Alex Thorne was thinking. No matter how polite he tried to be, or how tolerant, Sarah knew that he was being just that. It should have frustrated her, especially since the more she saw him the more clearly she saw the future that trembled before the two of them like an apparition on the desert.

He had choices. Everybody had choices, and it was those choices that fashioned the shape of the future. Each decision made narrowed the path taken. What Sarah saw were the possibilities that lay beyond those choices. She saw what might be instead of what would be.

At least that was the way she'd always thought of it. When she'd first encountered Alex, she'd seen both joy and grief, a beginning and an end. She'd seen the major pathways he might take. Something he would do might lead him to her. The same thing, or something else, might lead him to harm. She couldn't say what, and more importantly, she couldn't tell him what decision to make. With his resolution to stay, both possibilities shimmied into better focus. The dread crept as close as the anticipation.

"I did this on purpose," she said as Alex held the front door open for her. He smelled like soap. Sarah liked that. She liked the economy of his movements, the way he tilted his head to listen to her, as if what she said were important, even though she knew how uncomfortable he was with her. "I wanted to give us a little time to talk, away from the office."

"To begin the courtship?"

Sarah made it a point to grimace. "I don't interpret 'em. I just have 'em. I'd be as happy as you if nothing came of that one." She wasn't being entirely honest. She'd never considered falling in love before. Well, not since Billy Peterson in junior year of college, anyway. But now that it was an option, she couldn't say she minded terribly. She could do worse than Alex Thorne.

"What are our chances of escaping the inevitable?" he asked, his voice colored with a healthy dollop of skepticism.

They'd reached the rental car he'd left on the lot. After several false starts against the hot metal, Alex unlocked the doors and opened one for Sarah. She offered him a bright smile, wondering if he heard as much history in those words as she did. She wondered what the woman had been like who had hurt him.

"I don't know," she admitted, sliding into the seat. "I've never been in this situation before."

He joined her, but waited to introduce the key to the ignition. "Oh, I have," he announced with dry humor. "My ex-wife had visions, too."

Sarah brightened. "She did?"

He scowled. "Yeah. She saw dollar signs over my head and camera lights in her future. That was her idea of Kismet."

Sarah couldn't help a knowing grin. "And you fought her off until you were too weak to struggle anymore."

She was glad to see that Alex Thorne could take a little heat. Tilting his head slightly, he offered her a particularly dry smile. "You *do* have ESP," he said, and finally turned on the ignition. "Where are we going?"

At that, Sarah blinked. "Uh, my house."

She should have anticipated this. Alex was having enough trouble getting used to her as it was. The last thing Sarah needed at this point was to betray the full extent of her limitations. If she hadn't been so distracted by the premonition, by the Bartonberry account that lay open on her desk like an unsolved homicide, by the surprising warmth of Alex's eyes and the way his hand felt wrapped around hers, she probably would have had the problem covered.

No, she wouldn't. She would have jumped to her feet just as quickly, the impulse propelling her instead of logic, like always.

Alex turned with a particularly pained expression on his face and Sarah bluffed. "I'd rather not discuss the problems of my company in public," she said. "We can get some lunch delivered and sit out by the pool. Now, turn onto Bell, and I'll direct you from there."

"Does this have to do with the wedding-in-the-chapel part of the premonition," Alex asked dryly, "or the villain-lurking-in-the-bushes part?"

"It has to do with business," she insisted, unable to quite face those knowing eyes.

"Sarah, I don't want to insult you—"

"You're pretty gun-shy," she accused, head up, eyes challenging as she tried to deflect him. "Aren't you?"

"I'm *very* gun-shy," he admitted, refusing to be deflected. "But that doesn't have anything to do with why I don't like this idea."

Finally Sarah sighed, slumping back into the seat. "I don't know how to get to anywhere else," she admitted.

Alex blinked. "You're kidding."

Sarah shot him her first glare. "Some people have a bad sense of direction. I have no sense of direction at all. Are you happy?"

But Alex persisted. "How long have you lived in Phoenix?"

She shrugged. "Two years." He probably knew every street name in Denver and where they intersected.

"How do you shop?"

Sarah groaned. This was one area of her capabilities—or lack thereof—that had always bothered her. In the glaring light of Alex's competency, it frustrated her anew. "I walk. Now, can we please go?"

Alex wasn't finished shaking his head. "I'll pick the place," he decided. "I can usually find my way around."

"Of course you can."

That's why the gods had picked Alex for her, she thought with sudden, inexplicable frustration. He was a male Connie, all common sense and logic. It was a darn good thing he had such beautiful eyes, such a nice set of shoulders, such a surprising smile. It might offset that insurmountable pragmatism of his.

"I don't suppose you're left-handed," she tried.

"Sorry."

She sighed. "I didn't think so."

The gods weren't giving her a soul mate. They were giving her a new baby-sitter.

Alex turned the car left onto Bell, and Sarah was immediately lost.

Alex felt like one of the moon walkers. He'd just landed in a completely alien atmosphere, and he didn't know which way to step first. There were so many questions he wanted to ask Sarah. Not just about the company, but about her, about Connie, and about Ellis, who never mentioned the founder of Sunset Designs without a certain amount of awe in his voice.

Before him, Alex saw a gamine with a brain that seemed incapable of any recognized pattern of thought, a grown woman who got lost in her own neighborhood and yet convinced a gathering of very intelligent people that she could foray into the future and bring back treasures.

It wasn't that Alex didn't believe in intuition. He'd shared a pretty surprising communication with his sister over the years, a sixth sense of danger or excitement or pain that had united the two of them more than with the rest of his family. But that communication had been honed out of trouble. He and Lindsay had suffered together; they had forged their bond out of long years of love and struggle. Alex considered it a natural outcome of their special relationship.

He really didn't know how to take this capricious lightning that struck from the woman across the table. Could she really have a gift so startling? Did it have the right to exist without effort, without the years of sharing that became the currency exchanged for such an ability?

Lindsay would say yes. Lindsay, though, was a psychologist, a student of the vagaries of the mind. The unknown excited her. She lived for possibility. Alex was a craftsman, stolidly plying his trade, his brain a tool best suited to a well-defined task. He wasn't sure he could allow Sarah her magic. CPAs weren't a breed of animal that found comfort in the great unknown.

But he couldn't say he disdained her intent. He'd known her for two hours and could already feel the tendrils of her bright, winsome charm wrapping around him. He didn't really want to believe her, but he wanted her to believe in herself.

"What do you think of the company?" Sarah asked between bites of enchilada.

Alex wanted to smile at her. She had an appetite like a lumberjack. All that prophesying must tax a woman's strength. He took the time to swallow his first mouthful of *fajita* before answering. Around them, the cool white-tile restaurant was beginning to fill up. Laughter echoed from the bar, and a party of vacationers with New York accents took over the next table.

"I've only had two hours so far to look at it," Alex reminded her.

Sarah flashed him an unrepentant smile. "That's not my fault," she said. "I was going to try and talk to you last night at the hotel. I even left a message, but you didn't answer."

"I didn't get in until late," he retorted. "But if you're psychic, you should have known that."

She set her fork down, obviously well used to the challenge. "Your sister's overdue for her first baby and went into false labor. You stayed until she went home from the hospital. I know."

Alex actually paused, snagged by her trick. Then he saw the grin peek through and shook his head. "I told Ellis."

His reward was another of those quicksilver smiles. "How is she?"

"Frustrated. I'm glad I'm not her husband. Lindsay can be a real bear when she wants to."

"I'm sure when you're pregnant someday, you'll understand what she's going through," Sarah baited him.

Alex had the good grace to grin. "This is the payback. She was unmerciful when I was recovering from my last football season. Something about, I was around for the fun, the least I could do was pay the price."

"Which was what you said to her."

He liked the playful sparkle in her eyes. "Something like that."

Alex expected another comment from her on the subject, something akin to Lindsay's outrage at his very male goading. But when Sarah returned her attention to him after polishing off her rice and beans, she surprised him again.

"Why football?" she asked.

Alex lifted an eyebrow. At his size, that had never been tops on any list of questions he'd been asked. It had usually been the other way around, like Hector's question. Why accounting?

"Why not?" he countered, distracted by the way she tilted her head when she concentrated, consumed by the dreamy soft blue of her eyes.

She always looked as if her mind were absorbed by more than she was saying, as if inner voices diverted her. It should have warned him away. Instead it intrigued him. Alex was never going to get anything done on this job if he stayed around her. Already he was wondering what it would be like to kiss her.

"You're basically a left-brain person," she said. "Very logical, practical. You like computers, don't you?"

Alex tried to concentrate on the question. The slightly distasteful frown Sarah proffered betrayed her own feelings on the subject. Alex grinned in return. "Some of my best friends are computers," he said.

That was actually an accusation Lindsay had made once when she'd tried to unravel a program he'd been teaching her. Since that had been scant months after the Barbi debacle, he'd seen no reason to disagree with her. Now, three years later, he still didn't.

Computers, no matter how stupid, how exacting, how frustrating, always gave back just what they got, no more, no less. They never let prejudices or greed or infatuation or even hormones get in their way. Not like people. You never knew what you were going to get from people—if you got anything at all.

Especially women, he thought, looking at the woman who should have reminded him so much of the late, unlamented Barbi.

Sarah nodded, as if he'd been perfectly serious. "I'd think that with your education and talents, you'd be more inclined to avoid sports. Especially something as punishing as football." Zeroing in on him with those sweet, wide eyes of hers, she frowned. "Is it really worth that kind of sacrifice?"

Alex directed his attention to his lunch when he answered. It was a question he'd often been asked, one he'd considered in a hundred different ways both before and since his retirement. Was it worth the aching knees and accumulated hospital time? The Mondays lost to whirlpools and physical therapists and the rest of his life squeezed into the spring months until football passed him by? Was it worth the years it had taken to move beyond retirement?

Alex felt Sarah's eyes on him, like warm light. Interested, concerned, empathetic when she shouldn't have known how to be. He knew he'd give her the same answer he always gave. And yet he was surprised this time at the sudden stab of loss her question incited.

For a moment those years rose in him like blood from a newly opened wound, bright and hot and life-giving even as they drained away. Impressions of friends and fans, of road trips and games and thundering crowds, of biting winter afternoons and the endless repetition of practices. And in that moment he suffered again the cost of walking away.

"It was for me," he said as he always did, bare fact always an easy shield behind which to hide. But when he lifted his eyes to her, ready to push the memories back, he was silenced by the wonder in her eyes. The pain. She understood, and he hadn't said a word.

She saw it. In a bright flash, almost like film playing at fast forward, Sarah saw the camaraderie, the exertion, the struggle . . . the pain. She saw the exultation of achievement echoing from an empty stadium. Sarah saw a man with the strength to fight for what he wanted and the courage to walk away.

More than a baby-sitter, she thought. Someone who has had it all and given it away with grace. Someone with a passion buried deep beneath the calluses he's formed. A harsh ache ignited in her chest for the pain that had escaped him. An awe bloomed for his determination.

"Ellis wasn't as gracious about quitting," she said.

Alex shrugged, returning his attention to his *fajita*. "Ellis didn't have as much to go back to."

Sarah nodded. Ellis, the rising mercurial black star of Penn Tech. The brightest new rookie, and the sudden has-been when his leg was broken in the first game of his third season in the pros. Ellis, who came from the ghetto, became no more than an illiterate ex-football player with no skills and fewer prospects.

"How did you meet Ellis?" Alex asked. "He never told me."

Sarah smiled, her food temporarily forgotten for the memories. "When he won his suit with Penn Tech for having graduated an illiterate college senior, he took the money and went to University of Virginia. He was a thirty-year-old freshman when Connie and I started. And he still couldn't read. He ended up sleeping in our bathtub a lot. He sneaked in there when cramming got too rough and just fell asleep. I never saw anything like it."

Alex chuckled. "Yeah, he slept in my tub a lot, too. Usually when he was really hung over. He said that it had been the coolest place back home in Bed-Stuy, and that he'd just gotten used to escaping there."

Alex leaned into his chair then, eyes assessing and controlled, the moment of betrayed pain neatly tucked away. He was again in control, buttoned down and purposeful. "And when you got out, Ellis invested in Sunset Designs," he said.

Sarah set down her own cutlery, already missing the other Alex, knowing that he wouldn't allow himself back out yet. "It's Ellis's law school money. It's also our way of having some street smarts on this team. Neither Connie nor I excel in the cutthroat school of business acumen."

It had been a standing joke among the three of them. Sarah had the insight, Connie the common sense and Ellis the passion. He'd been the one who'd pushed Sunset into reality.

Ellis had always had a need to seek, an unquenchable hunger for more that fed his rage as well as his enthusiasm. After he'd lost football, his rage had been impressive. Football, he'd said, had been his release. His catharsis. There were still times when Sarah thought he hadn't found a suitable substitute.

"What do you do with it all?" she asked.

Alex frowned. "With what?"

Sarah waved a hand. "All that . . . emotion. The passion of the sport. Ellis talked for hours about the incredible highs, the surges of energy, the . . . the lust for what he did. What do you do with that now?"

Alex shook his head a little. "You did it again."

Sarah lifted an eyebrow. "You'll get used to it. How *do* you deal without that kind of release?"

His smile was dry. "I live vicariously through others."

"I'm not sure Ellis would agree with you."

"I *know* he wouldn't."

Passion, she thought, buried deep and rigorously controlled. Peeking out in the guise of consternation, betrayed in little frowns and the softening of those honey-brown eyes. Slipping through when he wasn't watching.

It was there, she realized, caught beneath layers of pragmatism, waiting to be mined, waiting to be tapped like a hive until it flowed over her like sweet, hot nectar. Until it surprised her, overwhelmed her.

Sarah couldn't help smiling with delight at the thought of well-composed Alex wild and abandoned. And all for her. The taste of honey was already sweet on her tongue.

Honey. Hives. Pollination.

Bees.

"That's it!" she cried, suddenly scooping up her purse.

Alex looked around. "What's it?" he asked.

"The Bartonberry logo. A stylized bee. Why didn't I think of it? Do you have a pen?"

She was flattening out her napkin, the shape already formed in her mind. When Alex handed over a gold pen, she arced lines in the center of the paper, suddenly oblivious to Alex's bemused frown. She'd been struggling with this idea for a week, and one lunch with Alex had provided it.

"We have to get back," she said, her eyes on her work as she scribbled away.

"I thought you wanted to talk about the company," Alex objected.

Sarah flashed him a quick grin. "Well, I guess you'll have to come by my house after all. I have to get this down to design. We're a week behind on it as it is."

She didn't even see Alex pull out his wallet and cover the check. Sarah was involved with intersecting semicircles and complementary colors, already seeing the logo on natural-food packages all across America.

"That's it," she announced with finality as she clicked the pen closed. The napkin disappeared into her purse and would have been followed by the pen if Alex hadn't reached over and gently plucked it out of her fingers.

"From my sister," he said. "She'd kill me if I lost it."

"Sorry," Sarah apologized brightly, a feeling of well-being suffusing her. Everything would work out. Alex would find the mistake, Bartonberry would love the design, and the company would settle back into regular chaos. For the minute she didn't have to even think far enough ahead to consider marriage or disaster. "Are you ready to go?"

Alex was already on his feet. "Don't forget your shoes."

Surprised, Sarah looked down. She'd instinctively slipped them off and wound her feet together, the usual position for creation in her office. With a guilty grin, she retrieved her shoes and followed Alex.

The heat struck them the minute they walked out the door. The sun was blinding, the streets shimmering and the low buildings in the neighborhood crouching beneath the stunted trees for shade. Sarah barely noticed. She was still flushed with her inspiration.

"Thank you, Alex," she said when they got to the car.

He turned without opening the door. "For what?"

Sarah blinked up at him. "I got the idea for the logo from you. And you can't imagine how hard I've been trying to come up with something."

Alex didn't seem quite sure how to react. Giving his head another one of those little shakes, he nevertheless smiled. "You're welcome," he said. "For whatever I did."

She saw that he still didn't understand. He didn't even realize how important this moment was to her. Sarah couldn't think how to explain it any better, so she showed him. Stretching up on her toes, she wrapped her arms around his neck and kissed him.

Chapter 3

Ellis, what did I ever do to you to deserve this?"

Alex wasn't in the least appeased when he heard Ellis's chuckle rumble over the long-distance wire.

"You tellin' me you don't appreciate my good friend Missus Wizard?" the ex-wide receiver demanded.

"I'm saying that you could have warned me before shoving me headlong into *The Twilight Zone*." That wasn't what was really bothering Alex, but he wasn't about to admit it to his gloating friend, no matter how many hundreds of miles away he was. "I bet you knew all about those premonitions she says she has."

The new round of laughter neatly answered his question. "Boy, I always said you was the marryin' kind. If you live long enough, anyway."

Alex took to rubbing his eyes. The light was soft in his suite, the furniture muted Santa Fe pastels, the only sounds he heard were those invading from the pool outside his window. Still, it all seemed too loud and irritating. And Sarah had made him promise to come over for dinner.

"Do you know the worst part?" he demanded. "After hearing all that, *I* was the one who insisted on staying. I *still* can't figure out how that happened."

Ellis made commiserating noises. "Yeah, Sarah can do that to you."

"You might have warned me that your good friend was a little different," he accused.

"Different?" Ellis demanded with too much humor. "What's so different about her?"

"Oh, that's right," Alex retorted. "I'm talking to a man who blessed his football with chicken skins. You wouldn't recognize different if it fell on you."

"Don' be makin' fun of my mama, Alex. She *gave* me those skins."

Ellis's mother was a bona fide Haitian priestess. Alex wasn't sure whether she practiced one of the religions unique to the Caribbean or had just made up one that appealed to the same sense of theatrics her son had inherited.

"I bet your mama likes Sarah."

"You kiddin'? They're soul mates."

"Well, I'm not. That entire place is just a little too Zen for my tastes. I can't wait until my partner finds out I'm down here investigating a 'premonition.' He'll have me committed."

"What'd you tell me when I had to quit football? Broaden your horizons, you said. There's more out there than pigskins and cheerleaders. Well, that's what I'm tellin' you. Do you some good."

Alex growled. "It's giving me a headache. It's bad enough working a job like this when everybody talks the same language. I have people there I'm not even sure are from the same *universe*."

"Don't hurt her. She's my friend." This time, Alex heard the concern escape into his friend's voice. Hurt her? Alex hadn't even managed to anticipate that far. He couldn't seem to drag himself past the immediacy of her, the stunning sensuality of her spontaneity.

Alex thought of the kiss they'd shared. She'd surprised him with it, impulsively wrapping herself around him as if it had been the most natural thing in the world. Kissing him with no more intention than gratitude and celebration.

Somewhere in that kiss his intentions had changed. His surprise had given way to pleasure, and pleasure had evaporated into hunger. Alex had found himself enfolding her with arms that ached. He'd curled impatient fingers into the silk of her hair and devoured the taste of her lips.

Honey. He could swear he had tasted honey on her. Her scent lingered on his clothes, a light aroma that reminded him of summer and mornings. He could still feel her vibrant body against his chest, her breasts straining and soft. And, just as he had out on that broiling parking lot where only a moment before he'd been suffering no more than the heat, Alex was struck with the harsh ache of sudden desire.

Within seconds, the room that had been so cool and quiet had become an oven, and Alex needed to move.

"The only thing I'm going to do," he grated out, knowing already that he was lying, "is check the company books and get myself back to Denver."

"Just make sure to watch your back," Ellis warned.

"Goodbye, Ellis."

"Alex? I mean it."

"So do I. I'll call when I have news." Without waiting for Ellis to reply, Alex hung up.

A swim. He needed a swim.

Jumping to his feet, Alex stripped out of his work clothes. Suit pants and tailored shirt hit the carpet and, for once, stayed there. He pulled on his swimming gear and doused himself in a cold shower until it was safe to be seen outside.

And then he stalked out to the pool and dove in.

People on deck chairs turned when they saw him coming. A few flinched from the scowl on the powerful features, and the tight set of the sleek muscles. One or two of the women took appreciative breaths and strolled over to intercept him when he surfaced.

But Alex hadn't come to socialize. He'd come to work off the sight of Sarah's eyes when she'd backed away from that kiss. The confusion, the vulnerable yearning that had softened them to the color of morning clouds. The languor of desire that widened the pupils and pulled him unforgivably close to kissing her again.

"Bartonberry," she whispered distractedly.

"Bartonberry," he'd answered, and the moment had been broken.

But it returned now, her startled face materializing beyond closed eyes, her erratic breathing sounding now to him like the slap of water as he cut through it.

Hormones. That's all it was. It was all it had been with Barbi, a raging case of infantile star ego exacerbated by the predilection for females of the blond persuasion. He'd been horny and he'd been full of himself and he'd fallen like a ton of bricks for the woman with the biggest eyes and the bounciest assets.

Alex's fingertips touched the side of the pool for the fourth time, and he flipped into a turn and headed the other way. He didn't see the heads above the water, following his progress like the sirens watching unwary sailors.

It wasn't ego this time. He'd learned that lesson the hard way, through courts and cameras and abstinence in the face of fame. But he'd been putting most of his energy into the business in the past few years—and Sarah had nailed it on the head. He liked computers. He trusted computers. Computers didn't have eyes the color of morning and lips that begged for kissing.

Computers didn't seduce you with their joy.

Alex dated nothing but businesswomen in Denver. Savvy, ambitious, intelligent women who enjoyed the outdoors and fit comfortably into social and official occasions. He'd been looking for a while now for a wife, a partner, a companion to share his life. He'd met each woman with a kind of anticipation.

Not one of them had elicited this kind of anxiety.

Not one of them had been a blonde with big blue eyes who was everything Alex did *not* want in a wife.

Not one of them had looked at him the way Sarah had when he'd talked about football, as if she'd walked off the field on the last day right alongside him.

Lindsay would probably have something to say about this. Maybe when he got home, after Lindsay had the baby and felt better, he might sit down and talk to her. He might ask her what this weakness of his was, and how to avoid it in the future.

But right now, he had to work it off or screw up the job he'd come to do.

It took almost an hour to dissipate the ache. Alex could feel his shoulders tighten and his knees start to tremble with the exertion. A pleasant lethargy began to invade his body. Pulling himself up to the edge of the pool, he swept his hair back with both hands and vaulted out. He didn't see the gazes follow him with growing disappointment as he bent to scoop up his towel and walk back to his room.

He heard the phone ringing even before he reached the door.

"Hello?"

"Thirty-five!"

Alex frowned. "Excuse me?" Then he recognized the voice.

"It rang thirty-five times," Sarah said. "I was getting worried. Are you all right?"

"I'm fine, Sarah. I was swimming."

The silence on her end of the line was a taut one. Alex realized that she really had been worried.

"Oh," she almost whispered. "I'm . . . sorry. . . ."

"Another premonition?" he asked, settling onto the bed without thinking of the wet suit.

"No," she said quickly. "Nothing new. It's just that I haven't really paid attention to it much today. What with everything . . ."

Alex understood perfectly. He'd been dealing with "everything" himself. "I'm fine," he repeated, wondering if he was going to have to make a habit out of that statement. "I'll be over in—" quickly he scanned the clock "—a half hour. Okay?"

She didn't answer him right away. Alex found himself leaning into the phone a little, wanting to hear her assurances.

"Sarah?"

"I'm sorry, Alex. I don't mean to hover. It's just a big responsibility...oh, well. Get changed before you ruin the bedspread."

Alex looked down, startled. "You—"

"Heard the bedsprings," she answered. "I'll see you in a few minutes."

What surprised Alex was that he wasn't really surprised. He was grinning—and he was looking forward to seeing what kind of gypsy caravan Sarah Delaney lived in.

Fruitcakes. He'd definitely developed a taste for fruitcakes. Shaking his head one last time, he got to his feet and headed for the shower.

"I told you he'd be there," Connie was saying.

"I know," Sarah sighed, settling into her favorite wing chair. Her feet—shoeless—were curled up beneath her, and she had a glass of iced tea in her hand. Outside her windows, her garden sagged from the heat. Not a leaf rustled. To the north the sky was sketched with naked mountains. The evening was stark in its golden light, the setting sun magnifying the desert colors, the harsh desert lines, wilting the greens and hardening the reds. Sarah closed her eyes against it and pressed the glass to her forehead to ease the ache.

"I don't know what to do, Connie," she said, hanging on to her friend's voice like a lifeline. "I'm not handling it right and I can't seem to...I don't know."

"You've said it yourself," Connie reminded her. "You're never a hundred percent right. Let's say you're having an off day here."

"I wish you were right," she said. "This is so hard. Premonitions feel bad enough without kissing interfering."

There was a pause as Connie digested Sarah's words. "It affected you that much?"

Sarah had to smile. Images tumbled. Sensations skittered along nerve endings. Her chest swelled with the intimate memory. Her belly tightened.

Connie needed no more than the suspicious silence for her answer. "I'm still not sure that your keeping such a close eye on him's going to save him from anything."

Sarah tested that thought and came away unconvinced. There wasn't a reason to explain her need to keep Alex close—not one she could successfully discuss with the pragmatic Connie, anyway. She just understood that, even only knowing Alex no more than a few hours, she already wouldn't forgive herself if something happened to him and she could have somehow prevented it.

She'd lied to him. Well, she'd fudged a little. She'd said there had been no new premonition. If it all happened that cleanly, she could have better explained. But the truth was, since that kiss in the parking lot, she'd felt a greater sense of urgency—and a growing impatience.

But for *what* she didn't know. It wasn't as easy as saying, "Watch out for that falling tree branch, Alex." It was more as if the air were disturbed around her, charged like just before a lightning strike. The kiss had stirred it up further. It had agitated the delicate balance until the possibilities roiled in her like acid—like an ulcer on an empty stomach.

She was anxious to keep Alex close to her, but she couldn't tell whether it was to further a destined relationship or prevent a potential disaster.

Or it could have simply been because she liked the way he kissed.

It was getting all too complicated. And it was getting in the way of the reason she'd asked Alex to come down in the first place.

"Earth to Sarah."

Snapping to attention, Sarah took tighter hold of the receiver. "I'm sorry, Connie. I'm trying to hammer this all out."

"Don't try," her friend suggested. "Logic isn't exactly your long suit. Just go with the flow, like you always do. *Which* reminds me, what provoked the Bartonberry logo? Design is in ecstasy."

"Lust."

Connie didn't so much as hesitate. "Uh-huh. Well, I have to get ready for my own date here. Maybe I can come up with a new bed sheet or something."

Sarah chuckled. "You told me yourself that Peter wasn't that kind of guy."

"Well," Connie retorted. "I figure if a CPA can inspire creativity, a computer system salesman should, too."

Sarah smiled. It was good to hear that kind of talk from Connie—from both of them. They'd put so much into Sunset that neither had had much chance for outside interests. Neither had had the time or energy. Sarah was glad they were moving past that. She wanted Connie to have a full life.

It would have been nice, though, to know this time whether Peter was the one to provide it. Sarah hadn't paid enough attention when he'd courted the company as a representative from Landyne Systems. Now that Connie had begun to see him away from business, Sarah would have to reassess. Maybe she'd have a chance when she saw Peter again.

"Have a good time," Sarah said. "I'll see you tomorrow."

"You, too, hon. Tell Alex 'hi' for me. And tell him to watch out for himself."

"He's a good man," Sarah said. "Isn't he?"

"Yeah," her friend answered. "He's a good man. I hope he's a smart man, too. See you."

Sarah sat for a long time without moving, the phone receiver still in her hand, the tinny beeping lost to her. She didn't know what to do. She knew what she *wanted* to do, but that might not have anything to do with what she *should* do. She wanted to ease into love with Alex just like sliding into the comfort of the whirlpool on her patio, steeping in it until it drove everything from her mind. But if she did that, the rest would become muddied. The clarity that enabled her to see farther than most people saw would dim, just as it had with whatever was happening with her company.

The light outside changed to mauve. The garden rustled, and somewhere a coyote anticipated the moon. Inside Sarah's house only the grandfather clock in the front hallway spoke, counting out the marching seconds with comforting familiarity. Linear progression, logical movement. A straight line. Except that Einstein didn't think time moved in a straight line. Sarah felt her life curling back in on her, bending and warping with the whims of whatever it was that held her sway. The past skidded close, and the future leaned back until it almost touched. And Sarah was caught in the middle, not knowing how to keep both of them in their places without sacrificing the insight she'd gained over the years.

How did she move in a logical progression when the next step she took could cost Alex his life? How did she act toward him so to settle the future into place? And in the end, did it matter what she did? Did she really have a choice? Or was she doomed to fall in love with Alex Thorne only to lose him?

Without thinking, Sarah lifted her forefinger to her lips, as if she could still feel the imprint of Alex's mouth there. As if she could rub the scent and taste of him onto her finger and then observe it.

It had been a long time since she'd become lost in a kiss. It had been a long time since she'd even wanted to. But out in that parking lot, where the asphalt sent the temperature soaring, her own temperature had risen, too. Her cheeks had flushed. She wouldn't have been surprised if her nose had flushed, as well. She'd stepped away from him, stunned and shaken and suddenly alive. And the only thing she could remember—except for the sweet ache that still refused to recede—was that all she'd wanted was more.

Out in the hallway, a bell chimed. Her finger still playing against her lower lip, Sarah didn't hear. She faced the fireplace, but she saw the crimson oleander that had edged the restaurant lot. She heard the stagger of her own heart. She smelled the clean soap of Alex's hands.

The doorbell chimed twice. Sarah looked up, then she jumped to her feet. It didn't occur to her to hang up her phone. By the time she was halfway across the floor, she'd forgotten she'd even been on it.

Alex took her breath away all over again. Sarah couldn't help but smile. "Welcome to Castle Gonzo, as Ellis calls it," she greeted him, thinking that he looked very handsome in his blue oxford-cloth shirt and khaki chinos.

Alex stepped inside and came to a halt, his eyes widening at the sight. "This is—"

"Not really what you'd expect," Sarah answered with a nod as she turned to follow his gaze. "I know."

Of all the decors she could have chosen, Sarah guessed this was the last one her friends would have anticipated. Connie still looked for beads and Jimi Hendrix posters, but then Connie knew Sarah's parents. Ellis had said he wanted postmodern, and Randolph had begged for more color. But Sarah had known from the time she was ten what her house would look like, and it did.

"Sarah," Alex said with some awe as he stepped further into the living room where Oriental carpets covered dark hardwood floors. "Did anybody tell you that this is Phoenix?"

Right alongside him so she could get a whiff of that crisp scent of his, Sarah grinned. "Connie says that I'm the only person nuts enough to put an English country house in the desert.''

Alex didn't look as if he totally disagreed. He couldn't seem to get over the whitewashed walls, exposed beams and tile fireplace. And that didn't even take into account the chintz furniture coverings and the French doors that led into Sarah's struggling garden.

To Sarah it seemed cooler this way, the dark tile and wood floors soothing after the harsh glare of the sun. She liked the flowers, the Regency period furniture, and the framed Pre-Raphaelite prints on the walls. To her it was peaceful, settled, comfortable. Nothing jarred in her house. Nothing surprised, and that was the way Sarah liked it.

"My mother says that I'm finally rebelling," she said.

"Against what?" Alex demanded, still looking around. "The circus?"

Sarah watched him as she answered, "The commune."

She loved to see the way she impacted on him. He turned on her and squinted a little as if to verify her statement, tilting his head as if to ease its way.

"You lived on a commune."

Sarah nodded. "Until I was sixteen. My parents were the original hippies—I, their little flower child. Our first family vacation was to Woodstock. Would you like a drink?"

"Oh, yes."

"You might want to sit down, too," she suggested diffidently.

He looked at the sofa as if expecting a rabbit to pop out. Even so, he eased himself down.

"I always wondered what happened to all the old commune people," he marveled, almost to himself as he settled back, eyes still to the traditional decor. "I guess they're forming design companies in the Southwest."

"Not all of us," Sarah said, and headed into her kitchen. "Beer or bourbon?"

"Beer. Where are your parents?" he asked.

"John's in Costa Rica building dams for the Indians," she said, reaching over to flip on the range before she burrowed into her refrigerator in search of Alex's beer. She found it instead in the freezer section, but evidently she hadn't put it there too long ago, because it hadn't solidified yet. "Blue is—let's see—last I heard she was in an ashram in Nepal. Then she goes back to Bangladesh."

"Blue?" he asked from the other room. "Your mother's name is Blue?"

"Not exactly June Cleaver," Sarah acknowledged, shoving the freezer door closed before anything fell out. "But she taught me a lot."

"Yeah," she thought she heard him mumble. "Fortune-telling."

"Beer," she announced with a broad smile as she returned. His legs crossed, one arm thrown over the back of the sofa, Alex filled her couch with a leonine grace. He looked so strong sitting there, as if nothing could hurt him. Immobile, implacable, with eyes so knowing and logical nothing should be able to trick him.

Still, Sarah knew that that wasn't the whole truth. It worried her on levels she couldn't name and stole some of her smile. "What about getting somebody else to do it?" she asked, dropping into her chair.

Alex looked over at her with a half frown. "I've been drinking beer since I was sixteen," he said.

Sarah didn't notice the humor that warmed his eyes. Waving away his jest, she leaned forward, her glass of tea still clutched tightly in her hand. "Don't you understand? This isn't a party game."

Taking a moment to pop the tab on his beer, Alex shook his head. "I thought we were going to talk about the business."

"I *am* talking about the business," she insisted. "How much do you think I can accomplish if you get yourself killed because you won't listen to me?"

"A comforting thought." When Sarah moved to object, Alex raised his own hand. "The warning has been given. Now, since I'm not going anyplace but back to Sunset Design in the morning, why don't you tell me what makes you think the company has problems?"

Sarah wanted to shake him. He was humoring her. She could see it in the patient set of his brow. She could hear it in the tone of his voice. Well, it would serve him right if he went out of her house and walked into a truck. Then maybe he'd believe her.

"If you do get killed," she threatened, "I get to put the inscription on the tombstone."

Halfway through his first sip of beer, Alex lifted an eyebrow. "What's that?"

Sarah smiled sweetly. "I was thinking of something along the lines of 'He wouldn't listen.'"

Alex laughed, a deep, throaty rumble of surprise. "It's a deal," he promised. "Now, let's get down to business."

Still, Sarah didn't want to move. There was more she needed to say, that he needed to understand. But she could see by the look in his eyes that he wasn't ready to listen. Throwing off a shrug, she popped back to her feet.

"Come on in the kitchen while I work," she suggested. "We can talk there."

Her kitchen was as homey as the rest of her house, with its red-tile floor and hanging bundles of dried herbs. She knew it wasn't as neat as it could be, but that was because she was cooking. And cooking, as Blue had often taught her, was akin to a drama, not a chore.

Sarah attacked her cooking in a style more like grand opera.

"Anything I can do?" Alex asked, slowing to halt behind her when he saw the pans piled on available surfaces and fresh foods cluttering up counterspace.

Sarah took a moment to try to assess. The pasta needed to go in, and the sauce was about to be put together. And the salad. Had she boiled the eggs?

"Would you like to make the salad for me?" she asked, still looking around the kitchen as if waiting for it to instruct her.

"Show me where everything is."

Sarah managed to unearth the lettuce and tomatoes and cheese, and discovered, after two false starts, that she did in fact have hard-boiled eggs, but she was having trouble remembering where she'd left the salad bowl. Alex chopped while she wiped up egg and looked.

"You said you had an uneasy feeling about the company," Alex said, tasting the tomato he was cutting and then following it with a sip of beer.

Buried deep in her cabinets, Sarah nodded. Then she remembered the pasta. Backing out, she headed over to where the water was trying to boil away.

"It's been creeping up for the past couple of months," she said, sliding the fettuccine into the water. "Nothing definite, and nothing we've been able to prove. Hector's getting pretty tired of my constantly coming down to accounting to double-check things." Staring at the range top without really seeing it, Sarah shrugged. "I don't know of any other way to do it. I even had Thaddeus install more safety backups on the computers, especially since I don't trust the things anyway. Have you seen the garlic?"

The sauce. She had to get it put together before the pasta finished. Reaching into the fridge, Sarah grabbed butter and cream and Romano cheese. And garlic. Just a little. But she thought she'd already taken that out. Brushing her hair away with a free arm, she turned back to her cooking island.

"The problem couldn't be in the plant in Virginia?" Alex asked, handing over the garlic from where he'd found it on a stool.

Sarah looked up, surprised. "Oh, thanks. I wonder why I put it there." When he passed the cloves to her, his hand brushed hers. A sweet tingle snaked up from his fingers, provoking a fleeting smile of surprise in Sarah. "No," she said, turning away, trying to think past the glow in her hand. "Virginia isn't the problem."

Cutting slabs of butter, she slid them into the pan and then pulled the flour over. Behind her, Alex returned to his chopping.

"Why not?"

Sarah shrugged. "I couldn't tell you. I just know. It's here somewhere . . . but my pepper isn't."

"I think you put it in the flour jar."

She looked. "Oh. Well, what do we do?"

"I checked with Thaddeus today," Alex admitted from where his pile of vegetables grew on the countertop. "And it looks like he's made things about as fail-safe as he can. He had alarms built in for unusual spending of any kind, and a good control schedule for inventory. He even changes the codes to get into the inventory and accounting programs once a week."

Sarah had never had a man in her kitchen before. Even standing with her back to Alex she could sense him there, like a wall of energy behind her, a sharp new scent in the house, an aura of strength. Stirring in the cream, she fought another smile and lost. She should be thinking about her company, and all she could focus on was the surprise of companionship, the seduction of electricity. He was distracting her, deterring her, and she was finding it more and more difficult to care.

"Is there anybody you suspect?" he asked.

Sarah almost didn't hear him. She was crumbling bacon and eyeing how many pine nuts she wanted to use, finding it difficult to focus on anything even so simple with her new discovery filling her. She was scooping up the nuts when his words sank in.

"Suspect?" she demanded, whirling around to find him facing her. "I don't suspect anybody."

Alex frowned at the nuts clustered in her palm. "I thought you were going to get me a bowl."

"Oh," she breathed, wiping hair out of her eyes and looking vaguely around. "Okay." Sarah bent to open drawers as she continued. "I thought *you'd* figure that out anyway. Can't you find problems with an audit?"

"Not necessarily without some kind of nudge in the right direction," he answered from above her, the knife making regular thunk-thunk noises on the counter. "It's rare for accountants to come across deliberate problems on a regular audit."

"But Ellis said you've ferreted out three, uh, embezzlers in the past year." Her voice had a little echo to it that made her want to chuckle. Alex sounded so far away, almost like a dream. A fantasy.

"Two of them were fingered by their co-workers. Another walked up to me the first day of a requested audit and turned himself in. Said he knew all along that we'd come for him. Embezzling is embarrassingly easy to do, I'm afraid."

Embezzling. Sarah hated that word. She hoped she'd never have to use it again. It implied distrust, deceit, maliciousness. The idea that somebody in her company could be intentionally doing that physically hurt Sarah. For a moment she paused, crouched on her haunches before the dim recesses of her cabinet, bothered by the dark.

"When did you first begin to suspect something?" Alex was asking, still chopping. "Was there a change in income or outflow recently?"

"No," she said, his question spurring her to continue rooting through her pots and pans. She was going to need the colander for her pasta. Pulling it out, Sarah stood to put it in the sink. "There wasn't anything different. That's the puzzling part. We're beginning to test new markets again, but we do that every so often so we don't get stale."

"New markets?"

The sauce. She'd almost forgotten to add the nuts . . . the nuts. What had she done with the nuts? "Sure," she answered, looking over the countertops for the nuts she'd set down somewhere. "We're looking at toys and computer animation systems for video."

Alex seemed to be watching her rather intensely as she ducked for a quick peek back along the area she'd just searched, to make sure she hadn't dropped the nuts there.

"Toys?" he asked. "Isn't that kind of a stretch?"

"No. We're thinking of designing something along the stuffed animal variety. We're creating new . . . Alex?"

"Yes?"

Turning on him finally, Sarah took a wave at her hair and frowned. "You didn't see where I put the nuts, did you?"

Alex never said a word. He simply walked over and slid open the cutlery drawer. There, nestled in an untidy little stack just shy of the cleaver were her pine nuts. Shaking her head, Sarah shot Alex a grateful smile and scooped them up.

"Thanks." Dropping them onto the counter, she drained the pasta into the colander. "Remind me to show you the Snarkalump we've just put together. She's a real charmer."

Pine nuts, a dash of nutmeg and the Romano. Sarah tasted the concoction and closed her eyes in contemplation. Once again her senses were unaccountably torn between the task at hand and the insistent tug of Alex's presence. It was as if he'd changed the color, even the texture, of the room. It was less placid, less pale—almost as if Sarah had decorated it to focus on the sharp accent Alex provided.

There was so much more to him than that accountant's temperament and athlete's body. He had a core that she could feel when she closed her eyes, pulsing away beneath his deceptive exterior. A heat, a fine, strong passion that needed release.

Sarah smiled secretly, her eyes closed, her tongue still preoccupied with the smoky taste of her sauce, her body singing in a way it hadn't in her life. And for a moment she did no more than savor the delicious sensations in her kitchen.

"Sarah?"

His voice sounded so puzzled. Sarah opened her eyes to see the bemused expression on his face. It made her smile all the more, provoking an urge to settle her hand against the hard line of his jaw. She didn't though. "What, Alex?"

"What about the bowl?" he asked.

"Oh," she said, looking around. "Did you need a bowl?"

Chapter 4

Sarah didn't get much work done the next morning. When she closed herself in her office with Vivaldi and her tea, instead of dreaming up colors and shapes, all she could produce were eyes. Honey-brown eyes, the color of sunshine on brandy. Warm, patient, kind eyes that tended to frown when puzzled. And they'd frowned a lot the evening before.

They'd frowned when Sarah had kept forgetting to find the bowl for his salad, which she'd finally served from a pot, and then again when Sarah kept losing her ingredients and finding them in unlikely places. Alex had frowned when he'd heard about the commune and then again when he'd discovered her extensive collection of classical and Zydeco music.

Sarah liked Alex's frowns. A small gathering of lines between his eyebrows, they spoke volumes in polite silence. He wasn't rude about Sarah's eccentricities, and he didn't make fun of her like some people did. He simply seemed to be trying to comprehend her, like a physicist coming to grips with the theory of chaos. Those frowns meant that at least he was trying. At least he was still intrigued enough to ask questions and be surprised by the answers.

"If that's a premonition you're having, I hope I'm included."

Startled, Sarah looked up to find Connie leaning against the open door. "Oh, hi. I was just thinking."

"Uh-huh." Her friend sauntered in and plopped into the chair across from the desk, crossing her legs ankle to knee in a manner more reminiscent of school than business. "If that's thinking, I'd like to know what fantasizing looks like."

Sarah came very close to blushing. Instead she finally took her first sip of tea. It helped her escape her friend's sharp scrutiny.

Settling more deeply into the chair, Connie grinned. "I'm glad you finally remembered to hang your phone back up last night. I was close to calling out Phoenix's finest again, especially with all the doom and gloom you've been preaching lately."

Sarah winced. The incident had provoked another frown. "That would have been the last thing Alex needed. Especially since he was the one who found the phone."

Her statement was met with an arched eyebrow. "He was?"

Sarah nodded sheepishly. "He sat on it. I told him it wasn't a big deal."

Connie grinned like a pirate. "I *should* have called the police. Can you imagine what he would have said when they'd shown up?"

Sarah grimaced with the thought. "Thanks, Connie. You're a big help."

Connie considered Sarah a moment, her grin fading to bemusement, her head tilting to the side, her brown eyes concerned. Sarah knew what was coming even before Connie did. Still, she let her speak her piece.

"You're getting a little starry-eyed for only twenty-four hours, aren't you?"

"It's that thrill of danger," she retorted casually, her eyes on her teacup, somehow not even wanting Connie this close yet. Connie was her dearest friend, her family during those years when she'd had none, but Connie was also her common sense. Sarah was still savoring the newness of Alex Thorne in her life. She didn't want Connie to list the reasons why she shouldn't.

Danger. Alex. Thirsty. Drink.

Now what made her think of that?

"I'm enjoying myself," Sarah said, trying to ignore the bees of association that buzzed in her brain. "It's been a long time since I've done that."

Connie smiled. "Since Billy Peterson, junior year. Yeah, I know. Well, just remember what old Aunt Connie says. Look before you leap. Especially where men are concerned."

"How's the computer-animation system looking?" Sarah asked in a deliberate effort to change the subject.

Connie paused before answering, just to let Sarah know she wouldn't let her off the hook. "Like a dream. Thaddeus is composing psalms to it. We should have everybody checked out on it within a month . . . everybody except you, that is."

Sarah shook her head. "You know better," she said. "I get a headache just hearing you and Thaddeus talking about it. All I'd have to do is take it out for a spin once and I'd crash the whole system like a Formula One in the far corner at Indy. And then where would our investment be?"

"I've taken the precaution of insuring it against anything," Connie reminded her. "Especially you."

"For a nominal fee, I'm sure."

Connie rolled her eyes. "Nothing is nominal with that bunch. I know the process is revolutionary, but you'd think we're renting out the Stealth Bomber for a weekend jaunt."

Thirsty. Liquid.

"How does Peter feel about losing out our account to Datasys?"

Connie's shrug was offhand. "He tries not to let it get in the way of a good game of golf. Besides, he's dating me, not Thaddeus."

"When you guys decide to progress past sports and megabytes," Sarah said, "let me know. I'd love to have him over."

Connie offered a dry grimace. "And have you scare him off by telling him he's destined to bear my children? Not yet, thanks. Give the man a chance to get used to me, first."

Liquid. Thirsty. Drink.

Sarah was on her feet. "Where is he?"

Connie looked around. "Who?"

But Sarah was already headed for the door. "Randolph doesn't like him. I guess he didn't get him any tea."

With a reluctant sigh, Connie stood and followed. "Just once I'd like to be able to follow a conversation with you to its logical conclusion."

"There is no logical conclusion," Sarah goaded over her shoulder. "Didn't you ever read Samuel Beckett?"

Connie shook her head.

Alex couldn't keep his mind on business. He wanted to blame it on the heat. Between his size and his metabolism, he'd never been able to comfortably tolerate any climate too familiar with the words "arid" and "hot." By the time he'd left the hotel that morning, the temperature had already been hovering in the nineties.

He could look out the window and see the clean, dry colors of the desert harsh against the white of the computer-room walls. It made him want to sweat, even in the climate control.

It made him think, surprisingly enough, of how cool the white had been in Sarah's house.

What an experience that had been, like a fast slide down the rabbit hole. He'd spent the entire evening struggling to keep up with her conversation and trying to justify the waterfall of words and ideas that bounced around the room like bright, fragile bubbles with the soft, quiet interior of her home.

Sarah had said that she'd decorated it for the child in her. She'd always yearned for the romance of an English country house, where flower gardens filled the air with scent and added color for the eye. Where the furnishings had been handed down for generations in the same family. The only thing that had been handed down in Sarah's family had been a recipe for zucchini bread, which she couldn't follow anyway.

She was president of one of the fastest growing companies in the Sunbelt, and she couldn't even follow the directions in that recipe. Sarah said she made all her meals up as she went along, sometimes trying to recreate dishes she'd tasted in restaurants and sometimes setting out on her own. If last night was any indication, the process was as much a surprise as the outcome. By the time they'd sat down to dinner, her kitchen had looked like an explosion at Spago's, but Alex had to admit that he'd rarely had such delicious food.

Then there was Sarah's garden. Alex looked out the window to see the silent wind dance through the wan trees. He ignored the computer readout in his hand thinking instead of the flowers so diligently planted and tended in Sarah's backyard: impatiens and oleander and begonias and geraniums, and any number of plants he didn't even recognize in a riot of color in the pallid landscape of summer. Quiet testaments to perseverance and inspiration from a woman who couldn't otherwise keep the same thought in her head for more than seventeen seconds.

He saw again the dreamy, guileless sensuality on her face as she'd stood before him in the kitchen with her eyes closed, smiling, as if savoring something delicious, as if hearing music he couldn't. He'd come unforgivably close to pulling her into his arms and forgetting the pasta and the premonition and the company.

''Here it is, Alex.''

Alex looked up to see Thaddeus ripping another stack of paper from the printer. His hair seemed a little wilted this morning, and he was dressed all in black, like some circuit-riding preacher. Alex wondered how he could stand the clothes in this heat.

"Are you sure you want to hit the warehouse already?" Thaddeus was saying, his attention still on the printout he was gathering.

Hauling his briefcase onto the table and snapping it open, Alex nodded. "I might as well. It'll give Hector a chance to get his figures ready for me."

Thaddeus looked up. "Ready? What do you mean? We all just went through that stuff."

Alex shrugged. "He's trying to pull together this month's figures, too. Whatever Sarah thinks is going on may be new."

At Alex's words, Thaddeus sketched a quick sign with his fingers that looked as if he were warding off the evil eye. Alex allowed an eyebrow to slide north.

"I don't know that many superstitious computer jocks."

Thaddeus looked a little more uncomfortable as he handed over his paperwork. "Don't tell Sarah. I don't think she'd understand."

Alex shut the sheets into his briefcase and then turned to lean against the desk. "Voodoo only works on people who believe in it."

Thaddeus assumed a defensive position, his arms crossed tightly against his chest, his weight on one leg, his eyes furtively checking out his assistants where they bent over their keyboards on the other side of the room. Ever since Alex had proven that he was not only computer-literate but sincerely impressed with Thaddeus's own work with the company system, Thaddeus had warmed considerably. He now gave every impression of a man about to give sage advice to the newcomer.

"I'm not some ignorant native squatting by a camp fire," he objected, leaning close to Alex. "I'm one of the best hackers in the country. I'm telling you, man, by the time I was sixteen I could break into any defense department computer and rearrange firing codes if I wanted. I tapped into NORAD once, like in the movie. Only I just left a message and got out. They never caught me." Now he tapped his forehead, his message intense. "Because I'm the best, y'know? The smartest."

He was making Alex feel old. "And?"

Thaddeus leaned in closer, and Alex thought of every vampire movie he'd ever seen. "And, there isn't anything in any research computer I've ever tapped that explains Miss ESP Delaney. Nothing that tracks like logic. But I've seen it anyway. I've seen her get those little spells and go all white, and then something happened. I'm telling you, it's downright spooky."

"No," Alex disagreed with an easy smile, trying to dispel the young man's images. "The idea of your getting into the defense department computers is spooky. Sarah is just . . . different."

Thaddeus flashed him a sharp grin. "So was Dracula. I'm just telling you, I'm a lot more comfortable with facts and figures. Give me a good binary system and I'm like a pig in slop. This stuff—" shaking his head, he let his eyes roll "—it's weird, man. Too weird."

Alex did he best to contain his grin. "If you're so uncomfortable, why stay?"

It was Thaddeus's turn to grin, the wide, brash grin that said that he owned the world. "Opportunity, man. Opportunity."

"See? He *didn't* get his tea."

By now Alex didn't even flinch. Sarah breezed in from the hallway, her feet bare and her white gauze dress drifting around her like a vapor. She had yards of beads around her neck and wore an embroidered vest of some kind. Earrings that sounded like tiny bells tinkled in her ears. Alex couldn't help but smile at the picture.

Right on her heels was Connie, her classy Yves Saint-Laurent suit a perfect counterpoint to Sarah's gypsy charm.

"Good morning," Alex greeted them both.

Sarah pushed back her flying hair and shot Alex a smile. "Randolph forgot you this morning, didn't he?"

Alex fought the urge to look around.

"Sarah's been preoccupied with whether you got something to drink this morning," Connie explained, shifting her own weight in betrayal of her impatience.

Alex shrugged. Beside him, Thaddeus shot him a look that translated into *See what I mean?* Thaddeus was expecting another display of extrasensory sparks, Alex imagined.

"No, I'm fine," he said. "I was just headed out."

Connie motioned to his briefcase. "Kim said you were headed over to the warehouse. Did you get somebody to drive you?"

Alex shook his head and lifted the briefcase as a signal of intent. He didn't want to be deterred by another surprise luncheon date. "No. I got directions. I called over and they're expecting me."

Connie nodded. Sarah shook her head, her eyes unfocused again, as if listening.

"You sure you're not thirsty, Alex?"

Alex tried a smile. "No, thanks, Sarah. I'm fine."

She kept listening, but couldn't seem to come up with the right message. "Liquid," she murmured, rubbing two fingers against her temple. Giving her head a final shake, she flashed Alex a smile. "Oh, well. You're going to be back later?"

"Probably the end of the day."

She nodded. "We'll most likely be here. Make sure you check in."

Preoccupied with the sight of Sarah standing there barefoot and exotic, her eyes wide and unfocused and alluring, Alex swung past her before he could be tempted to stay.

"See?" Connie was saying. "You can be wrong. That means that some of the other stuff might be off, too."

Sarah couldn't seem to take her eyes away from the empty doorway. She heard the swish of the elevator doors and then the whisper as it whirred into its two-story descent from the computer area to the lobby. And she listened to the voice that had nudged her into wondering about Alex's hydration.

Liquid. Liquid.

It was still there, still strong.

"We have to get back up to your office, hon," Connie said, walking over to open the glass door. "I saw Mr. Willoughby waiting out with Kim when we flew down here. He's going to want to talk West Coast distribution."

"Fluid!" Sarah cried, swinging on Connie. "Not liquid, fluid. Oh, God, Connie!"

She ran for the stairs. Out of force of habit, Connie followed right along, her heels clacking on the cement as they swept into the stairwell.

"Sarah," she panted, trying to keep up. "What fluid?"

Sarah didn't even hear her. She was obsessed with the picture of Alex walking off the elevator and down the white-stucco-and-red-tile hallway, purposeful, unaware, unknowing. Opening the door out onto the sunlight. Pausing to face the heat, maybe looking up into the washed-out blue sky of the summer afternoon. Thinking of how hot the car would be when he slid inside.

Sarah ran faster, the skirt of her dress skimming her knees and whirling around behind her.

Hector was walking toward the elevators as Sarah banged out into the lobby. His eyes widening silently, he sidestepped her and stood to watch. A couple of designers who had been heading in the front door scattered before her. Sarah didn't even notice. She was frantically searching the parking lot for Alex.

The desert heat seared her as she stepped out into the sun. The asphalt burned her feet. She saw the metallic-blue rental car and ran for it.

"Alex!"

He was about to slide into the driver's seat. When he heard her calling his name, he came to an uncertain halt, his hand still on the door, one foot poised in the car.

"Sarah?"

"Alex, get out of the car."

"What?"

Connie pulled up even with Sarah and stopped her. "Get back off the asphalt, Sarah. Come on."

"The car, Alex," she insisted, stopping scant feet away, close enough to see the beads of perspiration on his face. "Please, I need to talk to you."

"Sarah," he objected, finally noticing her attire. "Your feet. You're going to burn yourself." He began to edge away from the car.

"Then come over to the grass."

"Alex, please just come talk to her," Connie asked, doing her best to drag Sarah off the shimmering parking lot.

With a half shrug, Alex shut the door and followed them.

"What kind of fluid does a car have?" Sarah asked the minute the three of them had reached the grass.

Alex frowned at her. "Fluid?"

She was scanning the car, trying to see, trying to envision something she didn't understand. "I'm not mechanical. Are you?"

For a moment his gaze followed hers. "Yeah, I guess."

She nodded distractedly and turned back to face the confusion in his soft amber eyes. "What kind of fluid is there in a car?"

Still trying to understand, Alex shrugged. "Brake fluid, power-steering fluid, water for the radiator. Window-washing fluid."

The light broke. "Brake fluid." She sighed with relief. "That's it."

Alex was staring at her. "What's 'it'?"

The nausea hit then, the waves of rejection that always accompanied the revelation, as if her body had to literally purge the warning. Sarah looked away from Alex, down to the spiky green of the grass. She concentrated on simple senses, willing away the revulsion, the exquisite pain of the near miss. She battled the shimmer of his face, the sense of balancing on a terrifying edge that could have wiped him away like a strong wind.

Slowly the real world reasserted itself. Sarah heard the sibilance of the sprinklers on the far side of the complex, the drone of traffic, the chatter of birds. The world rushed back into her tunnel and filled it, and the weight of it tilted her. She took great, unsteady breaths.

"I almost . . . missed you," she whispered, dread coursing through her, closing her eyes and draining the blood from her face.

"Sarah? Sarah, what's wrong?"

She felt his hands on her, his arm encircling her and holding her up. She heard Connie move forward out of long-honed instinct and then pause, uncertain.

"You think somebody tampered with his brakes?" her friend asked incredulously.

Sarah leaned into Alex. His chest was so solid. So substantial. Still assailed by the suspicion that she was perilously close to slipping from the edge of the world, Sarah placed her hands against him, settled her head against the hard planes of him and rested.

"I think somebody tampered with his brakes," she answered. "I bet if you looked, there's a puddle underneath the car."

She felt the disbelief stiffen him, imagined the puzzled frown creasing his forehead and almost managed a smile.

"Are you okay, hon?" Connie asked, stepping tentatively closer.

Sarah realized with a start that for the first time in ten years, somebody other than Connie had pulled her back from the edge, Someone other than Connie had retrieved the harsh edge of reality and braced Sarah against it. It should have felt more uncomfortable, more unsuspected. Yet Sarah had never felt so protected in her life.

"I'm fine, Connie," she said, and lifted her head away from the heady scent of Alex's warmth. "I'm just hot."

"Then let's get inside," her friend insisted, taking over from Alex. Still stiff with uncertainty, he gave Sarah up and followed as Connie led them back into the building.

"Do you want me to call the police?" she asked.

"I don't know," Sarah answered. Connie held open the front door, and the cool air washed over them. Sarah gulped in lungfuls of it to help offset the sweaty trembling.

"Sarah."

Alex had made it through the door and then stopped. Sarah and Connie turned back to him.

"I'll be up in a minute," he said. "I want to check this out."

Sarah's head shot up and her heart faltered. "Don't do anything stupid, Alex. Leave the car alone."

"I'm not going to drive it," he assured her, his hand returning to her arm. "I'm going to check the brake lines."

"We'll be up in the office," Connie informed him. When he nodded, Connie led Sarah into the building.

Randolph was waiting with tea. He dispatched one of the salespeople to handle the impatient Mr. Willoughby and kept a personal eye on Alex out in the parking lot. When Alex returned with the just-arrived Phoenix police in tow, Randolph showed them all in.

"Oh, Miss Delaney," the officer, Sgt. Valdez, greeted her with a smile. "Good morning."

By now back to business, Sarah abandoned here work and stood up in a friendly manner. Immediately she grimaced. For some reason the carpet was brutal against her feet.

Connie saw her look down at her feet and shook her head. "I keep telling you to leave your shoes on," she said, then betrayed herself with a sudden sheepish expression. "God, I sound like my mother."

"Are your feet okay?" Alex asked.

"Just a little tender," Sarah admitted, motioning everybody to chairs before reclaiming hers. She remembered now. The parking lot. She could feel a few blisters forming on the more tender skin, but it wouldn't do any good to confess. Not only Connie, but Alex, too, would probably end up chiding her. Curling her feet under her, she turned instead to find Randolph waiting in the periphery.

"How about iced tea this time, Randolph?"

Alex certainly looked as though he could use it. He'd probably be happier with a beer, as hot and bedraggled as he looked. There was a smear of grease on his once-crisp white shirt, and his hair was shoved back as if he'd been spiking his hands through it.

"Was I right?" she asked quietly.

Settling into the chair across from her, he nodded. "I wouldn't have even noticed the puddle."

"Mr. Thorne says that you think somebody's trying to threaten him," Sgt. Valdez suggested diffidently. He'd remained on his feet, but Sarah knew better than to insist on his comfort. She was well acquainted with the officer. A short, burly man with ruddy complexion and coal-black hair, he stood at attention, notebook in hand. Sarah also knew just how much she could admit to the officer. He was definitely of the American school of pragmatism. See it, feel it, believe it.

Sarah couldn't fault him. There were things she didn't want to believe until she saw them, either.

"I don't know if it's connected," she demurred, her gaze drifting toward where her fingers tested the cotton of her dress. "Mr. Thorne is here conducting an audit for the company, yes. When he left today for the warehouse, I saw a puddle under the car and . . . well, suspected that it was more than an oil leak."

To her left Alex stiffened just a little, but Connie sat back in perfect ease on the other side, her eyes comfortably on the police.

"Why do you say that?" Valdez asked.

"I'm . . . mechanical," Sarah lied baldly.

Even Connie had trouble with that one. So, unfortunately, did the officer. "Uh, Miss Delaney . . . no offense . . ."

"Mechanical," Connie broke in with a tight smile. "Not electronic. Sarah noticed the puddle when we went out to, uh, remind Mr. Thorne about something. He's probably more used to this kind of thing than we are, though. Maybe he made somebody nervous by showing up for an audit."

"Really," the officer murmured, chocolate eyes suddenly sharp as he assessed the people present. "You think something illegal's going on?"

Again Sarah smiled and hoped that the sick dread didn't show in her eyes. Again Connie did the answering.

"I certainly hope not. Mr. Thorne is helping us make sure."

Heaving a sigh of frustration, the policeman shut his book. "No likely suspects?"

Connie shook her head. "None."

The policeman looked as though he were all too familiar with the scenario. Few companies who caught embezzlers prosecuted them. It was bad for public relations. Valdez's expression betrayed his belief that this was already one of those cases. "Not much to go on, I'm afraid. The brake line could have been cut, but it's a hard one to prove. No injuries, no suspects, no certain motive . . . best I can do right now is take all the information and tell you to be careful."

"And call if somebody dies," Alex said with a wry grin, evidently equally as familiar as the policeman with the situation.

Valdez shot him a returning grin. "I'd settle for anything concrete. Just to be sure, I'll check to see if anybody saw anything suspicious out in the parking lot."

Randolph returned with the iced tea just as Valdez was leaving. Randolph went ahead and passed three glasses around and then confiscated the fourth for himself before heading out to his desk.

"Mechanical?" Alex demanded from where he leaned against Sarah's desk.

Back in her chair, Sarah giggled, taking a long sip of the chilled liquid to quench the parch in her throat. "It seemed the easiest way to explain things. Officer Valdez doesn't believe in hocus-pocus."

"He did seem to recognize you."

Crossing her legs and settling more deeply into her chair, Connie snorted.

Sarah shot her friend a delighted look. "My house is also on Officer Valdez's beat," she explained to Alex. "I have some trouble remembering how to work my house alarm system."

Alex raised a hand. "Say no more."

There it was, that frown again, creasing his forehead, betraying his bemusement. But this time it was tempered by something more. Sarah saw the humor there for the first time, the resignation. And something else. Something she wasn't ready to label.

"Are you sure your feet are all right?" he asked.

Why was Sarah convinced there was so much more he wanted to say? She met his gaze with her own, basking in the honeyed depths of concern, feeding from the sharpening emotions. His eyes seemed to soften for a moment, as if he could tangibly touch her across the room and soothe whatever it was that he saw hurting.

It unnerved her. She was used to the concern of her friends. She wasn't used to the singular focus of this man.

She wasn't used to wanting to return her own attention solely to him.

But she did. Which was why she had to make the decision now and stick by it.

"My feet are fine," she said, tucking them even closer. "And you're going back to Denver."

Chapter 5

Alex decided that he must have ESP, too, because he knew exactly what Sarah was going to say before she said it. Much to her dismay, it made him smile.

"I thought we'd already settled that," he said, rolling his glass in his hands enough to make the ice clink against the sides.

"No," Sarah disagreed, leaning forward for what she must have known would be a fight. "You just ignored me the last time."

Settling further back against the desk and crossing his ankles, Alex nodded. "Well, that's probably what I'll do this time, too."

First Sarah glared at him. Then she glared at Connie, who was still comfortably ensconced in her chair.

Connie just shrugged.

"He was your idea in the first place."

"But what if I don't know the next time?" Sarah asked Connie, because, Alex realized, she always tested her reality against her friend's pragmatism. "What if something happens to him?"

"He's standing right here," Alex reminded her gently.

Starting at his intrusion, Sarah turned to him. Alex was struck by the suffering in her cornflower-blue eyes. If he hadn't known better, he would have sworn that he'd really driven off in that car and run into a brick wall.

What bothered him was that, instead of using his common sense, which had always been his strong suit, he caved in to emotion.

The sight of Sarah hurting from just the supposition of his injury infused him with the most irrational urge to protect her. To soothe away the tight set to her eyes.

She'd known him for all of twenty-four hours, and yet she took responsibility for him. Alex decided that her shoulders were too fragile for that kind of burden.

Pushing away from the desk, Alex strolled over to seat himself directly in front of Sarah. "And if I go?" he asked, setting his tea aside. "What do you do then?"

"I don't know," she retorted instinctively, backing away a little. "I don't care. It isn't worth your life."

"So you're going to let whoever it is get away with it simply because they tried to scare me off?"

Her eyes swelled with unshed tears. "Yes!"

Leaning forward, Alex excluded everything but Sarah in his gaze. "No. I'm not leaving, Sarah. You might as well get used to it."

She was picking at her dress again as if she couldn't keep her hands still, the agitation shimmering from her. "I'd never be able to live with myself," she whispered, begging.

"Neither," he said quietly, taking her hand to still it, "would I." Then he smiled, trying his best to lighten her load. "I'd be kicked out of the benevolent order of accountants if I caved in to one half-baked attempt to scare me."

"Half-baked?" she retorted in outrage, stiffening in his grasp. "If I hadn't guessed—"

Alex held on, thinking how her hand felt like a frightened bird in his, struggling for flight.

"Sarah, think about that for a minute," he suggested. "From what I gather, you've impressed most of your staff with your magical powers. I can't imagine whoever did it wouldn't consider the fact that you might at least anticipate this, if not finger him."

"You don't understand, Alex," she argued, now passive in his grip as she fought to challenge his gaze. The two of them were insulated by their concern, each for the other. A wall of energy surrounded them, throbbed between them. Their eyes met only the other's, intense, certain, distressed. "What I have isn't a constant. I can't always tune in and see. My abilities are like...like lightning striking. Sudden, without warning or reason. I can't control it any more than I can control the weather. I can't count on it even being right. And everybody in the company knows that."

She leaned forward, closing the space, intent and anguished. "Alex, if I were so impressive, I would have known the minute I met you that you were heading for my office. I'd have known what it was that's wrong with the company. I would have known who sabotaged your car, for heaven's sake."

Alex didn't know how to reassure her. He only knew that he had no choice, hadn't since she'd first leveled those pleading eyes on him. He had to see this through.

"That's okay," he said in his best tone of nonchalance. "We're going to need more for a conviction anyway. As far as I've heard, premonitions still aren't categorized as physical evidence."

Sarah straightened, furious at his levity. Alex refused to let go of her hands. "People do these things without ESP all the time," he assured her gently, offering simple support when logic wouldn't suffice. "We'll just have to go back to doing it the traditional way."

"Which means what?" Connie asked.

Alex was almost surprised to hear her voice. He'd been so engrossed in comforting Sarah that he'd completely forgotten about Connie sitting alongside him. Giving Sarah's hand a final squeeze before letting it go, he straightened and faced the pragmatic eyes of Sarah's partner. "I need a ride to the warehouse."

From that moment on, Alex looked on all the employees of Sunset Design in a different light. One of them had sent him a very personal message, and it would be in his best interest to find the sender before he or she found him again.

There were a thousand ways to embezzle from a company. Padding inventory numbers, writing checks to phantom companies, including the dead and long-gone on payrolls. Simple computer gymnastics.

Alex had once seen the senior computer programmer in an international bank walk out with millions of dollars by skimming a penny from each of the bank's accounts. He'd seen a payroll clerk pocket checks of departed employees that same clerk had conveniently left on the company books. Since the line workers were mostly illiterate, the checks had all been made out to "Bearer."

First Alex checked the warehouse, which took two days. The warehouse crew were brash and hostile and went out of their way to make Alex's life difficult, but only because they were insulted. Not because they were crooks. From what he could see, the inventory matched.

Next on the agenda was a visit with Hector in the accounting department to go over the company's fiscal policies.

Controls were in place that should have prevented the easiest kind of embezzlement. All checks had to be countersigned by Connie, and a check could not be endorsed by the person requesting it. One person in accounts receivable took in the money, and Jill recorded and balanced it. From what Jill said, Hector and Ellis had set up most of the safeguards in the company, and they'd done a good job.

Everything looked squeaky clean, just as Sarah had said. But somebody had tried to make him a traffic statistic.

Alex could tell that Thaddeus had decided to like him. He could also tell that Hector wasn't as sure. He certainly had the attitude down right. As smooth as a marble floor, Hector spoke as if he'd been studying up on the book of yuppyisms. He really wanted the American dream, and Sunset Designs was his avenue.

Hector was working his way through an MBA with a minor in computer science and loved to wax eloquently about how he would bring the company into the twenty-first century. It seemed to be the one level on which he could communicate with Thaddeus.

But beneath all that gloss was a very careful, very suspicious man. Alex was sure Hector saw him as a real threat, since anybody from Hector's department was prime suspect in playing loose with company change. And that, in turn, would reflect on Hector's managerial abilities.

Alex was amazed when Hector invited him out to lunch. Nonetheless, he went. Some of his most interesting information had been garnered over burgers and beer.

"Nice car," Alex said. He supposed he could have been more surprised.

In the process of fitting key to lock, Hector flashed a smug smile. "Leather interior, Blaupunkt stereo, cellular phone. My present to myself."

The locks snicked and Alex opened the door. New-car smell wafted out into the desert air, making Alex wonder if Hector had a can of spray with the scent for when it got older. A shiny red BMW 735i. No real imagination, he thought as he settled into the seat. A big layout, though, right down to the car phone and CD player. And Hector liked his Armani suits and Gucci loafers.

"You really seem to be doing well here," Alex said.

"And I'll do better," Hector agreed, slipping the key into the ignition. "Sarah's a rising star."

"Sarah?" Alex asked. "Not Sunset?"

"Sure, both. I already have headhunters sniffing at me, even before they know me. It's Sunset. The company of the century, and all guided by a woman who can't even boot up a computer. Like the man says, it's a great country."

Alex maintained a passive attitude. "It almost sounds like Sarah's success is a fluke."

"No way," Hector disagreed, turning the car into traffic. "You're talking about a woman with six patents. She's a certifiable genius. She could just use a little baby-sitting."

Alex's attention was caught all over again.

"Patents?"

"Sure, didn't you know? She invented the Great Perpetual Motion Machine."

That took Alex's attention away from Armani suits and stereos. "The what?"

Surprised, Hector looked over. "Haven't you ever heard of it?"

"Sure," Alex admitted. "That damn thing drove me nuts in the malls last Christmas. Sarah invented it? She doesn't seem the type."

"That's the great thing about Sarah. You never know where she's heading next. She's invented a safer child car seat, a trauma table for hospitals and a new cloth-dying process. And now she's getting into computer animation? All I have to say is that the opportunity for personal growth is maximized. If you know what I mean."

Sunset Designs was getting more and more intriguing.

It had been a long day. Mr. Willoughby had been back for a finalized proposal on West Coast distributorship, and several ad agencies had made tentative forays into securing the services of the fledgling computer-animation department. A new linen account had come in, and Midcentral Airlines wanted something flashier on their logo—by tomorrow, and some time after lunch Sarah had lost her earrings. She wondered whether she was going to need glasses. She had a splitting headache.

Of course, there was also the matter of the sleep she hadn't been getting the past few nights.

She'd been lying awake in the dark, listening to the birds, the highway, the bugs out in her garden chirruping in tidal chorus. Listening for the next warning.

It hadn't come. The company had gone on as if nothing had happened. Alex had gotten himself dusty and crabby out at the warehouse and returned to closet himself in the accounting department without anything to report. Connie had provided Sarah with pragmatic patience and Randolph had served tea and schedule updates.

Sarah, alone in her office and then alone at home, had brooded. It was already wrong. She had too big a stake in all of this to be objective. How could she expect the sight to be clear? She strained for revelation when revelation only came uninvited. She ached for prescience as the future lay dark and silent.

Every time Sarah tried to focus on a direction, her attention skittered away, as if it had struck slick ice. Her vision shattered, dissipated, waned. Frustration mounted and opportunity evaded her.

Sarah wasn't sure what time it was. She'd holed herself back up after the last meeting to beat out a new airline logo and had somehow produced the new sheet-and-towel design instead. She liked it, too, a kind of swirling print in the pale Santa Fe blues and brick-red that reminded her of the sunsets out in the mountains. It was too bad she wouldn't have a place to put it in her own house, where flowers bloomed on her linen.

But that didn't resolve the Midcentral issue. And it didn't do anything about her headache. Finally giving in to a yawn and a stretch, Sarah slid the new design away and retreated to her couch and her afghan. Sometimes getting a quick nap released the inspiration.

Alex. She saw him the minute she closed her eyes. She heard his voice easing her fears as surely as his hands had supported her.

Strong hands. Callused hands. Gentle hands. Football players should have hands like hams and grips like vises. They should be as subtle as steamrollers and blessed with the brainpower of armadillos.

Accountants should be small and mousy and as dull as television golf.

Yet Alex was none of these things. He had eyes that expressed more emotions than most men possessed. He had arms that cushioned instead of imprisoned. He had a sly humor that defused tension and an anger that smoldered rather than exploded.

He had a history that tantalized beneath his civilized exterior, and he had a primal energy that Sarah instinctively recognized.

She should have been thinking of airplanes. Instead she conjured up wide shoulders, slim hips, long, powerful legs. She tormented herself with what she'd known and what she could only anticipate.

What kind of body lay beneath his tailored suits? What would it feel like beneath her fingers? Beneath her lips?

No wonder she couldn't keep her predictions in line. She couldn't keep her hormones under control, either. Just envisioning herself in Alex's arms sent her blood pressure climbing. Remembering the one kiss they'd shared stoked the fires even higher. If she ever got around to really fantasizing about what lovemaking with Alex Thorne would be like, she'd land on the floor with a stroke.

The creak of the office door broke in on her musings. Sarah was surprised to realize how it irritated her.

"I hope it's important, Connie," she warned without moving. "I don't want to interrupt a good fantasy for nothing."

"I hope it's about me."

Sarah wasn't sure about the stroke, but she did land on the floor. Pushing her hair out of her eyes, she looked up to find Alex standing inside her office. The light from the anteroom haloed him, handsomely outlining the very attributes Sarah had been considering in such detail.

No, no stroke. She could see just fine. And her imagination was working even better.

"All right," she challenged, hands on hips, legs still splayed beneath her, head up. "I might as well ask."

Leaning by one hand against the door frame, Alex tilted his head, a smile nudging the corners of his mouth. "Go right ahead."

"Is it hairy or not?"

It obviously wasn't what he expected. For a minute all he could seem to do was stare at her. "Uh, Sarah—"

"Your chest," she clarified with a sneaky smile of her own. "Do you have hair on your chest?"

He was staring again. "You *were* fantasizing about me?"

She giggled. "Well, I don't fantasize about Connie, and Randolph's gay. And I'm afraid I don't fancy juvenile computer wizards. Just the conversation would kill me. So..."

"Yes."

"Good. There are some things a woman needs to know."

"Are you having another premonition?"

"I don't know," she admitted, her eyes bright and her chest suddenly tight. Settling herself more comfortably on the floor, Sarah flashed him her best smile. "But I'm certainly willing to try."

She should have felt at a disadvantage, sprawled at his feet like she was. Instead she felt...hungry. She couldn't keep her eyes off the clean cut of his slacks, the tight expanse of those shoulders of his beneath his shirt, the solid expanse of forearm exposed by rolled-up sleeves.

"Only if it has nothing to do with accounts receivable," he warned.

Sarah looked up to find his eyes in the shadows. It didn't matter. She could feel their heat, stirring chills in her, raising goose bumps.

"Do you know what time it is?" he asked, stepping on in.

Sarah took a look around. Out the window, Phoenix blinked fitfully beneath the trees and the stars struggled against the moon.

"I don't know," she admitted. "I lay down for a minute—" Returning her attention to Alex, she had to tilt her head back even further to find him. "Why don't you sit down?"

He took in her position. "On the floor?"

Sarah shrugged. "Why not?"

"I think I'd be more comfortable on the couch."

She grimaced at him. "Not into alternate experience, are you?"

Grinning, he approached and held out a hand. "*You're* the hippie," he reminded her. "I'm just an accountant."

For a moment Sarah couldn't move. Alex stood right over her, blocking out almost all the light, so that he seemed more a wraith than a man, a vision, a prescience...a promise.

Sarah shivered, the air that pulsed between them suddenly tumescent. They would be lovers. Not tonight, probably not very soon, but inevitably. He had just made that decision, and its force struck her like a physical blow.

Sarah didn't even remember taking hold of his hand. Suddenly, though, she was warm, warmer than she'd been in a long time—sweetened with a life she'd never realized she'd been missing. Alex pulled her to her feet, and she slid up against him. When he gasped with the sparks of their contact, she smiled.

They stood very still, Sarah's hand still in Alex's, her head back so she could look up into his eyes, her breasts grazing his chest. She felt his arm slide around her back, felt him draw her close. Saw the surprise in his eyes as he bent to kiss her.

Sarah's gaze held onto those eyes. Even caught in the whirlwind stirred by future needs and immediate desires, even as she felt the unbearably soft assault of his lips on hers, she sought the honeyed depths of his eyes beyond the shadow. She saw the impulse, the certainty and then finally, inevitably, the caution.

Alex's arms tightened around her. His fingers wove through hers. He coaxed his way past her lips and probed the soft, dark recesses of her mouth. Sarah held on to him. She invited him further, shamelessly, knowing now that she hadn't been wrong, that this was inescapable and right. She splayed her fingers against the crisp cotton of his shirt and longed to coax her own way past.

Groaning, Alex tightened his hold on her. His hands grew restless against her as his mouth covered hers with hungry demand. A heat welled from him, from the tips of his fingers as they strayed along her throat, from the solid wall of his chest where it met her aching breasts, from the steely length of his thighs where they fit against hers.

Sarah surrendered, sinking into it like a tired body into healing waters. She whimpered with the way that force leaped from him where he touched her, searing her skin and swirling deep into her to stoke her own heat. She arched against him, seeking warmth, the spark that crackled between them and shocked her nipples to rock-hard little nubs.

But just as the heat from Alex's touch exploded in her, as the knot formed in her belly that she knew wouldn't soon go away, he pulled back. He straightened and dragged in a lungful of air as if he'd been close to drowning. And Sarah, even knowing now that it wouldn't ultimately end here, felt lost.

Before she had the chance to see the regret that would surely appear in those brandied eyes, Sarah settled her head against his chest.

"You're a little gun-shy," she nudged, her eyes closed. "Aren't you?"

For a minute Alex didn't answer. Still holding her close, he winnowed his fingers through her hair. Sarah wanted to sigh at the unconscious sensuality of it. She kept her silence, her own arms now around his waist, her ear to the ragged cant of his breathing and the trip-hammer thud of his heart.

"I'm very gun-shy," he answered, although this time in an apology rather than a challenge.

Sarah nodded. "I don't think I would have liked her."

She felt the rumble in Alex's chest and knew that his chuckle was one of surprise. "You're being a lot more charitable than I was."

Sarah smiled, assimilating the steady beat of his heart. "She didn't hurt me as badly as she did you."

She still felt his fingers weaving sparks through her, spilling a delicious lethargy she knew was already dangerous.

"She didn't hurt me," Alex said with a curiously sharp edge to his voice. "She made me grow up."

Sarah shook her head, her hair rustling against cotton. "No," she said simply. "She made you grow old."

Alex didn't seem to have an answer. He merely held on to her, his hand against her head.

"Aren't you hungry?" she asked quietly.

Alex stiffened before Sarah recognized the double entendre she'd just delivered.

"I'm talking basic food groups, Alex. Dinner."

"Oh. Yeah," he admitted, his voice less strained. "I am hungry. Matter of fact, that's why I came in here about four hours ago or so. Where would you like to go?"

She could hear his heart slowing back down. A good, athletic heart, untaxed by brief challenge.

"What hobbies do you have?" she asked, not moving, counting his rate already at the low fifties.

Alex straightened. "What?"

"Hobbies," Sarah insisted, moving her head so she could face him again. She was going to need a chiropractor soon. "You still keep in shape, I can tell. What do you like to do?"

Even in the shadows she could see the size of his scowl. "Dinner ranks right up there," he retorted in a low growl. "Wanna join me?"

Sarah chuckled. "You remind me of Connie."

"I hope not," he said. "I would have been kicked off the team after the first session in the showers."

Sarah laughed and the tension ebbed. It was time to pull away, to form an orderly retreat to companionship for the time being. She didn't mind so much when Alex smiled like that. Or even when he scowled like that, because it was playful.

"I mean you're both so focused. I bet you taught yourself to ride a bike without any help."

"When I was four."

Sarah nodded. "Connie knew what she was going to do when she grew up from the time she was three."

Alex lifted an eyebrow. "She knew she was going to work with you? She must be clairvoyant, too."

Easing out of Alex's arms, Sarah shot Alex her own scowl and went on a search for her shoes. "She knew she wanted to own a business. Connie's an army brat. I think it was her way of rebelling against *her* life-style."

"Connie's an army brat?" Alex echoed in astonishment. "You two must have been some roommates."

Sarah grinned from where she was rooting around beneath her desk. "With about as much in common as Thoreau and Rommel. Connie's mother says I ruined her daughter. But then, Blue says that Connie ruined me."

"It must have been a disappointment to your parents when you didn't follow in their footsteps."

She'd found her shoes. Easing the bone pumps away from the pig's protective backside, she slid her feet into them and turned back to Alex. "No," she disagreed with a happy shake of her head. "What crushed them was the day they found out I had a stock portfolio."

Alex actually laughed. "You?"

Sarah wrinkled her nose. "Don't be so smug. I'm quite good at it."

"All that fortune-telling, no doubt."

Now all she had to do was find her purse. "Nope. That has nothing to do with it."

From where he waited, Alex crossed arms and settled against the desk. "What are you doing?"

"My purse," Sarah answered from under the drawing table.

"Don't you think lights might help?"

"I always leave it in the same place. Then I swear it moves around on me."

"Uh-huh."

She was crouched close to the floor, checking out the mauve carpet for her mauve handbag in the dark. She didn't find it. She did find Alex. She tripped over him.

Alex's hands shot out to steady her. "I'm a little hard to miss," he objected. "Even in the dark."

Sarah straightened and fought the urge to nestle back against his chest again. She so enjoyed the feel of his hands on her arms, hands that were a little tighter than necessary, that telegraphed Alex's unsuspecting attachment.

"Sorry," she said, even though she wasn't.

Alex's smile betrayed arousal and frustration. "You should be," he said, thumbs rubbing slow circles into her shoulders. "My patience isn't what it used to be."

His patience wasn't what he was talking about. Sarah's eyes widened. She found herself easing closer again, seeking that heat, that life....

"Sarah, you'd better be here—"

Sarah whipped around like a shot. First she saw her purse on the file shelves by the door, where she was sure she never put it. Then she saw Connie.

Connie stood stock-still in the doorway, her mouth open, her eyes wide. She had a large bag in her arm, and the tempting aroma of garlic wafted into the room.

"Chinese?" Sarah asked hopefully, completely oblivious to the picture she and Alex presented, still much too close to each other, still flushed and anxious.

"I'm...sorry," Connie apologized, backing stiffly away. "I interrupted."

"I lost my purse," Sarah explained, waving an arm in airy dismissal. "Now, bring that back in here."

Still disconcerted, Connie looked down at the bag in her arms, then at Sarah and Alex. "Oh...I, uh, have a meeting. I couldn't get you at home and figured you'd forgotten to get there again. Thought I'd drop something off."

"Well, stay and share it," Sarah said, and turned to Alex for confirmation.

He'd added toleration and patience to the other emotions in his expression. "Your purse is on the shelf," he said, letting her go with a final squeeze only the two of them knew about.

Caught dead center between the delicious promise of garlic and the surprising loss when Alex took back his hands, Sarah flashed him an uncertain smile. "Thanks, I saw it. Now, I just have to hope my keys are inside."

Before Sarah could say anything more to Connie, her friend shoved the bag of food into her hands and backed out the door. Sarah stared, not sure what it was that was so suddenly wrong in the little room.

"Connie?"

Connie grinned. "See you in the morning. Don't get lost going home."

And without another word, she turned away from the office. Sarah didn't understand. She turned to Alex, to see the same concern in his eyes.

"I'll...uh..."Dropping the steaming bag next to her purse, Sarah headed out the door.

She caught up with Connie at the elevator.

"What's the matter?"

Connie stared, her posture stiff and uncomfortable. "Nothing," she obviously lied. "I have to go, that's all."

Sarah answered with an epithet she rarely used. Something about prairie litter.

This time Connie's smile was a little more honest. "I'm sorry," she apologized, flexing her stiff fingers and raking a few through her carefully coiffed hair. "I didn't have any business being so stuffy."

Sarah took a step closer, still not satisfied. But she didn't say anything. She knew she didn't have to.

Connie's gaze slowly returned to Sarah's. Sarah could see defensiveness, protection, confusion there. "I know you," Connie said quietly, a hand out to Sarah's arm. "You dive headfirst into everything you do without looking. It's dangerous."

Sarah tried a conciliatory smile of her own. "I've always had you there to warn me about the shallow places."

Connie shook her head. "I can't follow you in this time," she warned. "You're on your own, and I'm afraid you're going to get hurt."

There wasn't any way Sarah could honestly satisfy Connie's concern. Her friend was right. Sarah did tend to jump in headfirst. She was in a position to get hurt. Badly hurt. But there was a certainty to her feeling about Alex that couldn't be communicated past her friend's worry. So Sarah reached out and gave Connie what she could.

"I can't say I'll be careful," she said honestly. "I can't say I won't be hurt. But I'll be all right, no matter what happens. It's a chance just like all the other chances we've taken to get where we are, and I think I'd like to take it. After all," she added with a sly grin, "you don't take any new ground without advancing."

At that Connie finally chuckled. She took back her hand and punched the elevator button. "Enough," she protested. "I know you've made up your mind when you start quoting *my* father. Just remember," she added, turning back for one last meaningful glance. "I'm there if you need me."

"I know," Sarah said with a final smile. "I love you, Con."

The door opened and Connie stepped in. Sarah knew she wouldn't know how to answer. She never did. Connie hadn't been raised by hippies to share the same words with friends that one would with spouses or lovers. Sarah did it without thought or prejudice. Connie was the closest thing she had to family, and she wanted her to always know that.

Raised by the Colonel and his brittle, correct wife, Connie still didn't know quite how to respond.

"See you in the morning," she said, and let the door slide closed.

Sarah shook her head and returned to Alex.

Chapter 6

For a long moment Alex didn't move from where he stood in the darkened office. He could hear the sounds of footsteps in the hallway and of traffic on the street. He could see the outline of desks and computers in the outer office. He could smell the faint perfume of Sarah against the assault of garlic from the bag. And he felt the heavy tension of Connie's surprise interruption.

Still, somehow, he felt disconnected. Unreal. It happened every time he was alone with Sarah. She drew him into the shadows with her smile and her bright, spontaneous excitement. She pulled him down, away from reality, away from sense, and let loose something in him that was better closed away.

Alex knew better. He'd been snared once, trapped as neatly as a fish in a net before he'd even recognized the calculation in his pretty wife's vapid eyes. He'd rued his capture quickly and paid for it at length. And yet, he was doing the same thing all over again, and he couldn't seem to make himself want to quit.

Sarah fascinated him. She was completely intuitive. She made him think of wood sprites, sirens, wholly sensual creatures caught between reality and imagination, able to dip their fingers into the well of dreams and pull one out whole. He thought of their fatal powers, their deadly allure, drawing men by their hands willingly to their deaths.

Damn. He dated pragmatic women, adults who walked carefully in the real world and debated it over drinks. He didn't tolerate bubbleheads anymore. He didn't take to flights of fancy. He'd made it a point not to after Barbi.

Yet here he was, mesmerized to a standstill by a woman who couldn't even keep track of herself, much less somebody else. A woman cared for by a host of adults, but who was oddly convinced that she was responsible for everyone around her because of whatever the gift was she thought she had.

Did he believe she'd really predicted the car situation? Probably not. She'd seen or overheard something and tucked it away. Like her purse, that memory was lost until someone had called it to mind. So much for the misty visions and unexplained feelings.

Besides, Alex was having trouble enough dealing with the tangible aspects of this attraction. He didn't want to have to consider what allowing hocus-pocus in would do to him. Intuition was something as simple as knowing a person well enough to anticipate him. Nothing more.

Nothing more.

"Alex? Are you still there?"

Alex started, looked up. Sarah stood in the doorway, little more than shadow and movement against the distant light. For a moment, for a brief moment, Alex thought to question her presence, to reach out a hand to test her substance. Instead, he shook away the fancies and approached.

"What was the matter?"

Sarah met his gaze, and Alex saw the light flicker across the blue depths like first sunlight on the sea. He found himself held still again, the memory of her body in his arms suddenly vivid. He could feel the sweep of her hair across his arm, the slender vibrancy of her against his belly, the surprising hunger of her mouth. And for a moment it was all he could do to keep from pulling her back into his arms.

He could still remember the moment he'd realized that they were going to be lovers. His body flushed with it. His imagination spun. His common sense went right into shutdown. With her woman's eyes, Sarah saw him too clearly. She threatened to unleash a part of him that best belonged tied down tight and secure.

"Oh, Connie's just being protective," Sarah assured him. "She's afraid I'm going to let you hurt me somehow.... Are you okay?" Sarah asked suddenly, stepping closer without bothering to flick on the lights.

At the last moment Alex reeled in his hormones and smiled. "I'm hungry," he said matter-of-factly. "I've been standing here smelling garlic and ginger and trying to decide if I really wanted to wait for you to come back before diving in."

Was it his imagination, or did Sarah relax? She stepped aside and turned back to where the bag waited. He guessed a moment passed. Reality intruded a little more.

Except that Alex couldn't keep his sense of fantasy at bay. He still half expected Sarah to have returned with holly leaves in her hair.

"You're right," she said, leaning over to peer inside. "It does smell great. Should we eat here, or at the house?"

"Here," he said a little too quickly. "I'd like to ask you a few things."

Sarah turned up to him. "You can't do that at my house?"

Alex answered by dipping into his pocket and rattling around for change. "Diet or regular?"

Sarah grinned her acquiescence. "You mean, harmful chemicals or carcinogens," she retorted with a bright grin. "Surprise me."

Before Alex headed off to the soda machine in the lunchroom, he flipped on the lights. Just to be safe. In case she disappeared on him in there.

"I guess no one's come forward to confess."

Alex shook his head while digging into a carton of Mongolian beef. "Not that I haven't given them ample opportunity." Casting a careful glance across the table, he continued. "You're willing to admit that somebody's doing this on purpose?"

"Doing what?" Sarah answered in frustration. "What would be worth killing a man over?"

"For some people? Pocket change. In this case? I'll be damned if I know."

She looked up at him. "You haven't found anything."

"Not a thing. The warehouse crew thinks you're Mother Teresa and the accounting staff is sure you're Nostradamus. Everybody is on their best behavior, and I haven't found one thing out of the ordinary."

"But something *is* out of the ordinary."

Alex saw the pain in those soft blue eyes, the hurt of a betrayed child, and found himself wanting to lash out at whoever had provoked it. "Something is out of the ordinary."

It took Sarah a second to break the contact, as if she were drawing on him for some kind of sustenance. When she did, she dropped her gaze to where she picked desultorily at her dinner. "What's your next step?"

Alex returned to his own food, unsettled by the unexpected sense of separation. "I'm settling into accounting for a few days. Doing checks of receiving and shipping, payroll, that kind of thing. Then I'll do some quick checks on companies you deal with."

"And if you don't find anything?"

He shrugged, his gaze back on her downturned head. "I'll do it again."

Sarah lifted her eyes. "What if—"

"I'm being careful."

With a frustrated huff, she slammed her plastic fork down. "Don't be stupid. A lot of careful people are... hurt"

"And a lot of companies are ruined by crooks. If you're so perceptive, Sarah, why can't you see that I'm not going to change my mind?"

That got a sheepish little grin out of her. "I can," she admitted, "but the feeling of danger keeps getting worse."

"In that case," he said. "You be careful, too."

"Me?" She seemed genuinely surprised. "These people are all my friends. I picked them because I connected with them."

"Connected?"

She blushed a little. "It's a Blue term. I just mean that I had to have a certain feeling—a kind of bond—before I could hire somebody. It's never failed me yet."

"I'm afraid that one of your friends has," he answered quietly.

Again Alex saw the bright pain and wondered how this self-absorbed artist could gather so many people in under her wing.

"It's so frustrating," she whispered, tears welling in her eyes, her hands restless. Climbing to her feet, Sarah paced over to the window and watched the thin line of lights that was the city. "I've tried so hard to see something."

"Is that how it works?" he asked, following to his feet, unsure of his place, his intentions.

She shrugged without turning. "It doesn't work any particular way," she admitted. "Sometimes I get a sense of something, like whether a person will make a good client. Or I see pictures. Like the time I saw Jared and knew he was going to marry Blue three months before he showed up on the doorstep. Then there are the times, like when I met you, I'm just... overwhelmed. Like being caught in a big wave with my head underwater. Those are the worst."

"You can't control it."

Sarah shook her head. "If I could, I'd be rich from the stock market." She offered a small chuckle. "Jill says that if I could get this thing to work right, I'd make a fortune for us both at the racetrack."

"Racetrack?"

Turning at the surprise in his voice, she nodded. "Sure, didn't you know? Phoenix has great racing. Greyhounds and thoroughbreds. Turf Paradise is just over on Bell." Stepping away from the window, hands deep in the pockets of her billowy cotton flowered skirt, Sarah grinned. "Unfortunately, I seem not to be one of those fortunate people attuned to the psyche of the horse. Or the greyhound."

Jill, Alex thought instead, sorting back through people. Accounts receivable. He'd have to check on her, too. And he'd have to get Sarah to talk a little more about her other friends. Offer unsuspected motives, opportunities, grudges.

Grudges, Alex thought with a mental shake of the head. Who could possibly have a grudge against Sarah? It would be like resenting springtime.

Nevertheless, somebody had tried to dismantle his brakes. There was at least one person with some kind of motive.

He got her to talk. Eased back into the couch, the lights off to better enjoy the show outside, Sarah offered information about her employees, praise for their work, sympathetic sketches of their lives, simple defenses for the people she trusted most.

There was Hal in design whose wife had cancer, and Maria in the secretarial pool who was putting herself and a brother through school. Sylvia, the sales manager who was the sole support of her single-parent household, and Joseph, a sales rep who was recovering from alcoholism.

All good people who had every reason to be grateful to Sarah. Any one of whom could have found themselves desperate for cash.

Alex ended up feeling like a heel. He listened to Sarah defend her staff like family, extolling and empathizing, and all he listened for was motive.

"What about Randolph?" he finally asked.

Lost in the jewel-studded night that danced outside her window, Sarah took a moment to look around.

"Randolph?" she asked, her eyes lost in shadow, her hair tumbled and shimmering. "What about him?"

"You said he's gay."

Sarah nodded. She wasn't making it any easier for Alex, who had never prided himself on his tact.

"Sarah," he said, "would he be a target for blackmail?"

It took her a minute to answer. A minute, Alex guessed, for the question to sink in. Suddenly she grinned.

"Do you mean does anybody else know?"

"Yes."

Sarah chuckled. "Only most of the legislative bodies in the United States. Randolph is an activist for AIDS funding. He helps run a hospice here in town."

Alex scowled at her delight. Sarah, a collector of people. A quiet champion without a cause. Wasn't there any dark underside to her motivation, he wondered. Any petty jealousy or prejudice or selfishness? She was so damn straightforward, so painfully honest and sincere. How could anyone take advantage of that? How could anyone deliberately hurt her?

Unfortunately, Alex had been out in the world long enough to know that there were people lined up for that kind of opportunity.

"He doesn't like you much," Sarah offered suddenly.

Alex saw that she considered him with tilted head and amused eyes. "Why?"

Sarah just shrugged. "He won't say. I think he's afraid you're going to hurt me."

Alex lifted an eyebrow. "Him, too? I seem to be a pretty popular guy all around."

Sarah offered a sly smile and an offhanded shrug. "Oh, I don't know. *I* like you."

He scowled. "Anybody else I should keep a lookout for?"

Sarah took a moment to think about it. "John," she admitted.

"John?"

"My father, remember?"

"Oh, yeah. The dam builder."

She nodded. "He's shown himself to be surprisingly protective, especially for a man who makes an appearance about once a decade." Her smile brightened again, impish and provocative. "But then, he's still out of the country. By the time he finds out about us, you'll be a daddy and I'll be designing from home."

Alex tried his best to quell the frustration at her words. "You see that, do you?"

She challenged him. "And a picket fence, and a boy for you and a girl for me. All that traditional stuff that made John cringe right up to the moment he left."

Alex didn't hear any regret. Any bitterness. He couldn't understand why. "Is that why you went to boarding school?"

"Oh, no," she said. "I went in when John and Blue headed off to save natives. They figured I should have some kind of structure to my life, since it looked like I was interested in more than natural foods and tie-dyeing."

"How often did you see them?"

"Since I was sixteen?" Sarah thought a moment. "Four times."

Alex sat stunned.

"No, that's not right," she amended. "Five. Blue and John came home for her wedding to Jared."

Five times. Five times in what, ten years? How could she survive neglect like that? How could she seem so outgoing and giving, when the people she'd relied on so much hadn't ever been there for her?

By adopting her own family, Alex realized. By vigorously defending the other psychologically needy. He thought of his own family, of the noisy holidays and the siblings always no more than a call away, of the months he'd spent locked in Lindsay's house and the strong bond that had tightened into steel with the tears and rage. He thought of his sister now, whole and happy, and how he fed on that like sunlight.

Damn. Sarah asked for no pity. She wouldn't have understood if he'd offered. Yet he wanted suddenly to hold her, to give her the security her parents had denied her with their frivolous affections.

"Well," he offered, struggling to pull something out from the story to praise, "at least their divorce was amicable."

"Divorce?" she asked. "Whose?"

Alex frowned at her. "Your parents."

"My parents were never divorced," she said simply. "Blue and John never got married."

"So explain it to me."

"Alex," Lindsay said with strained patience. "Why couldn't you wait a couple more weeks to have this crisis of faith? I can't really pay attention when this little beast is tap-dancing on my ribs."

"He'll play football."

"He will not. Are you sure you can't rely on cold showers a little longer?"

Measuring a short arc across the plush living area carpet, Alex turned in the other direction, a hand raking through his hair. "It's not that. I'm trying to figure her out, damn it. She just doesn't make any sense."

"Why, because she can come out of a bizarre situation in one piece? Seems to me both of us qualify for that privilege."

"But we had each other. The family."

"And she did it all on her own. Why are you so scared of her?"

He turned again, walking faster, his neck corded with tension. "She's never had a real family. She was deserted when she was sixteen. She hasn't seen her parents more than five times since."

"She was raised in a commune, Alex, not Mayberry. Her definition of family might be slightly different than yours. Does that bother you?"

That stopped him. He really considered it, wanting to be fair. "No," he answered truthfully. "But I couldn't be as unconcerned about it as she is. Why?"

"Because when a person looks up stability in the dictionary, the name Thorne is next to it. I'd say she's done a hell of a job with what she's had."

Now Alex smiled, and it was wry. "Makes you wonder what we've really accomplished with all we were given."

"I know what I've accomplished," Lindsay retorted easily. "Swollen ankles, stretch marks and twenty-four-hour bathroom stops."

Sarah didn't sleep again that night. But it wasn't the threat to Alex that kept her tossing and turning. It was the promise of him.

Each step taken brought them closer. The certainty of it ballooned in her chest until she could hardly breathe. She was falling in love with him. She could see him fighting and had a feeling she knew why. But time and time again tonight his eyes had betrayed him. His hands had strayed toward her as if instinctively seeking contact, communion.

Sarah knew she perplexed him. Alex was such a logical man, and this wasn't in the least logical. The last person he should want to love would be a butterfly who couldn't seem to roost in one place long enough to taste it. Yet, she knew better. The more she spoke to him or basked in his smiles and scowls, she knew that she might be the butterfly, but he was the earth. Patient and knowing and solid, waiting for her, settling her and giving her rest. Alex would be the person who made her whole.

Throwing off the covers, Sarah bunched up a pillow and threw her arms over it, seeking warmth even on this hot night. She burrowed her face into the marshmallow softness and thought of the unyielding strength of Alex's chest.

The last person she would have imagined herself with. A football player. A man who for fifteen years spent his autumns butting heads and scrambling for a ball. A man who came away from that with regret and insight, who saw his life in terms of routines and rituals, but who never suspected the fires he had banked beneath his pragmatism.

What was it she had seen in his smile, the past that so colored him, that aged his eyes and steeled his resolve? Whatever it was, it had to do with his silent astonishment at her family. Alex had a completely different image of community than Sarah had been given, and much of it had to do with trials that had tested his steely determination. Trials that had hurt him, had strengthened him, had solidified his commitment.

Alex would never understand Blue and John and Jared, who had all traveled together after Blue and Jared's wedding. He would never fully comprehend what the life had been like when free love had ruled and children were community property. Sometimes Sarah missed those days when she'd run barefoot in the fields and been able to call upon any of twelve mothers. But there were other times when she envied Alex the normal upbringing that so formed him.

When Sarah had children, she didn't think she would give them to anyone else to raise. Neither would she send them away. And she would give them a father, one father, who would be as devoted to them as she.

It was comforting to know Alex would be that father.

"I'd make a lousy father."

Sarah took a look at the expression on Alex's face and laughed. "I guess that means you don't see the attraction of a Snarkalump."

"Attraction?" he countered, turning the lumpy ball of bright blue fur over in his hands. "I don't even see the face."

"Exactly," she said with a nod. "It's kind of like a Yorkie or an English Sheepdog. It's what makes them adorable."

"*Does* it have eyes?"

Sarah took the toy from Alex and lifted a section of fur. The hand-sewn eyes were more reminiscent of a basset hound's than a sheepdog's.

Alex settled for a small frown. "It'll probably make you a fortune. After all, I was the one who said that the Great Perpetual Motion Machine wouldn't last out the month."

"That's because you're too regimented, Alex." Resettling the fur, Sarah packed the Snarkalump back into its box and handed it over with another two. "For your nieces."

He rolled his eyes. "They'll be insufferable. Thank you."

"Do you need another yet for your sister?"

"Thanks, no," he retorted. "She prefers to play with toy soldiers."

Sarah grimaced. It was two days since they'd shared dinner in her office. Two days in which Sarah had developed increasing difficulty in concentration. The staff had suspected premonitions. Sarah had to admit to herself that it hadn't been premonitions so much as visions. Fantasies. Memories of the taste and feel of Alex Thorne woven amid vague plans for the future.

Today she'd bumped into him in the accounting office when she'd wandered in the wrong door from the design department and remembered that she'd promised to show him the new toy line. It seemed more fun than coming up with a color scheme for Waldo's Restaurants, after all.

He smelled like soap, like citrus and cool breezes. Sarah wanted to close her eyes and take in the feel of him. But the gossip was already flying, and Sarah knew it didn't need any fuel. There was already an office pool going betting on whether Alex would win Sarah's hand or dump her in the dust, an image Sarah didn't particularly care for. Nobody would tell Sarah how the betting was split, but one look at each of her employees told the tale—the betting was heavily against her.

"Y'know," Alex was saying, bouncing the boxes a little in his hands as if weighing something. "Now that the Great Perpetual Motion Machine has been brought up, I've been meaning to ask you."

"I can get one of those for you, too." She smiled sweetly.

"Why didn't you tell me about your patents?"

Sarah shrugged, uncomfortable as always with that kind of thing. "You didn't ask."

Alex refused to retreat. "I would have thought a patent would be a pretty big deal. I'd think *six* would be cause for a media blitz."

"They were just ideas," Sarah defended herself. "I jotted some things down on napkins, I think, and Connie made sure I didn't give anything away."

"All of them?"

"No, the trauma table I did on one of those paper sheets when I was in the emergency room one time after falling off my bike. The table was too high to get up on, so I figured a way to incorporate a step stool and hydraulics."

Alex seemed capable of no more than a shake of the head.

"On a paper sheet."

She nodded. "They let me keep it."

He shook his head again.

"Sarah, there you are."

Both Alex and Sarah turned to see Thaddeus and Connie standing in the stockroom door, their expressions comically alike. Sarah didn't know whether to laugh or scowl.

"I'm stealing three Snarkalumps," she admitted, motioning to the boxes in Alex's hand. "Bribes for the accountant."

Connie swung a dry look in Alex's direction. "Enjoy them in good health."

"Cheaper than a cat," he retorted easily. "And you don't have to walk them."

It sounded as if Thaddeus swallowed his reaction.

"We're going to test-run the animation. Want to see a finished product?"

Sarah's grin flattened. "Are you going to explain it?"

"Put your fingers in your ears," Connie suggested. "It wouldn't look good if the company's president won't even look at her products."

"You know what computers do to me, Con." Sarah could see the polite bemusement on Alex's face. Of course, some of his best friends were computers. "I actually get headaches when Thaddeus explains how he programs. It frustrates me because I can't follow him at all."

"Computers only do what you tell them to."

"Computers," she retorted, "are relentlessly logical. I am not."

They had stepped out of the stockroom and now followed Connie and Thaddeus toward the computer animation office. Sarah knew she was dragging her feet. She was already nauseated at the anticipation of hearing them instruct her on how to program the images.

Rendering, they called it. One rendered a computer animation, and it was a process so complicated that one four-second television station identification took them up to two weeks' solid work. And they wanted her to understand it.

"If it makes you so crazy," Alex said as he matched her slow step, "why introduce it? It's still your company."

"Because I have Thaddeus. I knew that he and Connie would find the people needed to take care of the nuts and bolts. If I gave them the image I wanted, I could hide in my office until it showed up in three dimensions. It's a spectacular tool," she admitted. "I just don't want to see it work."

"You don't work with the computers at all?"

Offering a resigned sigh, Sarah looked up at Alex. "I'm the only person in the office who writes letters on a typewriter and submits expense reports in longhand. It's another part of being so very right-brained. I have no sense of linear logic. I can't take point A to point C by way of point B, and without that, I can't work a computer."

Alex, like all left-brained people, truly didn't comprehend. It was like the sighted trying to understand blindness, except that the blind to them had a legitimate handicap. The lack of logic seemed frivolous. "It just takes patience," he suggested.

"You were good at algebra," she challenged. "Weren't you?"

"Sure."

"I flunked. I could tell them every answer to every question, but that didn't count unless I could come up with the steps. I never could. It's like being dyslexic in a way."

Maybe "dyslexic" was a term he understood. Sarah saw that he at least pondered it now. Maybe that was better.

"In that case," Alex said with a grin, "I guess I'd better not let you stop off in accounting and shut down my terminal before we head on to the demonstration."

"I'll go in with you and offer support."

They passed the news on to the other two and then dropped off at the door to accounting. Hector looked up from where he was working in his glassed-in office at the back. Jill, bent over receipts and logs, never turned. Other than that, the office was empty.

Sarah followed Alex over to where his notes were spread out on the desk and waited as he took his seat. The sun rode high outside the tinted windows, flattening an already colorless sky. In the distance Camelback crouched between them and the downtown area. Trees drooped in the afternoon heat. Traffic was picking up as rush hour approached. Sarah could hear it as a vague grumble, and thought how glad she was she didn't have to brave that. She had a car, but it suffered from neglect, since she walked where she needed to go.

"It really is a pretty place," she said, looking out to the clean lines of the horizon. "But it's hard to appreciate it from here. A balloon or an airplane...no, a balloon. It's quiet and solitary and close enough to see the landscape. It's too bad you can't use a balloon for an airplane logo."

Behind her, Alex pecked at the keyboard without answering. Sarah really didn't expect him to respond. If he was anything like Thaddeus, he'd keep only half an ear for her anyway while he teased that thing.

Besides, she was having quite enough fun thinking about Alex and herself alone in a balloon above the Superstition Mountains. Sarah and Alex and the wind, maybe a hawk swooping close as it cut arcs in the hot blue sky.

Not that they could really take a balloon out by themselves. Sarah didn't know the first thing about flying hot-air balloons, except that you put more hot air in to make it go up. So she guessed Randolph would have to come along, too.

"Champagne," she said quietly to the window. "And maybe some fried chicken. Does that sound like a lunch for a balloon ride? I think it sounds like fun. I thought we could go Saturday, if you're not doing anything."

"Well, hell..."

Sarah turned halfway around. "If you'd rather have something else, I can ask Randolph. He'd know. He's always taking the balloon up for sunset flights."

"No."

Now Sarah was facing him. "Why not? Don't you like heights?" Alex didn't lift his eyes from the screen as he kept punching keys. "Look at this."

Sarah scowled at him, but he didn't seem to notice. "What's wrong?" she asked without moving. She didn't even like to face the screen. All those symbols and numbers seemed to taunt her.

"I was going to print out this month's accounts according to company. What you do is—"

"Alex."

He heard the warning and looked up.

"I don't want to know what you do. Really. Is there a problem, yes or no?"

His frown dissipated with the wry smile that crept in at the edges of his eyes. "Yes."

"Do you need help?"

The smile broadened a little more. "Yes. Can you get Thaddeus in here? I think he'll know what to do."

"Fine," she said with a nod. "Just don't start talking loops and dot commands."

"How 'bout viruses?"

She was almost out the door when he said it. Sarah turned around, her chest suddenly tight. "As in you don't feel well, or the computer doesn't?"

"The computer."

Slowly she nodded her head. Sarah understood the theory of viruses. Someone had programmed in a command to sabotage the computer. Beyond that, she didn't want to dwell on any of it. The bright balloon of her fantasies shredded and disappeared.

"I'll get Thaddeus."

Chapter 7

Sarah sat hunched over her drawing board, a silver marker in her hand as she outlined the hunter-green title she'd just designed for Sunset Toys. They'd had a logo already, one almost ready for production, but Sarah liked these bright balloons better, the one with stripes of pink and purple and orange lifting in front of the others with big checks of green and white. The logo was whimsical and fun. Just the sight of it made her think of fantasies and escape.

Outside her window the night pulsed, and inside, Debussy swelled from the speakers. Sarah wiggled her toes in the thick carpet and brushed a free hand through her hair. When the door opened into her office, she refused to look up.

"No."

It took him a moment to answer. "You know what I want to ask?"

Sarah went on outlining, the strokes of the marker sure and swift and exact. "Why do you think I left? You're going to tell me that Thaddeus can't seem to fix the system, and do

I want to call in somebody from the outside to assist?'' Now she looked up and knew that Alex could see her encroaching fear. ''Especially since Thaddeus might be the one who sabotaged it in the first place.''

Standing so solidly in the doorway, even with his tie loosened and his shirtsleeves hastily rolled up, Alex looked the picture of stability—of certainty. ''It's something you have to consider, Sarah.''

Sarah found herself wanting to run to him, to cower in the safety of his arms. ''I know,'' she admitted. ''But I can't have another outsider in this company. It would be too much.''

''And if it is Thaddeus?''

She offered an uncomfortable shrug, wishing she had more than the rationalizations she'd collected and dispersed the past two hours while she'd waited. ''The last time I was in there, Connie and Hector and Jill were helping. It can't be all of them, can it?''

''I don't know,'' Alex answered, coming closer. ''Can it?''

Sarah's head snapped up at that, her spine stiffening. ''No,'' she answered definitely. ''It can't.''

Alex's smile should have been amused. Instead, somehow, it conveyed sympathy. ''For the same reason the problem can't be in the Virginia plant?''

''Yes,'' she answered hotly.

Alex had reached the other side of the drawing board. His shadow fell over the balloons. For some reason, Sarah shivered. Like dancing on a grave, she thought distractedly, seeing the color sap from her drawing and wondering what it meant. Sunset Toys, the future of the company in shadow, in doubt? Maybe in trouble, and it was Alex casting the shadow.

Recapping her marker, she shoved the logo beneath the other papers piled on the table and stepped away.

''What do I have to do?'' she asked, still not comfortable facing the unyielding pragmatism in Alex's eyes. Make my problems disappear, she wanted to beg. Wave your strong, capable hands and take away the fear, the growing uncertainty that one of my friends is betraying me.

"What do you want to do?" he asked.

Stopping a few feet away, Sarah looked up at him. She knew he saw what she was feeling. She was hopeless at masking her emotions. His eyes shone in the scattered light from the arced lamp over her table. They were soft, like spring earth, as comfortable as steeped tea. Waiting, watching. Knowing.

"I want to run away," she admitted in a small voice. She was surprised when he smiled.

"Okay. Where would you like to go?"

Sarah tilted her head a little, trying to assess his intent, trying to brush away the tiny thrills of anticipation his invitation provoked.

"How can we?" she countered, trying for once to be the practical one. "The computer system is sick."

"And it has four doctors attending it who wouldn't miss us for a week."

Sarah sighed, feeling the weight of her own request, the series of events she'd set in order. Somehow it didn't help her to know that the person she was in effect accusing had initiated his own problems, had deliberately set out to hurt the company. Instead she felt that it was all her fault, born of her impressions, conceived with her unease. It was her fault that Alex was here, that he was in danger, that he would refuse to stop his search until one of her friends was exposed as a villain—or Alex himself was hurt.

Not for the first time in her life, Sarah wished her gift on someone else.

"Why don't you let me take you home?" Alex asked, taking her by the arms.

Sarah stiffened against the sudden desire to fold into him. "No," she said. "No, I don't want to go home."

"But it's late, Sarah," he objected. "And you can't do anything here to help."

Sarah looked up at him then. He was unconsciously brushing her arms with his thumbs, back and forth, gently, hypnotically. "Could we just drive for a while?" When he smiled, she felt the ground solidify at her feet. She felt her own weight ease a little.

"Where would you like to go?"

She grinned. "It doesn't really matter," she admitted. "I won't know where I am anyway."

Phoenix was an easy city to navigate. New enough to have wide boulevards, sensible enough to have a consistent street plan. Ten o'clock at night wasn't the time Alex would have thought he'd like to see the city, but he found that he was enjoying it.

The heat had died with the sun. A cool mountain breeze whipped in the window as they headed east through Scottsdale and past all the high-priced resorts that had been springing up. The sky overhead was clear, and the city sparkled like a new blanket of jewels. Alex could smell flowers of some kind on the night air and heard the restless rustle of palms.

Alongside him, Sarah leaned back against the seat, her eyes closed.

"How do you know where you're going?" she asked, not bothering to look.

Alex took a second to glance over at the distant columns and rowed palms of the Scottsdale Princess. Opulent and exotic, a far cry from the suburbs of Denver.

"Natural gift, I guess," he answered, heading instinctively for the mountains. He might not like deserts, but mountains were another thing altogether.

"I'm not completely directionally handicapped," she defended herself. "I can get around Richmond blindfolded."

"Then why move?" he asked.

"Because I was outvoted. Connie and Thaddeus thought we'd do better in the Sunbelt."

Alex couldn't help looking over at her in surprise. "So just like that, you move?"

The streetlights flickered over Sarah's face. Seen that way, she looked even younger, childlike. Just ingenious enough to have said what she did.

"We *have* done well here," she retorted without opening her eyes.

Alex battled the instinctive frustration her words provoked. Who had let this innocent out on the streets? Who had told her she could be an adult when she couldn't even seem to make decisions on an adult level? It would surprise him if somebody *wasn't* stealing her blind. She was too trusting, too open, too impulsive for her own good. And there was always somebody out there ready to take advantage of that.

"Sarah—"

He glanced over to see that her eyes were open now. Open and smiling, and more knowing than he'd given her credit for.

"No," she said with new life in her voice. "They didn't take advantage of me. I'm perfectly content wherever I live. And Phoenix is as lovely as Richmond, only in a different way. So if it doesn't matter to me, what's wrong with deferring to the others? They're my friends." Now her smile broadened, and Alex knew she had him. "They're also the gears that put this engine into drive. It can't hurt to keep them happy."

"What if one of them is the one doing this?"

Alex felt her stiffen, saw the smile die. The night seemed to chill a little without it.

"I don't know." Turning back to the front, she pulled a restless hand through hair that tumbled in the wind. "I won't know what I'll do until I find out what's going on."

They spent the next few miles in silence as the golf courses and Arabian studs slipped by, the city stretching out toward the hills beyond.

"Alex?"

"Yes?"

"What were you working on when the computer went dead?"

Alex hazarded another brief glance at Sarah and saw that her eyes were open and dark, facing the night like a personal specter.

"Accounts receivable."

Slowly Sarah turned toward him. "Jill?"

Instinctively he shrugged. "It's her department."

"And you think the breakdown was deliberate?"

"It sure looks like it."

"To keep somebody from looking at those records?"

"It would make sense."

Nodding, she looked away. "Who's capable of that?"

"I'd have to say damn near anybody in the office but you," he admitted. "You've collected quite a computer-literate staff."

"That's too bad."

"Yeah," he agreed, wishing he could somehow ease her dilemma. "I guess it is."

They weren't mountains like he was used to. These were more like hills dusted in chaparral and cactus. Even so, they lifted them above the city and silenced the night. Alex turned off onto a dirt road that twisted back toward Phoenix and shut off the engine.

Below them the lights in the valley spread out in a bath of glitter. The Southern Range blotted out the sky in the distance and the Superstitions ringed the night off to the left. Above, the stars mimicked the city for brilliance in a moonless sky, and behind them Granite Mountain was restless with night animals.

"This is beautiful," Sarah breathed without moving. "I don't think I've ever seen it like this."

Alex nodded, enjoying the light spring in her perfume even more than the clean desert scent wafting in from the windows. "Reminds me a little of the view of Los Angeles from Mulholland. Except that the air's clearer here. I wouldn't mind coming back when it's a lot cooler and doing some camping.''

"You wouldn't think of living here?" she asked.

"I like being able to go outside during the summer."

"Oh, it's not that bad," Sarah argued. "After all, there's very little humidity. That makes it feel cooler."

Alex laughed. "A hundred and ten degrees is still a hundred and ten degrees. After growing up in Portland, Oregon, anything above seventy is heatstroke range. Especially for me."

Alex saw Sarah look over at him, her head tilted a little, the breeze from her window winnowing through her hair. She sat quietly, her hands for once still in her lap. "What's your family like?" she asked.

It took a minute for Alex to answer. He sensed something from Sarah, some need he couldn't name that solidified around that question. She asked it easily enough, as if seeking no more than passing conversation. But even so, he heard an echo. A distant sigh that seemed wishful.

The idea made him want to shake his head. Now *he* was hearing things.

Turning a little in his seat so that he could rest his back against the door and watch Sarah, Alex crossed an ankle over his knee and slung an arm over the seat. Sitting next to him in the soft darkness, Sarah looked once again ethereal, half real and half dream, with the starlight dusting her hair and the night protecting her. He refrained from reaching out to touch her just to make sure.

"My family?" he asked instead. "Middle-class. Pretty normal. My father is an engineer and my mother taught second grade. I have one older brother, Mark, who's responsible for the nieces. Another brother, Phil, who's in the air force, and the one sister, Lindsay, a psychologist."

"The pregnant one."

He nodded, grinning. "The very pregnant one."

"Tell me about her."

Alex again saw something in her eyes seeping out beneath the shadows. "What about her?" he asked.

Sarah shrugged, her movements small as if in apology. "You and she went through a lot together."

Alex opened his mouth and then closed it again. "Did Ellis tell you?"

Sarah's eyes were ghostly now, almost eerie in the dark. Alex felt a funny chill snake its way down his neck. He hadn't said anything about Lindsay; he knew it. It wasn't something he shared easily. But Sarah knew. He could see it in her expression. Not inquiry, but certainty. Understanding before the words were even out.

Alex didn't tell people about what Lindsay had gone through, because it was no one's business. All the same, he told Sarah. And when he told her, he felt somehow as if it belonged between them.

"Lindsay's the one who always tagged along after me. Dated my teammates in high school and harassed me into teaching her to drive. We were always pretty close." He realized he was smiling, the picture of his determined little sister filling his memory. "She was married before. Widowed. Her husband, Patrick, had a lot of problems, and Lindsay took them all on her shoulders. She's kind of like that. Patrick was killed in a traffic accident. Died in Lindsay's arms. She'd been driving." Again pictures assailed him, sensations he'd forgotten a long time ago. The shrill of the late-night phone call, the smell of disinfectant and blood in the emergency room. Lindsay, stark and shattered, her head bandaged and her hands shaking uncontrollably. The oppressive, hostile silence of her home those next few days. The fury and frustration and terror that mounted as she slipped further and further away.

"After all she'd been through with Patrick," he said, his eyes still back on Lindsay's grief, her guilt and despair, "she couldn't handle his death. We almost lost her."

He didn't realize Sarah had reached over until he'd stopped speaking, until he felt her warm hand on his arm.

Alex looked down at the simple gesture, up again at the pain that must have been such a close mirror to the memory in his own eyes.

"That's what it was," she whispered, her eyes glittered softly. "I didn't know. It was horrible for you."

Settling his own hand over hers, Alex smiled, wondering at how easily he shared that private hell with Sarah. How comfortable it felt resting with her. Always before he'd brushed it off, distanced himself from it as if it hadn't hurt quite so much if he denied it.

But it had hurt. It had changed him. In the period of two months when he'd wheedled, cajoled and threatened Lindsay into hanging on to her life, he'd grown from a self-absorbed jock into an adult.

He'd outgrown Barbi and decided that he wasn't going to look back.

"Yeah," he agreed quietly. "It was. But it was worth it."

Sarah didn't seem to need any more than that. Alex could feel it in the tension of her fingertips. He saw it in the liquid emotion in her eyes. His own emotions rose and ebbed, as if called up and then drained from him. His memories danced between the darkness and the light, finally settling on the moment he'd stood up for Lindsay and her new husband, Jason, on their wedding day. Alex felt the old familiar tug of family affection that would never be spoken of in the Thorne household, communicated rather in gruff embraces and teasing, and knew that Sarah recognized it.

"Tell me about your family," he said in return.

For a minute Alex wasn't sure Sarah had heard him. She seemed to still be caught amid his words, unwilling to release his past just yet, unable to break the tie. Finally she took her hand back and used it to pluck at the folds of her linen skirt.

"My birth family," she asked, "or my celestial family?"

Alex grimaced. "I don't think we have time for that. How about just the people you ate dinner with on a regular basis?"

Sarah nodded, looking up as if to remember. "Well, that narrows it down to about forty."

"Forty."

She nodded. "Give or take a few. We ate on trestle tables. I helped prepare vegetables every night. We read passages from either the Upanishads or Thoreau before eating, and then sang after cleaning up."

"You really went to Woodstock?"

She nodded. "All I remember is being cold, wet and hungry. I kind of think of it as a refugee camp with music."

"How did you ever get from that to Zydeco music?" he demanded.

She grinned. "I never question the muse, Alex."

"I bet Blue taught you that."

She laughed. "No. Blue wasn't in the least musical. She was the quilter and herbalist."

Alex couldn't help but shake his head. He'd seen the tail end of the hippie era, touching its edges in high school, but he'd been too involved in schoolwork, too driven by football, to try to save the world. A typical self-centered, confused, frustrated teenage athlete.

"Is the commune still there?"

Sarah shook her head. "The last I saw of it, the land had been turned into a strip shopping mall. I haven't been back since."

"What about the people?"

She shrugged, the gesture a little stiff. "I don't know."

Alex kept his silence. He wanted to ask why, where had all those people gone who had sung with her and taught her and shaped her into the person she was. But something barred his way, some defense Sarah had erected with her hands where they lay clenched in her lap.

"Do you get together for holidays?" she asked quietly, her eyes straying to where she fingered the material in her lap.

"Holidays?" Alex echoed. "Sure. Whoever can, that is. What about you?"

Sarah smiled then, and it broke Alex's heart. She looked like a little child again, the girl who stood all alone at the edge of the crowd, too unsure of herself to join in.

"Blue celebrates Tet," she said, "and John prefers Ramadan."

"He's Muslim?"

The smile grew deprecating. "No. He just enjoys being singular. He has his chance now in Central America."

"What about you?"

She looked up with a wry grin. "Whatever strikes me," she said. "Since I don't have to check with anybody else's plans, it's easy to do."

"You don't have anybody else?"

Sarah shrugged. "Blue and Jared never had any children. I haven't seen my cousins since the various families reacted to the commune idea. I don't even think I'd recognize them."

"What about Connie?"

"She usually visits her parents. And, uh, we aren't comfortable in each other's company."

"What are you doing for Labor Day?" he asked, surprised at his own impulse.

Sarah looked up, her eyes dark and vulnerable. "What?"

"Labor Day," Alex insisted, fighting the urge to pull her into his arms and salve her isolation. "Or don't hippies celebrate that?"

Sarah's smile regained some of its sparkle. "Power to the people," she retorted. "Sure we do. I'm not doing anything, as far as I know. But I wasn't angling for an invitation."

Alex nodded, reaching over to take hold of her restless hand again. "You got one anyway. Lindsay's house for a barbecue."

"Pregnant Lindsay?" she asked. "Aren't you being a bit frivolous with your invitations?"

"By September she'll be dying for some company."

"I don't know," she countered coyly. "Do you think I'll get along with a woman who thinks I'm probably just another Barbi?"

Again Alex opened his mouth. Again he closed it. Sarah was smiling a sly, triumphant smile that told him she'd just won the round. He'd never mentioned Barbi's name to her. True, Ellis could have told her that. But he hadn't told anyone Lindsay's reaction to Sarah.

And Sarah had just told him.

Why did that make him feel so suddenly defensive? He wanted to ward her off, like Thaddeus with his evil-eye sign. Like Ellis battling evil spirits with chants and feathers. Sarah's sight endangered him, and it wasn't from guns and bandits.

But the attraction was stronger than the fear. Alex couldn't pull away.

"You're not a thing like Barbi," he countered easily. "You can count more than ten without taking off your shoes."

Sarah's bright laughter cleared the lingering past like a fresh breeze. Regrets and half-understood longings were swept away, and the night bubbled once again with her animation.

Alex stroked Sarah's palm with his thumb, thinking how very soft and small it was. How graceful. Alex had always thought of hands as tools, engineering marvels constructed for strength and dexterity. He'd never thought of them as artwork. But Sarah's hands were works of art. They danced, they soared, they sang in flight, their punctuation leaps and pirouettes.

They couldn't belong to anyone but Sarah.

"Hey," she said, suddenly squeezing his hand back as she straightened. "Did we eat dinner yet?"

Alex looked up at her. "What?"

"Aren't you starved?"

He didn't even think to lie. "Yes." And he knew that she understood he wasn't talking about food.

He heard her breath catch. He saw her eyes go a little wide. Her hand stilled in his and fluttered like a bird startled in its nest. His own body responded. Tautened. He felt it in his gut, a hot ache that coiled in anticipation.

"Alex—"

Before Sarah had the chance to object or ask, Alex kissed her. Leaning forward, one hand in hers, the other catching her along her jaw where he could feel the startled stumble of her pulse, he trapped her words.

She tasted like sunlight, like sweetness and warmth. Her mouth was pouting full with lips as soft as velvet. Her skin was smooth and fragrant. Alex curled his fingers into the hair that tumbled alongside her throat and stroked its silk. He tasted her soft groan and shuddered, his body anxious and demanding. Feeling her hand at his own jaw, he let go of the other. It lit against his chest and ignited a dark fire.

Alex reached for her, pulled her closer. Tremors ran through her. A bird caught in a heavy hand, a flower in a hard wind, she seemed at once to quicken and die in his grasp. Alex fought for control. He tried his damnedest to reel in his senses.

But Sarah was so soft, so alive, her body responding even before she realized it. He could feel her breasts tauten against him, felt the nipples constrict through the light sweater she wore. Her fingers raked him slowly, like a cat kneading its claws. Her breath quickened into whimpers. Her lips opened to him.

So soft. He gathered her into him, easing around on the seat, fitting her more neatly against him. He kissed her cheek, her throat, her ear, soaking in the fresh-flower smell of her hair as it tickled his nose. He drew his hand along her shoulder, toward the throb at the base of her throat, lower. Sarah arched into his hand, lips parted, her breath fanning his cheek. Alex filled his hand with her breast, small and round and taut beneath the coarse cotton of the sweater. He felt her shudder, heard her gasp and knew that she was smiling.

And because of that, because she was happy, because he wanted her so badly that the hurt ricocheted through him like a high-caliber bullet, Alex let go.

"Dinner might not be such a bad idea," he murmured into the soft mass of her hair, trying to regain control. It had been a long time since his own body had betrayed him like this. A very long time since he'd considered trying to fold himself into absurd positions in the back seat of a car.

But that's just what he was doing now, and it wasn't fair to Sarah.

For a moment Sarah was silent. Still caught tightly in Alex's embrace, her cheek against his chest, she let her own breathing ease. "Are you sure?" she asked.

Alex wondered whether he'd hurt her. He lifted his head to see her swollen mouth, her languorous eyes and uncertain anticipation.

"Do you really want to tell our firstborn that we conceived him in the back seat of a rental?" he demanded, doing his best to smile. If Sarah was worth her salt as a soothsayer, she could tell just how much it took for him to be a gentleman. Even now his body clamored for release. For Sarah.

Sarah smiled back. "I wouldn't mind telling him we conceived him at the house."

Alex wanted to groan. Instead he lifted a finger and ran it down her nose. "Well, now, that's something completely different. Although, your friends are still back at the office trying to crack the problem."

Sarah couldn't have realized how wistful her smile looked. "They won't miss me. Seems to me we were going to have dinner anyway...."

His body bucked with the promise in her eyes. Damn. Alex was hanging on to his professionalism by his fingertips. He'd already lost his objectivity. One more look at those wide, wide eyes did it. Pulling Sarah into his arms for a last, serious kiss, Alex turned back to the steering wheel. "Not another word, or I'm going to run us into a ditch."

Sarah felt as if something had lodged in her chest and couldn't quite get free. She hadn't said anything to Alex since they'd started back, nor could she think of anything *to* say. The feeling of imminence was strong, a crescive anticipation that sent her thoughts flying and scattered her sense.

But was it the sight of just exhilaration? Sitting so close to Alex, watching the sure, steady movements of his hands as he guided the car back to her house and thinking of what those hands would be like on her, she couldn't tell. She had an overwhelming urge to giggle, to sing or move. Her body whispered to her. Her mind tumbled from possibility to improbability.

She'd felt it in him the minute he'd taken her into his arms. Heat, emanating from a source even he didn't suspect. Exhilaration, desire. His muscles sang like the rigging of a ship in rising wind. His jaw tightened so abruptly Sarah could almost hear his teeth grind.

Alex thought he knew himself. He imagined that he had a keen control over his body, over the less orderly preoccupations of his hormones.

But Sarah knew something Alex didn't. When Alex had taken her hand, had stroked her palm the way he would her body, she'd seen the surprise that hadn't yet appeared in his eyes. She'd heard the echoes of a cry that had yet to be voiced. She knew that he wouldn't recognize his own surrender until it had already passed.

It was with mixed emotions that Sarah opened the car door and stepped out onto her driveway. Equal parts anticipation and trepidation. Unholy exhilaration. Alex slammed his door and followed her across to the porch. Sarah sensed his tension, heard his quick tread and the shallow cant of his breathing. Her own wasn't much deeper. She fought off the urge to giggle. They both were probably going to hyperventilate before they even got inside.

Her heels clicking on the cement porch, she turned for her key.

"Oh, dear..."

Behind her, Alex slowed to a halt. "What's the matter?"

Sarah looked around, disoriented, still preoccupied by her body's rebellious reaction.

"My key."

"You don't have it?"

She looked back to the car, trying to think. "I must have left my purse at work." Just to be sure, she dug into her pockets, pulling from the deep folds of her denim skirt buttons and rubber bands and the watch she'd taken off to wash her hands sometime earlier that day. And her earrings.

"Oh," she marveled, looking at them. "There they are." They got set down on the porch along with her other treasures. There were, however, no keys.

Alex couldn't seem to take his eyes off the growing pile on the porch. "Those look like diamonds," he ventured, motioning to where the earrings glinted up in the light from Sarah's living room windows.

"Uh-huh," she nodded absently, following with two business cards and a handful of sunflower seeds. "Connie gave them to me for Christmas last year. To celebrate our success."

Giving her pockets one last pat, she wandered off into the yard.

"Sarah?"

"Just a minute." It had been Connie's idea to leave a key there. Tucked into a little holder burrowed into the planter she'd had built around her pine. Sarah just had to remember which corner. She found it on the third try.

"I used to leave it under the mat," she admitted, stepping past Alex to pull open the glass door and slide the key into her oak-and-glass front door. "But I kept taking the mat inside to clean it and leaving the key sitting out on the porch.''

The door swung open and Sarah reached over to punch in her security code to the alarm system. Then she returned the key to its holder and the holder to its hiding place. Alex waited on the porch right by where she'd left all her gatherings.

Sarah had almost made it back to him when it dawned on her.

''Uh-oh,'' she murmured, chagrined.

Alex looked up. ''Uh-oh, what?''

She lifted her head to listen and then shook it. Sgt. Valdez wouldn't be happy. ''Might as well just sit outside now.''

Alex watched her sit down on the edge of her porch, the big door still open, light spilling out into the yard.

''Sarah, what are you doing?'' he asked.

''Waiting. Have a seat.'' She was embarrassed enough already, without having to explain. He'd know soon enough, anyway—from the sounds of it, in about thirty or forty seconds.

''Well, at least pick up your earrings,'' he suggested, and bent to get them.

That was when the glass door shattered.

''What the—?''

Sarah heard a cracking noise from across the street somewhere. Alex whirled around with more speed than Sarah would have thought possible. Shards of glass tinkled onto her entryway and scattered over the porch. Sarah looked at the door and then at Alex, as if he could explain.

Instead, Alex jumped on top of her.

''Alex, really—''

There was another crack and Alex rolled them both off the porch into the flower bed.

''My geraniums,'' Sarah protested, struggling to get free. ''Alex, get up before the police get here.''

''Somebody's shooting at us,'' he whispered in her ear.

She instinctively tried to see. ''What?''

That earned her another close inspection of the topsoil she'd spread. "Hold still. We have to get to some shelter."

"Shooting at us?" she echoed stupidly, thinking instead that he did have a hairy chest. It was tickling her nose where he pressed against her. His hand was on her head, and his arms were around her, shielding her from whoever was out there. "Well, they'll leave in a minute."

"What makes you so sure?" he countered. "Premonition?"

"No," she admitted to his pectorals. "When I opened the door, I punched in the wrong code."

Alex lifted his head just enough to get a look at her. "What code did you punch?"

Sarah did her best to smile. "One that said I was being held hostage."

Once Alex moved, Sarah noticed the flashing lights.

"All right, pal," the loudspeaker barked even as three more police cars screeched to a halt. "Let her up and throw out your weapon now, or you'll be breathing through your forehead."

Chapter 8

"Hey, you're Alex Thorne!"

Gritting his teeth in frustration, Alex did his best to ignore the gun barrel tattooing his temple. "Yes," he grated out, his face pressed close enough to the concrete to smell the dust in the cracks. "I'm Alex Thorne."

His fingers were laced behind his neck, and he was lying prone and spread-eagled on Sarah's sidewalk. Police cars choked the streets, and neighbors were already spilling out from nearby doors to watch the show. And just above his right ear, at the other end of the .357 that seemed far too friendly with his forehead, a young policeman was inspecting the wallet he'd just pulled from Alex's back pocket.

"Why would you want to hurt Miss Delaney?" he asked.

"Alex Thorne?" one of the other cops demanded, approaching. "I don't believe it. Stand him up, Phillips. I wanna see this."

Phillips retreated just enough to let Alex up.

"No kiddin'," the other policeman said in awe as Alex did his best to straighten out a knee that had met with the corner of Sarah's porch on the way down. "We got us an all-pro here, boys. Why don't we see you on those beer commercials?"

Alex offered a wan smile. "Because crime pays so well," he said.

The gathering police laughed. The sergeant was looking way up at Alex, much as he might the Empire State Building.

"What happened?" one of them asked. "She punch in the wrong code again?"

Alex moved his hands just enough to remind his audience of his uncomfortable position. The sergeant who watched football immediately waved an at-ease and reholstered his own gun. Alex brushed the dirt from his shirt. He had a sneaking suspicion he still had geranium petals in his hair from the fast dive off the porch.

"Roy Waller," the sergeant introduced himself with a huge smile, hand now outstretched. "Pleasure to meet you, Mr. Thorne."

"Alex," Alex amended, shaking hands with the bantam-sized officer. "I'm never formal with a man who has the power to strip-search me."

"So, what happened?"

"Sarah punched in the wrong code," he admitted, hand to his sore knee, his gaze swinging to where he'd left Sarah. "But just after she did, we were shot at."

Sgt. Waller was at immediate attention. "Shot at? Miss Delaney?"

Alex didn't even hear him. He had his back turned to the sergeant as he searched through the gathering crowd.

"It came from across the street," he allowed, eyebrows puckering. "I doubt they're still around, but you might find something."

"I'd sure like to hear that from her," the sergeant allowed, pulling out a notebook.

Alex was turning in the other direction. "So would I," he admitted. "Anybody see her?"

Several nearby heads lifted. Conversations faltered.

"Miss Delaney?" Sgt. Waller called as if that alone would bring her from the shadows. He didn't have any luck.

In the time it had taken the police to swarm all over Alex as if he'd walked out of a bank, Sarah had disappeared.

"Where are you going?" Sgt. Waller asked.

Alex threw open what was left of the storm door and stepped into the house. There was no knowing what Sarah would do. He could still feel the shock echoing in him, the bolt of adrenaline when he'd recognized the sound of gunfire. He'd been through this before. As far as he knew, Sarah hadn't. If she had any sense, she'd still be flat out in the flower bed, shaking like a new baby in the cold.

Not Sarah. She'd not only managed to get to her feet without anybody noticing, she'd slipped away. At least he hoped she had.

Glass crackled beneath his feet as he walked across the foyer. "Sarah? Where are you?"

Silence. She wasn't inside, either. Following on Alex's heels, Waller got a good look at the shattered glass and the bullet hole in the far wall. He was impressed enough to send his minions on a search of the lawns across the street.

"Valdez was telling us about his visit to the Sunset offices," Waller admitted, crouched down to get a better look at the bullet hole. "Think this had anything to do with it?"

Just the mention of the company sent Alex's head up. He knew where Sarah had gone. "Damn her," he growled, whirling around on his heel and heading back for the door. "She needs a baby-sitter."

"Hey! Where are you going?"

"She's at the office," Alex allowed, punching his way past the shattered storm door. Outside, lights still throbbed. A Minicam had joined the crowd, and the reporter was smoothing her hair before the magnesium lights. Police milled over the lawn. A few looked up when Alex stormed out the door. When they saw the look on his face, they instinctively backed away.

"At the office?" Waller echoed incredulously. "What the hell's she headed there for? It's dark."

"Knowing Sarah," Alex retorted blackly, "she didn't even notice."

"Wait," Waller objected, a hand to Alex's arm. "I'll take you. Phillips!" he yelled. "Secure the scene until I get back! Doesn't she know about leaving the scene of a crime?" he demanded as he tried to match Alex's stride and lost.

Alex just snorted. "Have you ever talked to her, Sergeant?"

"No. I've just heard Valdez talk about her. She's kind of a favorite around the squad room. You can always depend on her to liven up the day."

Alex snorted. "I'll bet."

The two of them swung into a cruiser and Waller edged them past the Minicam.

"Police were called out to this quiet neighborhood..." the reporter was saying. Alex saw her notice him and then recognize him. Her recital faltered to a stop, but before she could assimilate the new information, Waller had the lights and siren going and had cleared the traffic.

"So, why did she go to the office?" he was asking.

Alex thought the siren was loud. The last time he'd heard one this close, he'd been sharing the back of an ambulance with a couple of paramedics. He couldn't remember the noise being so irritating. But then, he couldn't remember much about that ride at all.

"Because she's afraid that the person who fired those shots is a friend of hers," he admitted in a voice that was a little too loud.

Waller looked over in surprise. "Somebody at the company?"

Alex nodded, his attention on the green-glass-and-chrome building that was taking shape at the edge of Waller's lights as they turned onto Greenway Boulevard. "A group of them are at the office tonight working on a computer problem. I think Sarah wanted to make sure they're still all there."

WOW!

THE MOST GENEROUS

FREE OFFER EVER!

From the
Silhouette Reader Service™

GET 4 FREE BOOKS WORTH $11.80

Affix peel-off stickers to reply card

4 FOUR FREE BOOKS **4**

FOUR FREE BOOKS

4 **4**

PLUS A FREE VICTORIAN PICTURE FRAME

AND A FREE MYSTERY GIFT!

NO COST! NO OBLIGATION TO BUY!
NO PURCHASE NECESSARY!

Because you're a reader of Silhouette romances, the publishers would like you to accept four brand-new Silhouette Intimate Moments® novels, with their compliments. Accepting this offer places you under no obligation to purchase any books, ever!

ACCEPT FOUR BRAND NEW

YOURS

We'd like to send you four free Silhouette novels, worth $11.80, to introduce you to the benefits of the Silhouette Reader Service™. We hope your free books will convince you to subscribe, but that's up to you. Accepting them places you under no obligation to buy anything, but we hope you'll want to continue your membership in the Reader Service.

So unless we hear from you, once a month we'll send you four additional Silhouette Intimate Moments® novels to read and enjoy. If you choose to keep them, you'll pay just $2.74* each—a saving of 21¢ off the cover price. And there is *no* charge for delivery. There are *no* hidden extras! You may cancel at any time, for any reason, just by sending us a note or a shipping statement marked "cancel" or by returning any shipment of books to us at our cost. Either way the free books and gifts are yours to keep!

ALSO FREE!
VICTORIAN PICTURE FRAME

This lovely Victorian pewter-finish miniature is perfect for displaying a treasured photograph—and it's yours *absolutely free*—when you accept our no-risk offer.

Perfect for a treasured Photograph

Plus a FREE mystery Gift! follow instructions at right.

WE EVEN PROVIDE FREE POSTAGE!

It costs you *nothing* to send for your free books — we've paid the postage on the attached reply card. And we'll pick up the postage on your shipment of free books and gifts, and also on any subsequent shipments of books, should you choose to become a subscriber. Unlike many book clubs, we charge *nothing* for postage and handling!

Waller was definitely interested. "And if somebody's missing, you might have a suspect, huh?"

"We might."

They swung into the Sunset Design parking lot and screeched to a stop. Alex tumbled out before Waller had a chance to so much as switch off the engine. He wanted to know himself who would be there—or who might have just slipped away for food or rest or no reason at all. Would it be Thaddeus? Hector? Jill?

And if they had decided to try to slip back into the office without anyone noticing their absence, what would they do when they stumbled across Sarah as she hurried in with only their protection in mind? Alex went from a walk to a run.

She was standing with the security guard in the foyer.

"When?" she asked, disheveled and out of breath and whispery. Her small voice echoed in the marble foyer.

Alex wanted to shake her. He wanted to hold her. Without waiting for the sergeant, he stalked on into the building.

"Oh, they been gone a couple hours now, Ms. Delaney," the guard was saying. "Miss Connie was saying something about celebrating, but everybody else voted to go home."

Alex saw Sarah slump. He didn't know whether she felt defeat or relief. He felt frustration. Walking up behind her, he took her by the shoulders and swung her around. When he saw the hurt in her eyes, he realized how very afraid he'd been.

"Didn't anybody tell you never to walk off without letting somebody know?" he demanded, the fear metamorphosing into anger. The security guard flinched at the harsh growl, obviously uncertain whether to reach for his gun or not. Sarah, on the other hand, didn't seem to know what it meant to be intimidated.

"I'm sorry," she apologized, her eyes wide, her skin the color of old milk. "I didn't mean to leave you there like that, Alex. Really."

"Me?" he countered, incredulously. "I'm not talking about me. I'm talking about you wandering around in the dark within minutes of being shot at. You don't know that they weren't still out there someplace." He should walk out. He should damn well leave her to the police and all the trusty aides she'd collected over the years. Something was getting way out of control here, and Alex didn't like it.

Surprised, Sarah blinked up at him in a way that made him think of a baby animal caught away from its nest. Lost, troubled, uncertain.

"But they were shooting at *you*," she said.

"What makes you think that?" Waller asked on approach.

"Shooting?" the security guard echoed.

Alex couldn't take his eyes off Sarah, frustrated and furious and so relieved that he wondered that he didn't shake.

Sarah looked from Alex to the policeman. "Good evening," she smiled without moving from Alex's grasp. "Alex was with me."

Waller scowled. "We figured that out. Think you're ready to include the police in this little squabble now?"

"I don't know for sure it's about the company," Sarah objected lamely.

"Any other reason somebody would want to shoot Mr. Thorne, that you know of?"

Sarah and the security guard stared at Alex. Alex scowled. "Not in the past year or so, anyway," he said. "It's time to bring in the police, Sarah."

Even more tension went out of her, as if she were a balloon slowly deflating. "I know," she whispered. "But I hate to do it."

"In the past year or so?" Waller interrupted.

Alex decided not to dredge up old and unnecessary business. "Before we get involved in long explanations," he said, already feeling the trembling take hold of Sarah, "why don't we make a few quick phone calls?" It was all he could do to keep from shoving everybody back out of the way and pulling her into his arms. Damn her.

Sarah's head shot up. She was all set to object. Alex never gave her the chance. "They came a lot closer this time, Sarah."

"Okay," Waller agreed. "But I'm still going to find out about that year-or-so situation."

"It's not as interesting as it sounds," Alex assured him dryly, and guided Sarah over to the security desk where she could dial her friends.

"None of them live that far away," she demurred.

"Do you want the guard to get the numbers?" Alex asked, settling her into a chair.

"No, thanks. I know them all."

Alex shot her a sharp glance. "You know those phone numbers by heart?"

She shook her head, a hand instinctively up to brush hair from her forehead. "I know the numbers of everybody in the company."

"By heart?"

Sarah looked at him, and Alex saw the humor finally struggling to take hold. "Sure," she said. "Why not?"

And damned if she didn't.

"Connie?" she said brightly as if a policeman weren't standing over her shoulder taking notes. "Why aren't you here?"

The voice on the other end sounded just as happy, enthusing about whatever had gone on in Sarah and Alex's absence. Sarah nodded a couple of times, offered a few monosyllabic answers and promised to see Connie at work the next morning.

"The computer's fixed," she announced, hanging up. The life had disappeared from her voice. Alex could feel the tension of duplicity radiating through her. Sarah wasn't made for the double life. She should never have had to lie to her friends or ferret out traitors. But there should have never been a hole in her front door, either.

Alex hoped he was around when they finally did come up with the embezzler. He wanted very much to add his own small justice.

Thaddeus was home as well, and kept Sarah on even longer, extolling his own virtues. Unfortunately, they weren't as lucky with Jill or Hector. Neither answered.

"These people are all considered suspects?" Waller asked, scribbling away as Sarah hung up the final time.

"Nobody's considered a suspect," she objected miserably. "We haven't even found anything wrong yet."

Waller shot an incredulous look at Alex, who could only manage a shrug. "That's what I'm doing here."

"That's why you're getting shot at and sabotaged."

"It seems."

Waller nodded, and there was nothing hesitant about the opinion. "Then there are damn well some suspects someplace. Now, who besides these four?"

Alex looked down at Sarah. She looked up at him.

"Everybody," he admitted.

Waller sighed. "Is this a shorter story than the one about somebody wanting to shoot you?"

"Yes."

"Fine. We'll give it a run-through on the way back to the crime scene."

Sarah felt as if she were battling her way out of a fog. She was so tired she could barely sit up, and yet Sgt. Waller still refused to leave. Slurping at his third cup of coffee since setting himself up in her favorite armchair, the sergeant didn't seem to be in any hurry to finish his questioning. At the moment he was asking Alex about the previous sabotage, and Alex was patiently answering.

Seated alongside him on the couch, Sarah couldn't take her eyes off the front door. Especially at the hole in the front door, marking the exact spot where Alex's head had been before he'd bent down to get her earrings.

Her earrings. Oh, well, it looked as though she'd lost them again. Or maybe the dozen or so police technicians who had swarmed over her porch would find something. She really didn't care. Earrings didn't matter in the least when balanced against a life.

Alex answered some question and Sarah turned at the sound of his voice. He hadn't moved since they'd returned. He'd seated himself next to her and put an arm around her shoulder as if to shield her from the inevitable battering of police procedure. Protecting her, when he'd been the intended victim.

How could he be so calm, so authoritative and concise when he'd missed dying by inches? How could his anger have dissipated so quickly when it was her fault he'd been there in the first place?

Sarah felt weary, defeated. One of the people she'd trusted the most had tried to kill Alex. This had all gone beyond the company, beyond her or the trust they'd built up. This involved a crime so horrible that Sarah couldn't believe she wasn't able to somehow see it on the person.

But she hadn't even seen the danger. Completely submerged in the sensual delights of anticipation, she'd blithely led Alex right up to the porch and then provided the light to make him a better target. She hadn't had a clue, not a tingling or a murmur.

Why hadn't she insisted Alex leave like she'd wanted?

Why couldn't she do it now?

"You'll be hearing from the detectives a little later," Waller said as he drained his coffee cup and lurched to his feet. "But right now, you might as well get some sleep."

Sarah blinked at the officer, wondering whether he was joking. There was still glass on the floor and gouge marks from where they had extracted the bullet from her door, cups and saucers out and dusty footprints all over her rug.

She had just suffered a convulsion in her life, a shock that echoed along her nerve endings and whispered in the quiet confines of her house. Worse, she was responsible for it and didn't know how to prevent it happening again. And he suggested she sleep, as if the only thing she had to look forward to the next morning was exams.

"Maybe you'd have better luck," she said abruptly.

Waller swung around to her. "Pardon?"

She motioned to Alex. "Get him to go home."

Waller lifted an eyebrow. "That's what I just did."

"No," Sarah insisted, getting to her own feet, away from the solace of Alex's arms, away from the temptation to depend on him when it could hurt him. "To Colorado."

She was bringing Waller to a dead stop in the water. "But I thought he came here to help you settle your books. You want him to go?"

Sarah nodded. "Yes. Please."

Now Waller included Alex in his quizzical stare.

"Sarah thinks this will all get worse before it gets better," Alex explained without following suit. Comfortably sprawled back on her couch, with legs crossed and coffee mug in hand, he looked to Sarah as if he were settling in for the duration.

Waller buttoned his pocket back over his notebook. "Probably will. Want some protection?"

"No," Sarah insisted. "I want him gone."

Waller squinted at her. "Has he caused you any problems, Miss Delaney?"

"Oh, no," she said quickly. "No. He's . . . well, it's just that I'm afraid he'll be hurt."

Waller's only consolation was a shrug. "Might happen. But I think he can take care of himself." He was turning away before Sarah could protest further when a thought stopped him. "Which reminds me," he said, turning back. "You were going to tell me a story, Mr. Thorne."

This time Alex got to his feet. Sarah felt him close the space between them like a blanket of energy closing over her. It protected and nurtured her—and she was afraid of it, for his sake. The more she got used to it, the harder it would be to push it away.

"How about the abbreviated version?" Alex asked. "Sarah's beat, and I still have to get back to the hotel for an hour or two before heading back to her offices—" he must have sensed her objection forming, because he turned on her with a scowl "—whether she likes it or not."

"Something I can check out would be nice," Waller agreed.

"My sister works for the Special Assignment Crime Task Force out of Denver. Little over a year ago, she and an agent named Jason Mitchell got involved with a case that put her in jeopardy. He hid her at my place while he closed it, but the bad guys found her."

"And you?" Sarah asked, plagued by a sudden impression of numbness, surprise, anger. Desperation.

"Let's just say I didn't help much."

"That be the Esperanzo case?" Waller asked, eyes sharp. "Mitchell really put the nails on that guy's coffin."

Busying himself with a final sip of coffee, Alex nodded.

Waller nodded back with some satisfaction. "Couldn't have happened to nicer scum. I had a taste of the Esperanzo bunch down here, too. Sent Mitchell a personal thank-you note. You tell him for me when you see him, okay?"

"Happy to," Alex agreed.

"Her husband," Sarah said.

Both men turned to her.

"He's her husband, isn't he?" she said, sharp with the impression of hard, green eyes. Determination. Ferocity like a winter storm.

"Yeah," Alex admitted, the hand with the cup sagging a little in surprise.

Sarah grinned. "I can't wait to meet him."

Waller couldn't quite take his eyes off her. "So, does this mean he's staying?"

Sarah looked up at Alex and saw an equal determination. Not so hot, so visceral. Just as impenetrable. "Yes," she succumbed, feeling worse every time she did. "I guess it does."

"Good," Waller answered with a nod as he turned once again for the door. "Saves me from having to find him when I need him again."

"I'll be here," Alex promised.

"Here?" Waller asked, not turning back around again, his message implicit.

"I'm over at the Fountains when I'm not at Sunset," Alex amended.

Sarah let Alex walk Waller outside. She contented herself to collect cups and saucers and take them to the kitchen, considering the surprise revelations the brief conversation had brought. Trying to understand why that particular door should suddenly open up into a turbulent time in Alex's past when she couldn't manage to see what was in front of her nose.

It was so frustrating. And so frightening. Sarah wanted to protect him. She wanted to offer him half of what he offered her. Yet the wisdom she relied on as much as he did his mathematical tables was as faulty as a tattered gauze in a wind. Brushing close and then disappearing, never whole, never certain. Surprising when it failed, even more surprising when it didn't.

"How did you know?" she asked when she heard him step into the kitchen behind her.

"Know what?"

The tile carried his feet comfortably, the echo satisfying and whole. Completely against her will Sarah smiled to herself, even as she dipped soapy hands into the water to finish the dishes.

"Where I'd be," she said without turning, willing him closer, wanting to slake her thirst on the substance of him. "I'd only gotten there when you arrived."

"It made sense," he said gruffly. "As much as you make sense."

That did make Sarah turn around, because she knew something he didn't. "No," she disagreed. "It didn't make sense at all. I should have called, not gone over. I almost did, except that all those police were between me and the door.''

"And you didn't want them to know what you were doing before you had a chance to do it," he scowled without much humor, the light in his honey-brown eyes more troubled than even he allowed. "You scared the hell out of me, Sarah."

Sarah shook her head, wanting him to see. "Don't you understand?" she insisted. "Connie wouldn't have known. Neither would Ellis or Thaddeus."

"Sure they would," Alex retorted easily. "Hell, Sgt. Valdez probably would have known. It only took a minute to figure out where your first thoughts would be."

Still Sarah shook her head. "No," she said, and knew Alex wouldn't allow her conclusion yet even if she could prove it to him. "For an accountant, you're a very perceptive person."

Alex wasn't having any of it. "Accounting isn't just figures, Sarah. It's people, too."

She smiled and swiped at her hair. "But it's mostly figures."

Alex walked up then and lifted a hand to her forehead. "You have suds in your hair," he objected, wiping the moisture with gentle fingers. "Why don't you have a dishwasher like every other twentieth-century businesswoman?"

Sarah couldn't pull her gaze from his, basking in the sudden warmth of that sweet brown. The rapport, the last traces of gruff frustration, the growing wonder. "I like the feel of hot, soapy water on my hands," she admitted in a soft voice, her chest suddenly tight with his nearness.

Alex's eyes seemed to grow a little, his pupils dilating. Somehow nearness.

Alex's eyes seemed to grow a little, his pupils dilating. Somehow Sarah's own words hung between them like a promise rather than a simple admission. A plea that came colored with all the turmoil they'd survived this evening, from the moment she'd first courted Alex's sensuality to the moment she'd almost cost him his life. She couldn't help the words, the invitation that accompanied them. She couldn't stop it.

"We spend all our time distancing ourselves from the simple pleasures of the world," she said, hearing the breathiness in her voice and seeing its impact on Alex. "I bet you take showers, don't you?"

"Religiously." Funny, he sounded breathless, too.

Sarah nodded, never looking away, soaking in the heat from his eyes like a summer sun. Suddenly, she felt small and lonely and hungry. "I bet you'd be surprised by how delicious it feels to sit in a hot, soapy bath for an hour or so."

"We're not talking baths here, Sarah," he reminded her, as if reminding himself, as well. "We're talking dishes."

"Soapy water," she amended. "Hot, soapy water. It calms me. Soothes me. I like the slippery feel of it on my skin," she admitted. "The scent. I soak in the water and rub at my dishes and watch my garden, and all the problems of the world slip out of focus." Alex stood only a foot away, tense, taut, radiating a sensuality that struck Sarah like a tide. A hot, slow, pulsing tide that threatened to suck her under.

"Soap," he echoed in a strained voice.

Sarah nodded. "You should try it."

He didn't move. Neither did Sarah. The water on her hands evaporated, and the soap bubbles behind her popped in the sudden silence. Sarah didn't even know she was going to speak. Impulse and action were simultaneous and sincere.

"Or you could make love to me."

Chapter 9

Alex didn't move. For a long moment he didn't speak. The insects chorused outside, and in the hallway the grandfather clock ticked away in the silence. Sarah never flinched, never prodded or excused. She merely waited, as taut as he, as hesitant. As torn.

And in the stillness that stretched until it threatened to snap like frayed nerves, Alex realized he couldn't do what she wanted. What *he* wanted.

It wasn't the desire in her eyes. He'd seen that before and understood it. It wasn't the suggestion in her voice or the temptation in her request.

It was the pain. The residue of what had happened that night. Alex saw the betrayal eating at her, saw the erosion of her safe, bright world and knew that it was security she asked for. Comfort.

And he couldn't offer it the way she asked.

He'd dealt with pain before. He'd held his sister through a depression so terrifying it had almost sent her through that mirror of madness. He'd beaten off her despair and held back his own loss when his knees had kept him from walking onto the field again. He'd survived failing to protect Lindsay when she'd been at physical risk. But this wasn't the same.

This wasn't a violent emotion. Nothing about Sarah was violent or passionate or desperate. She was composed of pastels and displayed her emotions the same way—in shades of fear, hues of joy. She still looked hurt, confused, like a child who couldn't understand the capricious world of an adult. She struggled with betrayal and couldn't grasp it, and it was Alex who felt the rage.

Standing there before him, she looked not so much the sensual nymph she could be but the loneliest, the most fragile person he'd seen. And Alex was afraid that his own surprising emotions would shatter her.

His hand shaking from the control he had to exert over himself, Alex reached out to stroke her cheek. "I don't think that's such a good idea right now, Sarah."

Her smile was tentative—at once relieved and disappointed. "You mean you're turning down the first proposition I've made in my entire life?"

Alex pulled her into his arms, soapsuds and all. "I mean that tonight's not the right time. You need sleep and you need a little security, and I'll be happy to provide them both. But beyond that . . ." He could only shake his head, fighting the surge of need, of desire—using all his legendary willpower to fight the turmoil her innocent request had unleashed in him.

Her head tilted back, sending her hair tumbling over Alex's arms, Sarah sighed. "And what about you, Alex? What do you need?"

Alex figured that Sarah should have felt what his body needed. It was certainly telling them both in no uncertain terms.

Why did his common sense shut down when he had her in his arms? He'd been ready to throttle her when he'd discovered that she'd run off tonight. He'd been ready to tear the person limb from limb who might hurt her. And here, filling his arms with the soft, frothy feel of her, he wanted to bury himself in her until the rest of the world disappeared.

Only one other time in his life had he been that short-sighted. Only one time had he given in, and look where it had gotten him. He had ended up alone trying to deal with the rage of loss by himself. He'd been flayed raw and left out in the wind. He'd risked too much.

"I need to get you to sleep and then find out what the hell's going on with your company," he finally said, the smile aching on his face.

Her smile grew. "You're lying, Alex."

He shook his head. "Give me credit for once not making my decisions based on hormones."

Sarah proffered a pout. "Leave it to me to fall in love with a practical person."

There was a lurch in Alex's chest. He tried to discount Sarah's words or their import to him. She was just being Sarah, talking off the top of her head, ready to believe in signs and portents. Even so, the words sounded unaccountably sweet.

"Next time make sure you don't get into elevators with strange accountants."

For a moment they stood there, soaking in the silence of the kitchen, the surprising comfort of isolation, the soothing cadence of matched heartbeats. Even the confusion seemed to ease a little.

"Alex?"

"Mmm-hmm."

"You can call about the baby now."

Still six feet under the smell and sense and feel of Sarah in his arms, Alex forgot to move. "Baby? What baby?"

He could feel Sarah smile against his chest. "The one they're naming after you."

Still he didn't understand. Alex couldn't quite pull his attention away from her, from the emotions that still warred in him like high winds.

Then, suddenly, as if the shell around him shattered, the answer hit him. "Oh, my God," he gasped, straightening to attention. "Lindsay."

He didn't even wait for Sarah's affirmation to head for the phone. Nor did he hear her, left behind, as she shook her head in gentle amusement.

"She's fine, you know."

"Why didn't you tell me?"

Sarah looked up at the distressed outrage in Connie's voice and set down her pen. It was still too early in the day. She hadn't gotten much sleep the night before, the sun was too bright, and she had a headache from having to sit in with Thaddeus on a demonstration of the video-animation equipment. She wasn't at all sure she wanted to deal with Connie right now.

When Sarah looked up, Connie came to a dead halt on the other side of the drawing table. "Oh, hon. You look like hell."

"Randolph already told me," Sarah admitted with a listless swipe of her hair. Taking a final look down at the persistently blank sheet of paper on her drawing board, she finally gave up and climbed off her stool. Midcentral Airlines wasn't getting its logo today, either.

All Sarah could think of was loyalty and betrayal. Need and fear. Belonging and loneliness.

"Well, he was right," Connie said, walking up to take Sarah by the arm. Sarah followed her over to the corner without a protest. "Why didn't you call me? I could have been at your house in ten minutes flat. You shouldn't have been alone last night, for heaven's sake."

"I wasn't alone," Sarah admitted, sinking into the sofa and curling her bare feet up beneath her. Her sandals stayed with the pig. "Alex stayed."

It took Connie a minute to find her voice as she settled herself in alongside and poured Sarah a cup of tea from the Wedgwood service Randolph had left earlier. "Was he a help?"

Sarah managed a smile. "He was a gentleman. I asked him to make love to me and he said no."

It was obvious that Connie wasn't sure how to react to either end of that statement. Consternation, alarm and relief all swept across her features in quick succession.

"You're right," Connie admitted, handing Sarah's cup across. "He is a gentleman. I'm not sure Peter would have shown such restraint."

"I'm not sure you would have let him," Sarah retorted with her first smile of the day.

Connie grinned. "True."

"I didn't even know," Sarah confided in her friend, her voice torn between confusion and misery. "He almost died, Con, and I didn't even get a warning."

"You had a warning," Connie reminded her brusquely. "You told him five times to go back to Colorado. I don't see why you should feel guilty because he doesn't see good sense when it's staring him in the face."

Sarah shook her head. "I know when there's going to be a flash flood. I warned you the time the train you were going to get on derailed. I told Hector when his wife went into premature labor."

"And you stopped Alex from driving on bad brakes," Connie finished for her, impatient with Sarah's uncertainty. "Stop being responsible for everyone, hon. It's a no-win proposition. Now, you wanna know what's going on here?"

Sarah remembered her tea and took a sip. "I guess."

Connie nodded, now all business. "The police detective called. He'll be here at eleven. I've set up interviews with everybody he requested—he requested damn near everybody, you know."

Sarah shrugged uncomfortably. "I couldn't narrow it down."

Connie's smile was proprietary. "What about the four of us who were maybe seven blocks away just before the shots were fired?"

"Come on, Connie," Sarah objected, then dropped her gaze to her cup, guilty and ashamed for what she'd feared the night before. "Besides, I . . ." She couldn't quite bring herself to finish, to admit what she'd done.

Connie did it for her. "You checked. We'd already gone." When Sarah looked up, unable to keep the surprise and relief from her eyes, Connie grinned that old, brash grin of hers and took a long sip of her own tea. "For your sake, I wish we'd all still been stuck over that damn program. Unfortunately for all of us, Thaddeus managed to break through it about half an hour after you left. He really is a genius, by the way. We should pay him more."

Sarah nodded, distracted by the enormity of the situation, by the tarry stain of duplicity, by the lingering envy at the sound of Alex's excited laughter the night before. "Okay," she said instinctively.

Connie shook her head and reached over to nudge Sarah's teacup in the right direction. "Are you sure you want to be here today?"

Startled from the morass she seemed to be caught in, Sarah looked up. "I don't want to be anyplace else."

Connie sighed, the strain on Sarah's features now echoed on her own. "I'll have Randolph hold all your calls until the detective shows up."

"Everybody except Alex," Sarah amended.

Connie smiled and Sarah remembered all those times Connie had cheer-led and refereed and conducted clandestine operations between Sarah and dates. "Everybody except Alex," she allowed, and got to her feet.

"Thanks, Con," Sarah said as her friend opened the door to leave. "I don't know what I'd do without you."

Connie turned one last time before leaving and bestowed one of her sharpest smiles. "You'd get lost on the way to the store, wander up into the mountains and become so intrigued by the shapes and colors that you'd starve to death with a stick in your hand scratching out designs in the dust."

After Connie left, Sarah tried her best to keep her mind on the problem at hand. She owed it to Connie and everybody at the company who was being interrogated and disturbed. She owed it to Alex so that he could get away before something else happened. But as hard as she tried, her gaze still drifted back to the sunbaked summer landscape and her thoughts to the evening before.

To Alex and his polite withdrawal.

What had changed his mind? She'd been so sure when they'd walked up to her house that he'd wanted to make love to her. She'd felt his defenses ease a little, tasted the stunning power of his arousal. His eyes had brimmed with it; his voice had rasped with it. The electricity had snapped and popped between them on the ride home, shocking careless fingers and igniting gasps. The promise of what would happen had stolen words and stretched minutes into agony.

And then the shots had been fired. Somewhere between that time and the moment she'd asked him to make love to her, he'd closed himself off again.

She'd seen her request slam into him, felt the residue hum through him like a live wire. He'd battled himself like a storm at sea and barely brought himself back under control.

Sarah would have loved to talk to Alex's sister. She wanted to know what his ex-wife had been like, what Alex had been like with her. Had he completely surrendered to her charm, opened himself up and exposed the hot core he now protected so closely only to have it violated? Had he decided that it was too much of a risk to ever do that again?

Was Alex, who had battled through all those years in professional football, who had survived his sister's crisis and the loss of faith from a capricious spouse, afraid of the emotions he'd locked away behind that neat button-down job of his? Was he afraid of something more, something intangible that Sarah couldn't quite get a finger on yet? Something, maybe even Alex wouldn't admit to, that he'd unconsciously recognized the night before?

And was it fair for Sarah to expose his vulnerabilities, when just by doing so she could put him in more danger? She wasn't wise. She was frightened and uncertain and overwhelmed by the sudden magic of Alex in her life.

How was she supposed to be able to know what would protect him? Why should she have to be strong enough to ignore her own needs for common good? She needed Alex. She needed his strength, his love, his wry eye on life—she needed the passion he had only hinted at. Sarah wasn't sure she had the courage to forfeit that.

Sarah was absorbed by the palm trees dancing in the wind outside when Randolph returned with a fresh pot of tea and some banana bread.

"The police didn't ask to interview me," he said without much inflection as he traded teapots.

Surprised, Sarah looked up. "Why should they?" she asked. "You weren't here last night."

Filling her cup and adding three teaspoonfuls of sugar, Randolph handed it over. Sarah could see something was wrong, but for the life of her she didn't know what.

"Randolph," she said, accepting her tea. "Are you upset because I don't think you're embezzling?"

His smile was light and fleeting. With eyes the size of a cocker spaniel's, Randolph was a heartbreakingly good-looking man. He also had the knack for looking like the only person left on earth who had serious thoughts.

"I guess I'm wondering if you don't think I'm talented enough to do it."

Sarah's headache swelled. "Sit down," she said, the most preemptive command she'd ever issued to Randolph.

"Sometimes I forget to say it," she said sincerely, reaching out to take his hand. "But there would be no Sunset

Design without you. I guess I keep figuring that you know that.''

Rather than lighten his expression, her words puckered his features into even more serious consideration. "Then will you take my word for something?"

Sarah didn't even have to think about it. "Of course."

When he lifted his eyes to her, Randolph looked like an archangel in a Michelangelo painting. Sarah couldn't help but smile.

"Alex Thorne isn't doing you any good here," he said abruptly, neatly erasing her smile. "Send him back to Colorado."

Sarah couldn't think of a decent objection. "Randolph?"

"You're not paying attention, Sarah," Randolph insisted. "Ever since he's shown up, he's been hurting you *and* the company, and I think you'll find that everything will be back to normal when he leaves."

"But the attempts on his life . . ."

He shook his head. "You trust my judgment. Trust me now. It's not us, it's him."

The white sheet of paper on Sarah's drawing table never was filled up that day.

Alex had been in a fairly good mood when he'd arrived at Sunset that morning. He hadn't slept at all the night before, stretched out on Sarah's couch and listening to her soft breathing in the next room. He'd ached without respite and spent too many hours ignoring the reasons.

On the other hand, he was an uncle again. Lindsay had given birth to a healthy nine-pound boy they had indeed named Alexander. After Lindsay had seen the size of the baby's head and shoulders, she'd claimed the resemblance was just too strong to ignore. She was healthy, happier than she had ever been, and Jason had been as tongue-tied over his child as a schoolboy with an idol.

And then Alex had waded back into the problems at Sunset. He hadn't been able to so much as find a handhold on them. Someone had deliberately sabotaged the computer system to keep Alex away from accounts receivable, and so far he couldn't figure out the reason, which was why he was so frustrated.

After nearly eight hours poring over printout, screen and calculator, he hadn't found a thing. *Nada*. Zero. By the time everybody else left the department, he had gotten as far as deciding to check something else out and come back to accounts receivable when he was fresh.

"You look tired."

Lifting his head, Alex took in the sight of Sarah standing in the open door to the accounting department. She was in slacks today, pink ones, with a kind of gauzy peasant blouse tucked in, some kind of fringed shawl at the waist and a chintz duster over that—and bare feet. Dangly earrings tinkled at her ears and beads fell from her neck in waves.

"Just frustrated. I can't find even a padded expense account."

He'd moved on to the files of companies Sunset dealt with. As he talked to Sarah, Alex punched them up, one after another, for a cursory look. His eyes burned and his attention was minimal now. He knew it was nearly time to quit.

Sarah walked in and perched herself on the desk just out of view of the screen. "The police aren't any happier. They say everybody has a motive, but nobody has a motive."

Alex flashed a quick grin. "Helpful." He scanned Darrow, Ltd. and then brought up Datasys. "Did they happen to mention anybody's name in particular in connection with last night?"

Something wasn't tracking, but he couldn't decide what it was. Alex rubbed at his eyes and looked again. Still he couldn't decide why the screen bothered him.

For her part, Sarah drew imaginary pictures on the edge of the desk with a finger. "I wish more people had thought to have good alibis last night."

Alex saw the frustration in Sarah's eyes. It made him remember that it was Jill's department he'd spent investigating all day. "Jill didn't have an alibi, huh?"

Sarah sighed. "No. She said she wasn't home. But she swears she wasn't here, either. Beyond that, she says she can't tell us."

"What about Hector?" he asked.

Sarah took up exercising her toes at the end of outstretched legs and then got back to her feet. "Said he was so wound up after working through the computer problems that he took a long ride in his new car. His wife was asleep by the time he got home."

Alex tilted his chair back and braced a foot against the desk. "The seduction of a BMW 735. What do you think about Jill?"

Sarah wandered over to the window and looked out. "It's not Jill."

"You're sure?"

Sarah turned from the window, her eyes clouded and resigned. "No. Did you find something in her department?"

"No," he admitted, looking briefly at the blinking cursor that sat amid all the rows and columns of data. "There wasn't anything. Which means that either I've missed it and have to go over it again, or I was deliberately steered in the wrong direction."

Sarah was quiet a moment. Alex watched her, wishing he could offer her escape. Wishing he could soothe the strain in her small shoulders.

"What are you going to do?" she finally asked.

He shrugged, contemplating the screen and considering his state of mind. "Whatever it is, I'm going to do it tomorrow. I'm beat."

Sarah turned back to the window. Alex looked up to see the late afternoon sun gild her pale hair and warm her skin.

The night before when he'd checked in on her, the hall light had illuminated her sleeping features much the same way, making them younger, more vulnerable—making Alex feel old and tired and lonely standing in the dark.

"Balloons!" she cried suddenly, spinning around.

Alex instinctively looked to the window. The clear blue Arizona sky was faultless and empty.

"No," she said with a little giggle. "I mean let's go. Randolph's taking a sunset flight up today, and he invited me. Come along."

That fast the life was back in her eyes, the sparkling invitation that was so deadly. Her hair settled at her shoulders like wind-swept silk. Her lips parted in a smile of delight.

"Please?"

Alex did his best to scowl past all the enthusiasm. "I thought Randolph didn't trust me."

"He doesn't," she admitted brightly. "But he hasn't spent that much time with you, either. This could kill two birds with one stone."

"Figuratively speaking, I hope," Alex amended dryly.

Sarah's smile grew as she closed the distance to where Alex sat. "We can stop by for some chicken and wine and enjoy the sunset from the air. Come on, Alex. There isn't anything else you can do tonight. Celebrate your new nephew. Celebrate summer," she begged, setting her hands on his desk and leaning closer. "Celebrate life."

Alex scowled this time. "Hippies," he snorted. "Next you'll want me to go barefoot and wear beads."

Sarah giggled. "And grow your hair to your waist."

Damn it, she was infecting him, too. Suddenly he wanted to see her against the sunset, the breeze tousling her hair and the sun turning her hair into red gold. He wanted to take the computer and dump it into the nearest pit and walk away holding Sarah's hand and never look back.

Which was why she was so dangerous.

"One balloon flight," he agreed. "Accountants are only allowed so much fun," he informed her, shutting down the program and climbing to his feet. "It upsets their delicate systems."

Sarah snuggled close, her eyes bright and her arm threaded through Alex's as she guided him straight for the door. "In that case, we'd better make this good."

Sarah's voice sounded suspiciously smug. And Alex's chest went suspiciously tight just at the thought of it.

Chapter 10

Since a hot-air balloon rides wind currents, there wasn't much extra breeze. The air was still and sweet and cooling, lifting the balloon fast as the last heat of the afternoon rose off the desert. The sunset was lost to a band of muddy clouds that forecast some of the rare rain Phoenix was privilege to.

Preoccupied with the sea of collapsed material, a burner and a fan, Randolph had greeted Sarah like a partner and taken Alex's unexpected arrival with resignation. Now as they soared up over the edge of the Superstitions, Randolph relaxed a little and shared in the champagne.

Sarah was glad. She wanted Randolph's help and allegiance where Alex was concerned. She wanted as many friends as possible to help him. As much as anything, she wanted all her friends to like each other. Connie called it the one-big-happy-family syndrome.

"How long have you been ballooning?" Alex asked as he watched Randolph work the burner.

Randolph waited to finish a burn. Even after being up with Randolph before, Sarah was still surprised at the noise and heat every time he opened up the flame. It was like standing next to a coke oven. Then, sudden silence, with only the distant sound of sheep bells and one or two barking dogs drifting up from the desert to break through.

"I've been racing for about five years. Ballooning about ten."

Alex nodded, took a considering sip of champagne and a peek over the edge of the small basket. "Sure is a quieter sport than football."

"More expensive, too," Randolph added, then offered a dry grin. "Before you ask."

"You figured I would?"

Taking a moment to assess his drift, Randolph shrugged. "It seemed inevitable, especially in your line of work."

Alex took another sip of champagne, his eyes steady and noncommittal. Sarah could hear the gears mesh, could almost see the calculations being formulated. Across from him, Randolph was positioning himself, as well. It was as if swords had met in the first clash of a duel.

"Well, since you want me to ask," Alex said evenly, his tone doing nothing to ease Sarah's tension. "How much would one spend on a sport like this?" The little wicker basket didn't seem big enough or sturdy enough to withstand the calculated mistrust that sparked like static electricity.

"Let's just say that it's a good thing I'll never have children," Randolph admitted, his eyes away to the hills. "They'd probably starve. Of course, it's gotten better since I've started competing. I'm sponsored now."

"By Sunset Designs," Sarah offered.

Alex smiled. "Of course."

In the end Sarah wasn't sure whether her idea had been a good one or not. Randolph and Alex never did seem to relax around each other. The ride was a success, such as it was. The air cooled as the sun settled into the western mountains and the first lights of Phoenix winked on. The rain held off, but tantalized with the faint smell of moisture on the evening breeze. The sunset sky shuddered with gold, with peach and hot corals and deepening blue beyond the curtain of clouds that still piled up at the horizon. And Alex and Randolph were so preoccupied with maintaining polite conversation that neither saw it happen.

It was just as well. Sarah had looked up again, wallowing in the rich, brilliant colors of the balloon against the sunset, wishing she could somehow suspend this moment longer, floating, aimless, almost content.

As she looked, the sun, which had been dodging in and out of the clouds for a few minutes, disappeared abruptly, casting a long shadow over the bright stripes that swept up toward the sky.

A shadow. A chill. A sudden terror.

Sarah gripped the sides of the basket, afraid of falling, afraid of dying. Feeling the awful stain of prescience dull her sight and dim her hearing. She felt the world shift, shudder and right itself, and still Alex and Randolph went on discussing lift ratios and wind velocity. She heard the future whispering in her ear, dread suspicions of disaster, and no one's head turned at the sound.

Sarah wanted out of the balloon. She wanted away from the sinking in her stomach. She wanted anything but the knowledge that she couldn't say for sure what it was she was seeing. She just knew that this sensation had struck twice, and that it had to do with her logo, with Alex and with some kind of danger.

For the rest of the ride, she sipped at the warming champagne and did her best to ignore her nausea.

When they finally bumped to a landing, Alex helped Randolph subdue the wilting balloon and pack everything away before he and Sarah headed home.

But Sarah couldn't really say that she felt a sense of victory, even a sense of relief. She'd felt undercurrents during the ride that had nothing to do with wind and found her best attempts at joviality met with polite smiles. And somewhere in the guileless blue of the desert sky, the future had lain in wait for her. By the time she leaned her head back against the headrest in Alex's rental, she felt exhausted and jittery.

"How about a swim?" she asked suddenly.

Alex looked over. "We just went ballooning," he reminded her. "After which I was going to drop you off at home and go back to the hotel."

Sarah looked over, wondering if he could see the sudden, surprising intensity in her eyes. The currents stirred, muddy and indecipherable, and Sarah was suddenly afraid of them. For once she didn't want to be left alone with her sight.

"After a swim," she said, and heard the slight note of pleading in her voice.

Alex must have heard it, too. Taking a brief look over, he searched out her expression with some worry. "What are you trying to tell me, Sarah?"

She couldn't. Sarah knew simply that the path she'd chosen for tonight was inevitable and that it felt like the only choice. The only right choice for them both, no matter what happened.

She knew how much she needed him, and that made her wonder whether what she was feeling was merely selfishness or truth.

"I'm telling you that I'd like a little time alone with you," she said. "Away from the computers and the police and everything." Sarah wondered if Alex realized why she watched the far distance instead of him as she talked. "And I don't think it would hurt you to unwind a little, either."

Outside the car, night had taken control. Darkness blotted out the scenery, melding mountain into anonymous sky and desert into oblivion. Only the city challenged. A cloud of lights flickered in the distance, and neon punctuated the free enterprise of suburbia. No relief out there, no quiet. Only the echoes of too many people, the murmurs of struggle and competition. Sarah could feel it like the pulsing of her own blood. She wanted respite. She wanted immersion.

"I thought that's what we were doing," Alex said, pragmatically.

Sarah offered a fleeting smile. "Except that you and Randolph still don't like each other."

Alex didn't insult her by denying it. "You can't make everything happy and bright, Sarah."

Sarah shouldn't have felt so miserable. "I can try."

For a moment Alex did no more than drive, one hand resting on the top of the steering wheel, the other tapping the outside of the car door in time to the music that wafted gently from the radio. The lights swept him in waves, riding up the set planes of his jaw, over his pursed mouth, darkened eyes and tousled hair. Sarah waited, unsure what she wanted him to say, unsettled by her own uncertainties, silenced by the surprising depth of her reaction to the sight of his features, sharpened again and again in profile.

"We'll stop by the hotel for my trunks," was all he said. It was enough to shatter the tension like ice over a thawing stream.

Sarah felt the current beneath rise in her, bubble free and take her in a strange giddiness. She recognized the passion of certainty and smiled with the wonderful anticipation that tightened in her belly. He was coming home with her. He was going to swim and then later, maybe take a turn in the whirlpool. He was going to relax. And Sarah, her instincts as sharp as any woman's when it came to a man, knew that this was the time she would have her decision from him.

She would set the stage with age-old precision and hope he would seduce her.

If this was the way Alex Thorne relaxed, Sarah was going to have to rethink her seduction plan. Taking a few extra minutes to make sure she looked just right in her aqua-and-black maillot, she'd stepped out onto her patio to find Alex already in the water. Swimming. Eating up the pool in strong rhythmic strokes that didn't so much as pause at the end of a lap.

Easing her way into water that steamed into the cool night air, Sarah watched him work his way back to the other end of the pool and realized how he worked off some of the aggression he'd once brought to the playing field. And if he didn't stop working it off so well, there would be no aggression left for her.

She didn't think to question her decision. In the back of her mind she knew that what would happen tonight would further complicate things when the sun rose in the morning. She even knew that she was casting yet more threads of involvement that might keep Alex where he could be in danger. But the moment he'd decided to come over, when Sarah had felt the rush of exultation at his simple statement, she'd known what his words had portended.

If she could only get him to quit swimming sometime soon.

God, she thought, watching his muscles ripple in the translucent lighting in the pool, he's so beautiful. Sculpted, each limb in perfect proportion, each movement as fluid as flight. His shoulders were tight and broad, the water sluicing along tendon and muscle as he reached for each stroke. His legs scissored effortlessly. Resting at the side of a pool she'd only used for lounging, Sarah admitted to herself that she could watch him swim for hours.

Except that she couldn't. Just watching him tightened the ache in her chest. Imagining those fingers cupping over her that way made her anxious. He was afraid of his strength, his intensity. Watching him, it occurred to her that maybe she should be, too.

When he reached the far side, Sarah slid under water. She could barely see him, his body all shadows and planes in the ethereal world of water. Holding her breath, her hands out at her sides to keep her in place, she smiled.

Alex never saw her. One minute he was slicing through the water, his mind deliberately on nothing. The next he ran into something solid. Something solid, but very, very soft. Sputtering and startled, he pulled to the surface, only to hear the bright music of a familiar laugh.

"Sarah—!"

"Did anybody ever tell you that you don't know how to relax?" she demanded, looking all the more like a nymph with the water beading in her hair and on her skin. A siren, maybe, was that the sea fairy? Rising from the oceans and luring sailors to their deaths? If she popped up the way she looked now, Sarah could do it. Even in the shadows Alex was sure he'd never seen eyes so blue, so big, so guileless. So lethal.

"If memory serves," he retorted, trying very hard to keep his eyes off the way the droplets slid along her throat, down the deep V neck of her suit and back into more shadows. "You invited me to swim. I was," he insisted, motioning behind him, "swimming."

"If you'd been on your feet," Sarah countered equally brightly, "that would have been a marathon. And I would have been sitting in the dust back at the two-mile marker."

"Well, then, what did you have in mind?" He shouldn't have asked it. Just the words opened some kind of door in him that focused on those water droplets, sliding, glistening, gathering on her skin. Disappearing into the warm cleft of her breasts where they strained against the bright Lycra of her suit. If he wasn't careful, everyone in the neighborhood would get a good idea of what he suddenly wanted.

Sarah, however, tilted her head to the side as if in serious consideration. Only the cagey sparkle in her eyes betrayed the fallacy. "Food," she admitted.

Struck by the urge to laugh, Alex rolled his eyes. "You should be the size of a defensive tackle, the way you eat."

Sarah giggled. "I am the size of a defensive tackle," she admitted blithely. Gesturing to her very enticing curves, she grinned. "This is an illusion. Smoke and mirrors."

Giving in to temptation, Alex tested some of those curves with assessing hands. "Smoke never felt like this." The suit was sleek and smooth, the waist and hips beneath it soft and small, fitting neatly in his hands. It was all Alex could do to let go.

He didn't regain his space, though. The cool night air chilled his wet skin, and the water soothed his torso. Sarah's breath drifted in soft clouds toward the invisible night. Her chest rose a bit more quickly and her eyes widened. Alex couldn't drag his gaze from them, suddenly suspicious that he was losing his balance. That blue was so hypnotic, so bright that it could blind a sane man and soothe a madman. Her hair glowed in the reflected light; the shadows trembled over it. Her skin glistened and beckoned. She smelled like wildflowers and chlorine, and Alex found the combination oddly alluring.

His own lungs seemed to work harder. His heart tap-danced as if he'd just done a triathlon instead of seven lousy laps. And deep in his belly, where he kept his dread and anticipation, something flared, but it was too soon to tell the difference.

He knew better. He had more control than this. He'd tumbled into a set of guileless blue eyes once and still wasn't sure he'd found his way out. He couldn't afford to do it again. If he considered making love to a woman, it should be done out of desire, not desperation.

But he felt desperate. He felt separate and cold and isolated, and all the warmth he needed stood so close he'd only have to reach out to claim it.

But he shouldn't.

"What kind of food?" he asked, knowing how strained his voice sounded and hating himself for the weakness.

Sarah seemed to startle at the sound of his voice. Her lips parted, closed. A little sigh escaped.

"What I'd like," she admitted in a curiously small voice, "is pasta. Lots and lots of white clam sauce and garlic bread."

Alex wanted to shake his head. He wanted to move free of her. All he could manage was a wry smile. "And of course you have a pasta maker."

Sarah grinned. "Of course."

"And by the time you're finished cooking, the kitchen will look like a mortar raid on an Italian restaurant."

How could she look so enticing merely by smiling? "Something like that." Her eyes were knowing, intimate.

"How about an apple or something instead?"

"Chocolate cheesecake," she said, brightening by degrees. "I made it the other day, so the kitchen's already clean. Want any?"

Alex couldn't help smiling back, wondering if chocolate really was a substitute for sex. If it worked, he might end up hogging the whole cheesecake. "Sure."

Food was very sexy to Sarah. She always liked how it was used in the movies, when lovers fed each other fruit or cake or candy. Food seemed to represent the exchange of primal needs, interlacing nourishment with sensuality, survival with pleasure.

Sarah especially liked the idea of a man licking her fingers as she slipped a morsel of food into his mouth. As a teenager she'd tried that once with a boy named Mark Walston only to get her nail stuck in his braces. Alex, she was sure, would be much more adept at something like that. If she could manage to talk him into it.

Her body still hummed with his nearness. She could feel his eyes on her as surely as the rays of the setting sun, branding her with their heat and suffusing her with light. He'd been so close, so very close to taking her in his arms again. She knew it. She could feel it, throbbing between them on the night air like heat off a hot street. And then, as suddenly as hard frost, he'd closed himself away again.

Which was where the food came in. Sarah padded back out to the yard, humming.

The insects were singing tonight. Off in the distance an owl screeched. Traffic murmured and the breeze sighed. The rain promised earlier had evaporated with nightfall, but a few of the clouds still chased a half-moon and mottled the stars. Out on her patio the flowers slept, their aroma heavy in the cool air. The palm rustled fitfully and water slapped against the walls of the pool. And stretched out atop the water as if suspended on aquamarine light, Alex floated on his back.

At first he was all shadow, like another specter of the night. As Sarah's eyes became accustomed to the change in light, though, she began to pick out features. His eyes were closed and his face relaxed. His arms were outstretched and his body still. Sarah thought of the temptation in her hands and smiled.

Then she saw the scar. New enough to still be pink, slicing his torso almost in half, like a saber wound, like a violation.

Numbness. Surprise. Terror. Fury.

Sarah didn't feel the plate slip from her hands. The crash startled her, brought a hand to her mouth. Alex stiffened at the sound, gained his feet with a splash.

"What happened?" he demanded, already looking for trouble.

Sarah's eyes were still on the scar, the memory. "Oh, Alex . . ."

The distress in her voice brought his head around.

"You didn't tell me."

He followed her gaze. "This?" he asked, motioning to the livid scar as if it were a tattoo. "Gallbladder. Bad surgeon."

"You were shot," she countered instinctively. "Three times." Stricken by the sense of blossoming pain, dimming consciousness, mortality, Sarah lifted her eyes to his. "You almost died."

Alex shook his head. Pulling his hands through his hair to force it back, he vaulted from the pool.

"I'm glad you weren't around when it happened," he chided gently, gathering her into his warmth. "I would have been a lot more worried than I was."

Her hand instinctively reaching for the flaw in his flawless physique, Sarah lifted her gaze to Alex. "Why didn't you tell me?"

His smile was protective. "What for? The only time this comes in handy is when I'm trying to impress marines and hockey players."

"But I can't get a handle on you," she protested, frustration suddenly welling in her, her head resting against his chest, where it seemed so warm and inviting. "I think I do, and then there's something else, something important. Every time I tell you to stay, I find out something else that tells me you should go."

"Sarah," he said, placing a hand beneath her chin and lifting it. "I'm not leaving. No matter what you say, or Connie says, or even what the governor of Arizona could say, I refuse to leave a job unfinished."

"You refuse to forgive yourself for letting Lindsay down," Sarah retorted instinctively as the fragile material of her vision fluttered again, revealing sights, emotions, choices. "You were protecting her. They shot you and took her, and you're still trying to do penance."

"Isn't that a little melodramatic?" he asked, his eyes too dark to be unconcerned.

"Is it?" she answered. "You think it was your fault, don't you? You should have somehow overpowered those men with their guns and saved your sister. And now you're in another situation where you think you can protect somebody, and you won't hear of leaving when it might save your life."

"I won't hear of being intimidated by somebody whose claim to fame is a fast finger on the keyboard."

Sarah saw him clench up with the memory, still only a year old, still more raw than the scar on his torso. The resolution to make this time different grated through him like the track of a rusty knife.

"I don't want to tell your family that you died trying to redeem yourself," she protested in a whisper.

His arms remained around her, his hands splayed across her back. His chest rose and fell erratically beneath her fingers, and his heart thudded. "That's not the reason," he said, his jaw like steel.

Sarah challenged him, dueled with the bronze in his eyes, facing him without flinching, even as she felt the strength gather in him. "Then what is the reason?" she demanded, her voice small and afraid.

A new light flickered at the depths of the metallic brown. "A reason?" he countered in a strained voice. "You want a reason?"

The air sparked between them. The night thrummed, and in the distance a siren wailed and keened. Sarah forgot to breathe. It took all her energy to remain steady before that new, unholy light and nod her head.

"A reason," Alex repeated in an amused little murmur. "Well, I have a reason for you."

His reason tasted an awful lot like a kiss. Sarah never quite knew when she closed her eyes. She knew simply that one minute she was challenging him and the next she was surrounded by him.

His argument wasn't a gentle one. It was almost as if more than memories had been released when Sarah had touched his scar, as if the frustration and furious determination had somehow escaped alongside. Alex pulled her to him so tightly she couldn't breathe. His hands clutched at her, tangling in her hair and holding her to him. His mouth met hers with a bruising hunger. Sarah had asked for this. She had begged and cajoled and schemed. And when she finally met it, she was surprised.

His mouth was rapacious, nipping, sipping, plucking at her tender skin. He didn't wait for an invitation to invade, but sought her tongue with harsh strokes. Sarah gasped, sighed with wonder. She fought for balance, even caught tight in his grasp. She arched closer, his heat heady in the cool night. Stretched up on her toes, her head back before his assault, she admitted that no matter what she'd thought she'd orchestrated, Alex had surprised her. He'd taken it out of her hands and assumed control. And she was trembling with it.

"You want a reason?" he grated out, his mouth at her ear, his hand sliding up to cup a breast. "I'm bewitched. Damn it, I know better, but all I've been thinking of is doing this."

Lightning splintered in her with his hungry touch, the torment of his hands on her. Sarah's mind whirled with light and darkness and need. She opened her mouth and sipped at the water that slid over Alex's throat and drank at once his fire.

"I've tried so hard to stay away," he growled into her throat, spilling chills with his tongue. "Taken enough cold showers to drop the damn water table..."

Sarah nodded, panting, sinking into his touch. "I know...."

"Walked away when no sane man would..."

"I—" his mouth was working lower, tasting the upper swell of her breast and somehow sapping the air from her lungs "—know...."

Alex moved a hand just enough to slide a suit strap from her shoulder. Sarah bit her lip, curled her fingers into his back, lifted to her toes when her knees threatened to give out.

"I tried being mad at you."

She couldn't even nod. The evening air swept across her bared breast, cooling the moisture, tautening as Alex explored the nipple. She couldn't breathe, couldn't think, couldn't hold still. But she couldn't stand up, either.

"Alex—"

Somewhere in the depths of his hunger Alex must have heard the desperate note to her voice. Pulling himself together, he held where he was, his hand at her breast, his arm circling her waist.

When he lifted his eyes to hers, Sarah was halted by the volcano she'd unleashed. A molten energy, a voracious thirst that had only flickered in warning before, now glowed uncannily from his cat's eyes. And yet, still, the exquisite control to care.

"The whirlpool," she suggested breathlessly. "It's very... nice, and... I don't have to stand up."

Alex took a second to look over at where the water in the separate little pool steamed and bubbled in the shadows. Sarah saw the realization of how close he'd come to losing control stiffen him. Saw the recriminations pass without taking hold and the desire win out.

"Sarah," he managed, turning back to her, taking her into his arms. "I didn't bring a raincoat to this party."

A curious delight bubbled up in Sarah's chest. Her knees were still watery and her skin shuddered with anticipation. There was a melting in her belly that warmed her and a trembling in her hands. Even so, she giggled.

Outraged, Alex looked down at her. "This isn't something to joke about, Sarah."

"Oh, no," she agreed with a wave of her hand, unable to quite stop yet. "I know it isn't. It's just that I knew somehow you'd be the one to bring up the subject."

Alex was losing his patience again. "Is that a problem?"

"No," she insisted, lifting a hand to stroke his cheek. "It's so sweet. And so... left brain. It's all right," she assured him, lifting way up to deliver a little kiss of appreciation of her own, her breasts sliding up along his chest as she went. "I'm already taken care of, really."

His brows pursed. "You're sure."

Sarah smiled, happy and impatient and uncertain at once. "Next time it'll be your turn. This one's on me." Sliding deliberately back down, she held out a hand. "Now, it seems to me we're wasting some lovely moonlight."

Sarah loved her whirlpool. There had been many designs conjured in it as she'd drifted in the soothing rush of warm water. But it had always been a solitary pastime. As she stood before Alex, anticipating what her whirlpool would be like shared, she knew it would never be the same.

He wouldn't let her walk. Sweeping her up into his arms, Alex carried her past the shards of broken stoneware to the steps of the whirlpool and then slowly descended into the water. There was a seat, a ridge of tile that rimmed the edge and brought the water to Sarah's shoulders. Alex settled himself onto the seat and then eased Sarah down into his lap.

"I don't know what to do with you," he was saying, his eyes never leaving hers, his hands lifting once again to her hair. Wrapping his hands in it, lifting it from her neck, he brought her face to his. "You wouldn't know a wolf if he bit you."

Sarah wanted to move. She wanted to undulate against Alex so that she could savor the slippery feel of water on him. Instead she let herself be kissed thoroughly and deeply. Her own hands were on his shoulders, shoulders like concrete, like tensile steel that bent with terrible pressure. She kneaded him, opening and closing her fingers like a cat sharpening claws in the sunlight, the sunlight that shafted deep into her belly and burned.

"You'd probably cook pasta for him and then he'd eat you up, just like grandma..."

At first the kisses were gentle, a greeting of wonder, an exploration. As Alex's grip tightened and Sarah surrendered, the kiss deepened, quickened. Their tongues parried and parted. Teeth nipped and tested. Soft groans of hunger mingled, and passion rekindled.

"I should walk away...while I have a chance...."

Sarah felt Alex's hand fall again, felt it find her breast and knead it. She pressed into his touch, hungry and aching for him. She twisted in his hold so that she could arch against his chest, tormenting herself on the soft tickle of hair, on the sleek power of muscle. Her hands wandered, hungered. His hands commanded.

"I should lock you in your room...."

Sarah gasped, her head back, as he nipped at her throat. "You should shut up," she advised, as breathless now as he, "and enjoy your pasta."

He chuckled against her throat, a deep growl of pleasure, of surprise and hunger. Sarah pulled his head down to her. Alex swept the other strap from her shoulder and freed her breasts to the water. He slid a hand down her belly, over her thighs, her knees, his mouth still marking passage along her throat.

Sarah looked at her breasts, pale and full and glistening with water. She saw the golden tousle of his hair against her skin and the shadow of his hand beneath the water. She heard the harsh cant of his breathing and tested the set of his muscles. A whimper gathered in her throat. A fire crested in her belly and slid into her legs, following the path his hands had taken. As his fingers stirred the water that pulsed along her skin, she eased open her thighs to him. She stretched so that her breasts lifted from the water.

Alex cupped a breast in his hand, weighed it, caressed it. Pleasure tightened in Sarah. She fought for air. Her head fell back, her hair drifting in the water, her eyes to the night sky. She felt Alex take her breast in his mouth and she smiled.

Desire had been a fire in her. His tongue stirred it into conflagration. Sarah felt her legs melting, her limbs shattering. She clutched at him, rocked in his arms, hummed with the surprise of it. She begged him with her hands and her cries and her body, and he answered by slipping his fingers beneath the material of her suit and seeking out the fire he'd lit.

Abruptly Alex pulled away. Sarah stiffened, ready to protest, only to feel herself spun around to face Alex, to feel her suit slid from her and find herself fitted neatly straddling against Alex's hips.

His suit was gone, too. She didn't know how he'd done it. She didn't really care. Her body sang with the proximity. The water swept around them, and the steam dissolved the world into a dream. Alex wasn't smiling. His eyes were fierce and dark and hungry. Sarah shivered with the thrill of it. She fretted with waiting. She could feel his arousal against her, full and intimate, and instinctively eased against him. His body glowed in the soft lighting, the water glittering as it slid along his arms and down his chest.

Sarah loved Alex's body. But more, she loved his face, the handsome planes and steely jaw, the dark flavors of his mouth and the fire in his eyes. When she lifted her gaze to meet his, she found what she'd expected, and more. She found an incandescence, a hot, living ferocity that threatened to consume her. And knowing that it could, she smiled. She smiled and invited him to do just that.

From that moment grace was lost to hunger, finesse to desire. Alex let his hands loose on Sarah and she answered with her own. She writhed against him, moaning with the agony he incited, seeking more, seeking him. He gasped, growled, cursed as she tormented him. Lightning sparked and sizzled. The night air swept passion-heated skin and fanned the flames. The desert sang around them and the moon danced with the clouds.

And when Sarah began to splinter, her body coming apart at the magic Alex's greedy fingers stirred in her, he took her under the arms with hands as strong as passion and lifted her onto him.

She scrabbled at his back. She danced in his arms. She offered his soft, seductive mouth her whimpers and cherished his groans. Her body was full with him, taut and hot and anxious. Their bodies arched, sang, lifted into the night. Sarah's eyes flew open. Her head fell back. Her body convulsed around Alex and welcomed him home, and she cried out, soaring, spinning, singing in his arms. And even as she did, she felt Alex follow her, his hands clenching, clutching, his voice hoarse and surprised and awed.

Later, resting spent and sated in his arms, Sarah knew that she had finally seen the real Alex Thorne, the soul she'd so long suspected. Her practical, left-brained accountant had the steel of a general. He also had the fire of a revolutionary.

Chapter 11

Oh, Sarah, you didn't.''

Never bothering to look up from where she was working at her drawing board, Sarah scowled. ''You're the third person who's said something like that this morning,'' she objected to her friend. ''Am I *that* obvious?''

Flashing a wry grin, Connie stepped into Sarah's office. ''Hon, the whole place can tell when you've broken a nail. This is just a bit more monumental.''

Sarah didn't like the sound of that any better. ''Could you please not make it sound so historic? I'm hardly an innocent.''

''You're not exactly Sadie Thompson, either.'' Reaching the board, Connie leaned over it, her eyes avid. ''So, how was he?''

Sarah went right on sketching, the idea completely formed and needing only expression for life.

When she didn't get an answer, Connie looked down. Then she moved around to get a better look.

''What's that?''

Sarah spared her friend a brief look. "Oh, a life jacket." She went right on drawing, close to completion.

Connie sighed. "A life jacket?"

Sarah nodded, lips pursed, eyes intent. "For airplanes. There was a thing on one of the shows this morning about how difficult it is to get into one of those life jackets the airlines give you. I had an idea..."

Connie looked stunned. "You never watch those shows."

"Alex does." It didn't occur to Sarah that this was a terribly odd statement. From the strangled noises alongside of her, it seemed that Connie thought it was.

"There, see?" Sarah said, motioning to her drawing. "Only the one strap, attached to everything. What do you think?"

"What was he like?"

Looking up from her sketch, Sarah blinked. "Who?"

Connie scowled mightily. "Alex. Are accountants as boring as their stereotype?"

Sarah could feel the blush build along her throat. "Hardly."

"Well?" her friend demanded, leaning in for the lowdown. "Defend his honor."

Facing Connie's renewed enthusiasm was unnerving. Sarah knew darn well that when her friend got that look in her eye, there would be no dissuading her. They wouldn't be getting back to the life jacket without some kind of news briefing. "I will give you," she offered, "one euphemism."

Connie scowled grandly and propped chin in hands. "Go on."

Sarah sighed. "You know how I describe my premonitions?"

Connie looked a little bemused. "Like lightning striking. Why?"

"Because, it applies to Alex, as well. And," she finished with an unexpected giggle of delight, "last night I found out that lightning can strike the same place twice."

"Alex? What am I hearing about my friend Sarah?"

Startled by the sound of the familiar voice on the other end of the line, Alex straightened. "Ellis?"

"Damn right, this is Ellis. Ellis the avengin' angel if you been free with Sarah."

Leaning back in his chair, Alex raked a hand through his hair. The computer room was overflowing this morning with people training on the new animation system. Keyboards clacked and screens beeped and twiddled. Country-western music filtered from somebody's earphones, and one of the women was wearing sharp heels that clicked briskly across the floor. Alex wasn't at all sure he was in the right place to be having this conversation. As a matter of fact, he wasn't sure where this conversation *would* be appropriate. He had been trying so hard to sort out what had happened last night that he hadn't slept at all.

"I'm waitin', boy."

Alex winced. Ellis sounded much like he used to before trashing hotel rooms. "Did Sarah say something?"

"No, Sarah didn't say something."

"Well, she and I were the only two there last night. Where did you get your information?"

"A concerned third party—who thinks you might be using your less cerebral body parts to do your decision making, if you know what I mean."

Alex knew just what they meant—whoever "they" were. He'd spent the entire night wondering the same thing. After all the times he'd made it a point to walk away, all the cold swims and colder showers, why should he have picked last night to go into hormonal overload? What had it been about Sarah's eyes when she'd seen his scar that had broken his resistance?

"Seems to me," Alex said, rather than face the truth, "that you were the one so anxious to get me married off."

"Married is one thing," the voice threatened in no uncertain terms. "Taking advantage of a vulnerable woman is another."

Alex was all set to protest, the memory of Sarah's knowing smile hovering close enough to distract, when she wandered in the door.

He stopped, frowning at the difference he saw in her. She was a little mussed, her flowing linen dress floating around her calves like a breeze and her eyes wide and distracted. She made it several steps into the room before slowing to an uncertain halt and looking around, bemused. Without missing a beat, every person in the office pointed down the hall.

"Wrong office," they chorused with the precision of long familiarity.

Her eyes sharpened a little and she smiled. "Thanks," she acknowledged with a little wave, and walked back out the door. Barefoot. Humming.

Vulnerable as a kitten on a highway.

Alex couldn't quite deny Ellis's charge.

"Fine," he surrendered. "Come right over and push my face in. It'll be a pleasure."

Surprisingly Ellis did no more than chuckle. "Don't handle the guilts well, do you, boy? How's the company coming?"

Allowing a sigh, Alex sat back up and leaned his elbows on the desk he was commandeering from one of Thaddeus's assistants. The lack of sleep throbbed right between his eyebrows, and he rubbed at it with two fingers. "The police came and went. Sarah admitted that she wasn't sure she was going to prosecute the embezzler if that wasn't who was doing the shooting—I assume you heard about that, as well—"

"I did."

"The rest of the evidence is negligible. So I'm back on my own. Right now I'm rechecking the accounts receivable, and then I'll go back to the records of companies Sunset deals with."

"How much longer, do you think?"

"A day. A week. A year. Who knows? I'm not really breaking records here."

"Not those, anyway. Take care of her, man. She's fragile."

That was as much acquiescence as Ellis was going to give. He was probably the closest thing Sarah had to a big brother, and Alex knew all about how big brothers felt. There were times he still wasn't sure he wanted to admit how grown-up Lindsay really was. And Lindsay usually at least acted like an adult. Sarah meandered through her world as if oblivious to it. She tended flowers and drew pictures and couldn't remember to put on her shoes.

And she had the greediest hands he'd ever known.

"All right, Ellis," he gave in. "You've made your obligatory call. Now go back to your books and let me get back to my problem."

"Take care of yourself, too, my man."

Alex hung up the phone thinking that he was becoming sorely tired of everyone telling him to take care of himself. Most of all, he wished that concern would stop coloring Sarah's eyes every time she saw him, as if she were watching someone she loved with a terminal disease. He could take care of himself. He could take care of *her*. But he couldn't take much more of the worry in her eyes, the pervasive fear that melted the blue into a kind of sweet fire. It made him want to hold her, to shield her. It made him want to love her.

Damn. He knew better. He should never have given in the night before, should never have even agreed to sharing the pool with her. He was having trouble enough concentrating on his work without remembering how the concern in her eyes had transformed into vixenish laughter just with a kiss. How she'd seemed to brighten, deepen, sweeten with his touch. Her eyes, so ingenious and spontaneous, had suddenly glowed with a feminine power that still stunned him.

Alex could see her, wreathed in the spirals of slowly rising steam, her hair gleaming and her skin so soft it looked translucent, and he couldn't get over the idea that somehow she'd worked magic in that yard of hers. Reality had

seemed to dissipate before his eyes, the worries and respon-
sibilities and good sense suddenly the intangible in the misty
night she'd created. Only sensuality and emotion had survived. The sweet slope of her breast, the bright cascade of
her laughter, the instinctive choreography of her passion.
The piercing torture of her concern for him.

Instincts. She lived on instincts and intuition, something
Alex had never trusted. Immersed in the magic of her universe the night before, he had forgotten to question. This
morning he remembered.

*Get the hell out now don't make me do it don't make me
do it*

Startled, Alex pulled away from the keyboard. Where the
hell had *that* come from? He'd been punching up some of
the smaller files in accounts receivable when suddenly the
message had appeared on his screen. A message that hadn't
been there yesterday when he'd left. A tiny frisson of warning crawled up his spine. The warning was meant for him.

"Thaddeus?"

The redhead looked over. "Yeah?"

"Come on over here a minute, will you?"

It took Thaddeus even more time than Alex to react.

"Oh, boy. I hope that's a joke."

Alex shook his head. "I don't think so. What can we find
out about it?"

Still facing the puzzling message, he shrugged. "The terminal where it originated. Time it was entered."

"Show me how."

It took them a few minutes.

"Alex?"

"Yeah."

"It originated here."

The two of them looked at each other. Alex hadn't moved
from the room all day. Thaddeus had spent the majority of
it fine-tuning the animation program with the staff. And
whoever was threatening Alex had been in the room with
them.

"This computer?"

Thaddeus shrugged. "A computer in this room. Alex, everybody in the building's been in here today."

"Was it entered today?"

"Nine-thirty this morning."

Nine-thirty, as everyone had milled around after Thaddeus's bells-and-whistles routine with the new animation program. Everyone. As much as he tried, the only one Alex could remember sitting at a computer was Thaddeus, who had finished the program alone.

Alex felt a small mental nudge, an urge to call out one particular name. He couldn't say why and didn't like it. He wasn't in the business of divining guilt like water. Until yesterday, he hadn't ever had the desire to.

Alex paused, lost for a fraction of a second in the past. Troubled by ripples of memory.

"Alex?"

Startled, he turned back to find the mysterious message once more taking up the screen in front of him.

"Yeah?"

"If you don't mind my saying so," Thaddeus said in a quiet voice, "that message sounds just a bit off balance."

His eyes on the frantic words, Alex couldn't help but think the same thing. "Print it out for me, Thaddeus," he said. "And then don't say another word, okay?"

Thaddeus looked as if Alex had asked for the firing squad. "What are you talking about?" he demanded. "Aren't you going to do anything about it?"

"Sure," Alex promised him, wishing the message didn't nag at him. Wanting the lingering suspicion to disappear. "Catch the son of a bitch who wrote it."

"Don't say anything to Sarah," Alex suggested. "She wouldn't take it very well."

Thaddeus snorted. "She'll probably tell *you*. And then she'll do a Vulcan mind-meld with the computer and find out who infected it with bad vibes."

"Sarah?" Alex countered with a raised eyebrow. "Never. She hates computers."

Sarah was surprised to notice that the sun had gone down. She'd been immersed in her work, as usual, doodling with ideas and letting her mind drift toward inspiration. Randolph had stopped in a while earlier to check on her before he'd gone home, and Jill had asked if she'd like to go out to dinner. Thaddeus, infected with an unholy zeal over the new program, had spent the majority of the afternoon breezing in and out of her office, doing his best to reignite her headache.

The one person she hadn't seen that afternoon had been Alex. Thaddeus placed him in the computer department, where he was poring over reams of material and muttering to himself. Stretching out the kinks from her legs, Sarah smiled. She'd like to see Alex muttering to himself. He probably had that little frown between his eyes, the one that still showed up when she surprised him.

She loved him. The admission didn't stun Sarah. It seemed as natural as daybreak, warm and bright and alive in her. In a period of days, Alex had measured the emptiness in her life and filled it without even knowing it. Within a matter of minutes, he had reawakened her as a woman.

Sarah lowered her eyes a little, still amazed at what had happened the night before. People had always accused her of practicing magic, but last night it had been Alex who had woven the magic. Just the brush of his gaze against her skin had dimmed the night. The strength in his voice, in his arms, had reconstructed time. Sarah had first fallen, and then floated and finally soared, and it had all been borne on the wings of Alex Thorne's passion.

He wouldn't be comfortable with it, yet, Sarah could tell. He'd been so quiet when he'd woken too far into the night to go home and Sarah had insisted on his staying. Breakfast had consisted of his watching the morning news reports with a bagel in his hand while Sarah watched him. It had been a careful truce, a polite withdrawal. Only Alex didn't realize that Sarah had no intentions of leaving it there. Sometime in the night, when they had showered and then shared her bed, fresh and clean and newly insatiable, she'd discovered a very definite taste for lightning.

She knew he was approaching before she even heard him. He stirred the currents before him, like a ship pushing through still water. Sarah brushed her hair back, setting her earrings to tinkling, and fought the blush the mere thought of him provoked.

It was nice to be in love, truly better than she'd ever hoped with half terror and half anticipation. As alive as she felt, Sarah was surprised she hadn't really tried it since college.

Of course, the way she'd felt in college hadn't been half as nice.

Her heart tumbled at the cadence of Alex's footsteps on the carpet. Her chest constricted and her smile drew a life of its own, perversely refusing to die. Sarah did her best to sit still, but by the time he opened the door, she was almost on her feet.

Then she saw him and faltered. "What's wrong?"

Startled, Alex looked up. "What?"

Sarah tilted her head, gathering impression. "You're worried about something. What is it?"

He scowled. "There's nothing wrong," he told her, pulling a hand from his pocket to furrow it through his hair as he walked in. "I'm tired. I'm seeing numbers when I close my eyes and hearing computer-generated music—which, by the way, is highly annoying."

Sarah couldn't help but smile. He did look tired. His shoulders were slumped beneath his snowy shirt, and his tie looked as if it had suffered a few yanks of frustration. Even his gait, usually so commanding, slowed.

"Zydeco," she said brightly.

Alex squinted.

Sarah giggled. "It sounds about as far from computer noise as I could get." Shrugging, she hopped off her stool. "I think that's why I like it."

She won a grudging grin from him. "Didn't Connie feed you yet?"

"You make her sound like my nanny."

Alex maintained an unrepentant air. "Zookeeper," he acknowledged, settling an elbow on the edge of her drawing board and leaning close for emphasis. "You could make a mint on tours through here just to see the exotic species. Did you know that your computer's being used to bet on horses?"

"Jill. I know. But it's personal."

Alex waved off the protest. "So's the program one of the sales staff has in to predict the end of the world. Do you know that you even have a keypunch operator who prays to her monitor the whole time she's working?"

Turning her back on Alex, Sarah bent to begin gathering together her paraphernalia. "Not to it," she told him. "For it. She thinks it's possessed by the devil, and that if she prays while she works on it, she'll stay safe."

There was a small silence of disbelief behind her. "I know this is a stupid question, but why does she still do it?"

Sarah straightened, one shoe in hand, to find a strained look on Alex's face again. "Because that's the trade the women's prison taught her."

"Of course."

Back down on her hands and knees to hunt up the other shoe, Sarah heard a heartfelt sigh escape Alex as he moved around to perch on her chair. "And you expect me to find the odd man out in this bunch," he objected wearily. "The way things have been going, I have the most horrible feeling I'm going to end up finding out that *I'm* the embezzler."

Sarah's head popped out from behind a couch. "That's silly."

Alex shot her a rather pointed look. "So is a company CEO playing hide-and-seek with her personal apparel."

Sarah checked under the couch. Nothing there but the pen she'd lost the other day.

"Where *is* Connie?" he asked.

Sarah popped up again and instinctively looked around. "I don't know," she admitted. "Haven't you seen her?"

"Earlier. I just figured she'd be here checking up on you, since it's almost ten."

That brought Sarah to a stop. "It is?"

She wasn't quite sure how to define the look in Alex's eyes, somewhere between amusement, consternation and dread. Was that what a man looked like when he fell in love? she wondered. It didn't seem nearly as nice as what women felt.

Her shoe was between the curtain and the window. The jacket to her dress was falling down the back of the bookcase. And when she turned around for her purse, she found Alex holding it out for her. Smiling, but not looking quite happy enough.

Slipping her shoes on, she skirted the outheld purse and dropped a kiss onto Alex's lips. "Are you going to feed me?"

Again his expression shifted. Again there was a certain amount of consternation to be seen. "Only if all you want is food."

Sarah chuckled. Alex's words conjured up the night before, and it hovered between them, hot and intimate and sweet. Sarah blushed, her gaze slipping a little. Alex stiffened, quieted. The air between them shivered with remembered emotion, pulsated with banked desire. It was palpable, like a heavy breeze, like the smell of roses in a late garden. Like the swell of a taut silence.

"You frighten me sometimes," Sarah whispered honestly.

Alex's eyes narrowed in surprise. He went very still. Sarah knew it was what he feared himself.

So she smiled for him and lifted her hand, cupping his solid, square face. "You woke something in me that I didn't even know was asleep," she admitted. "Something I'm not sure I can control."

She never took her eyes from his, the golden brown bathing her in its curious sunlight. Alex took her hand into his and then pressed it against his lips.

"I know," he said.

Sarah wanted to tell him to keep her hand, to never give it back or let it go. She wanted to always feel as safe and whole as she did right then.

"It's different than with friends," she said. "Isn't it? You don't risk as much with friends. You don't open up as much."

Alex's smile was crooked and sweet. "You don't fall in love with friends," he told her. "When you fall in love, you risk falling on your face."

"Oh, well," she retorted with a silly grin. "What's a scraped nose or two?"

Sarah had wanted support, declarations of undying love. What she got was a small shake of the head. "It hurts a lot more than that," Alex said, and she could feel the shattering loneliness.

She saw him walking away, making the choice that would return her life to its equilibrium, and wanted to cry out to stop it.

"Oh-oh, I'm going to have to stop checking up on you."

Sarah and Alex spun around to find Connie striding in the door, purse and briefcase in hand.

"No," she objected lightly. "Don't blush on my account. I've just been on a close encounter myself, so I'm not in the least embarrassed." Setting down her things on the bookshelf, she bestowed a wry smile. "Although maybe you should be. You two are putting a strain on the air-conditioning system, and it's only seventy degrees outside."

"You must have had a nice time," Sarah marveled at her friend. "You're heading into warp drive."

"I've been showing off our latest retirement investment," Connie admitted, then turned to take in Alex. "Did you know that our girl has done it again? I should thank you for not going home last night. You've inspired the Delaney Life Jacket."

"Life jacket?" Alex asked.

"Delaney?" Sarah asked, scowling. "Why not Sunset?"

Connie leaned against the doorway and considered Sarah with patient eyes. "What does the sun do when it sets?"

It took Sarah a minute to follow her train of thought. "It goes down."

Connie nodded, appeased. "Which is what we don't want the people who buy these to think they're going to do."

"Oh."

"What life jacket?" Alex insisted.

Connie threw a little wave in Sarah's direction. "After watching a piece this morning on airliner life jackets, our girl here decided to make a simpler one. The patent attorney is already salivating."

"Why Delaney?" Sarah asked. "Why not Mason?"

Connie took on a look of even greater patience. "Because you're the star, honey. Nobody connects Mason with anything but office memos."

Sarah still wrinkled her nose. "I'm not really sure if I want to see my name every time I look under an airplane seat."

Connie gathered together her paraphernalia. "Well, I have an appointment with an underused pillow." Stopping as she filled her arms, she turned to Alex, fixing a smile on him. "So, tell me. Does this mean I'm finally off the late shift? It's been playing hell with my social life, y'know."

"Connie," Sarah objected, "I told you you didn't have to always check up on me."

When Connie turned to her, she saw the sum of all their years together in her friend's suspiciously soft expression.

"I'm the one who found your house," she said dryly. "I'm obligated to see that you use it at least every so often." Shifting her gaze a little, she considered Alex. "Are you going to take her home, or do I?"

"No," he said, the purse still dangling from his hand. "It's on my way."

Connie shouldered her own purse. "Well, see if you can watch something tomorrow morning on the common cold. I'd sure like a condo on Maui."

Sarah blushed. "Connie!"

But Connie was already out the door.

"She's a little wired," Alex commented, watching her brisk retreat.

"She's in love," Sarah said, retrieving her purse and preparing to follow. "I think she's even more excited by the life jacket."

Alex turned a bemused expression on her. "You really redesigned the life jacket?"

Sarah smiled. "You're really going to feed me?"

Ultimately Alex didn't get the chance to watch television at Sarah's the next morning. He didn't wake at Sarah's at all. He fed her and took her home, hearing the silence pile up between them in the dark as they approached her house. He wanted to make love to her again, to lose himself in the silk shower of her hair and drink in the little sounds of pleasure she made. He wanted to think he could open himself to a woman and feel safe. But it wasn't that easy. It never was.

So he pulled up to her house, ready to make his apologies—a long day, a headache, a call to Lindsay—only to find Sarah asleep beside him. Tousled, pouting, childlike. And he ended up carrying her inside—after digging her key out from underneath tree roots as he balanced her in his arms, that is—and putting her to bed. And then, astonished at how much he ached at the sight of her, he locked her back in and went on to the hotel.

Saturday morning found him at the keyboard in an otherwise empty office. He didn't mind; it was easier to get his work done. But his mind wasn't on work. As he punched up the companies Sunset dealt with, either supply or delivery, he thought of mistakes. As he scanned data and checked addresses and authenticity, he thought of opportunities.

Barbi had been a mistake. He'd invested everything in her, diving in headfirst only to find himself on dry ground. As naive as a love-struck kid, he'd done more than share, he'd bestowed, bequeathed. He'd given it all away before he realized he wasn't going to get anything back. And if that episode taught him nothing else, it should have taught him to be cautious, especially around blondes who made him feel protective and possessive.

Yet here he was preoccupied by another set of wide blue eyes. Here he was flagrantly courting disaster. No, he amended, he'd already gone past that. He'd made love to her. He'd surrendered to that guileless smile and irresistible passion, and couldn't think how to get free.

He wanted to back up, to regain his safe footing. But it was too late. He'd already tasted what it was that had been so exhilarating about falling in love the first time. When he'd made love to Sarah last night, he'd remembered how good it could feel to fall hard—and how very terrifying. He was falling in love with her and he didn't know what to do about it.

The first time he dialed her number, it was busy. Looking up at the clock on the wall, he saw that it was only about ten. Probably Connie checking up on any new inspirations. Doing his best to shake off the urge to try again, he turned back to the computer.

She wasn't really like Barbi, he reminded himself. Behind Sarah's distracted, seductive eyes hid a brain that sparked genius. Beneath that soft, slightly vague exterior lay a creation of whimsy and wonder. Alex couldn't imagine Sarah having enough focus to betray anyone, much less the man she loved. He couldn't imagine coming home to find her in bed with his oldest friend.

But he hadn't been able to imagine that of Barbi, either.

Alex was so distracted by contrasts and comparisons that he almost missed it. He'd been filing through each of the companies that Sunset did business with, checking the picture of each company against his own mental picture of legitimacy. Some he checked in directories, some he recognized from doing other audits in the textile industries. Some he made notes to follow up on. Then he reached one that brought pencil and eye to a halt.

It wasn't anything glaring. Nothing obvious or concrete, just an out-of-town address—and a date on which transactions commenced that corresponded neatly with the start of Sarah's "feelings."

Nothing. Perfectly kept records, goods delivered, payment made. All on time, all without comment or complaint, which in itself was unusual. But it wasn't that information that brought Alex to a halt. It was lack of data. An address, a phone number for questions, a name for addressing inquiries. No notes about sales visits or problems with the product. A curious flatness that was like a furnished apartment without personal touches. A neatness that sprang the catch on Alex's suspicion.

And the mailing address was a post office box. Perfectly legitimate, but also inescapably convenient for the felon. Post office boxes were favorite addresses for frauds. He'd seen this same data the other night and put the discomfort down to exhaustion.

Alex picked up the phone and dialed. The Los Angeles number was temporarily disconnected. He'd have to call Ellis and have him check up on things. But first, he'd call Sarah.

Busy. She really liked to talk. Alex brushed aside his own impatience and dialed again, rubbing at his chest.

"This better be life 'n death," Ellis growled in greeting.

"It's a lead," Alex answered, and was satisfied to hear Ellis scramble for coherency.

"Who is it?"

"I don't know," Alex admitted. "Who buys the computer programs at Sunset?"

There was a short pause. "It's always been Thaddeus," he said. "It's kinda like his religion, y'know?"

Thaddeus, the bright-eyed wonder boy who looked like Spike Jones. The wunderkind with a brash sense of himself and his capabilities. Thaddeus, who knew the progress of Alex's investigation because he was so anxious to help. Alex really liked him.

"Ever heard of a company called Datasys?"

Another pause. "Wholesaler, isn't it? Connie once said they'd gone to them because they could come in cheap, what with Thaddeus there to set up the programs and teach 'em. You think it's Datasys?"

"I don't know," Alex admitted, rubbing at his eyes and unaccountably thinking of calling Sarah again. "I have a hunch."

"Oh, catching, huh?"

"An accountant's hunch, Ellis. That's different."

"Sure it is, boy. Sure it is. So, what do I do?"

"Check out Datasys on that fancy mainframe you have at the law school. I want to know who owns it and where it's licensed."

Ellis had a note of awe in his voice. "You really think this is it, don't you?"

For a moment Alex considered the information before him, the stark figures and data, and thought again of Sarah. "Yeah," he finally admitted. He was rubbing again, worrying at the weight that seemed to gather behind his breastbone. "I think we're on the right road. Call me when you get it. I have to call Sarah."

"Oh, man, don't burst the lady's bubble yet."

Alex hung up anyway. He suddenly wanted to check with Sarah, to find out what she knew, find out what she'd want to do.

He dialed Sarah's number again. Once more it was busy. He was in the middle of a string of oaths when he remembered the night he'd goosed himself on her telephone receiver. She'd left it off the hook again.

Frustrated, he looked up at the clock. Ten-thirty. He thought of calling the police, but then considered all the times they'd been there already. Her house was only a few blocks away; he'd go himself to satisfy his curiosity, ease the impatience.

Shutting down the computer, Alex stood and headed out the door. Damn her for a child. Couldn't she for once be responsible? He needed to talk to her about what made an innocuous-looking company suspect. He needed to ask who had authorization over what, who ordered the software, who gave approval for the money they put out on computerization. He needed to be there when she found out who it was who was hurting her, because he had to protect her.

The day was another scorcher, the heat slicing through his T-shirt and matting his hair. Even the air conditioning in the car didn't seem enthusiastic on the short ride to Sarah's. Alex took the corners a little too fast and screeched when he pulled the car to a stop in Sarah's driveway.

Her door was closed. Alex rang the bell, a hip against the newly replaced glass door, an eye along the neighborhood. Sarah didn't answer. He knocked. A couple doors down, a man watering his lawn did a little nonchalant eavesdropping. Alex pulled a hand through his hair and thought of going for the key. First he'd try the door.

It figured. She'd left it unlocked. If he did hang around, Alex was going to have to teach her a thing or two about personal safety. He pushed the door open and strode into the cool entryway only to find it as hot as the street. Alex faltered to a sickened halt.

"Sarah?"

The room was a shambles. Cushions were ripped. Windows were shattered. Books and papers covered the floor in ragged hillocks. The lamps were all broken, and the lovely old grandfather clock was gouged and scored.

Dread shot through him. Finally remembering to let go of the door, Alex stepped inside.

"Sarah!"

Chapter 12

The police arrived within minutes. Sirens screamed and the shudder of strobe lights strained the white walls. Even though he knew she wasn't there, Alex kept tearing through the debris.

This wasn't a burglary and it wasn't vandalism. This was a violation. Everything Sarah owned had been destroyed, her lovely antiques shattered, her prints slashed, her flowers uprooted and lying in untidy clumps over the lawn like piles of plague victims. Her bed had been ruined, the mattress ripped and the soft floral linens as mutilated as the real flowers outside.

A sudden, spilling rage took Alex. He heaved overturned furniture out of his way and clawed through the scattered papers. Panting, furious, frightened. Sarah wasn't home, and her house was a wreck.

It was Valdez who answered the call. Valdez the pragmatic, the rule keeper and protocol follower. Valdez, who stood in the living room as if he'd just witnessed a natural disaster.

When he saw Alex, he took an involuntary step backward. "Miss Delaney?" he asked. Behind him two more officers stepped into the mess.

"She's not here," Alex grated out. "No sign of her. I'd been getting a busy signal for half an hour and just figured she'd left her phone off the hook again."

Valdez looked around, almost at a loss. "No sign of foul play."

"What do you call this?" Alex retorted, chopping at the ruined room.

But Valdez shook his head. "I mean . . . uh, blood."

Alex paled even more. "No," he said quietly, raking a hand through his hair and looking around again. "No blood."

Valdez answered by turning on his backup. "You two get to the neighbors and find out why the hell nobody heard anything. Put out an APB on Miss Delaney. You know what she looks like."

"There was a guy out watering his lawn when I pulled in," Alex offered lamely, the rage sinking into frustrated impotence. "Maybe he saw somebody."

With a general nod, the two walked out, making it a point to close the door behind them. As if it could somehow offer some kind of protection now. Alex wanted to laugh.

The police again. Good heavens, now what could they be there for this time? It seemed she couldn't walk up the sidewalk anymore without running into a brace of blue uniforms.

"I'm sorry," she said, pushing open the door with her hip. "Did I trip the wrong code again?"

Sarah didn't even get a chance to set down the bags. Before she could turn back from shutting the door behind her, something very big barreled into her.

"Where the *hell* have you been?" Alex. He had his hands on her shoulders—hurting her, he was holding on to her so tightly. He looked so angry that for the first time he frightened her.

"Alex?" she said in a very small voice, her bags crushed against her chest between them, the beautiful morning outside forgotten. "What's wrong?"

"I asked where you were," he demanded fiercely, giving her a little shake. "Damn it, you wander around like you're in a fog and just expect everything to be like a tea party. Don't you even lock the door when you go out, for God's sake? You just let anybody in here?"

Sarah was truly afraid now. Rage and frustration welled from him like hot poison. It washed over her, chilling her in its wake. Overwhelming her with its size.

"Alex, you're hurting me."

She might as well have slapped him. Her words stunned him into silence. Sarah saw it then, the surprise, the hurt, the spark of self-directed anger that had triggered all this.

"What's the matter?" she asked, dropping the bags without thinking about it, without hearing the fragile crush of eggshells at her feet. Her own hands came up, afraid now for him.

"How long have you been gone, Miss Delaney?"

For the first time Sarah realized that there was somebody else in the room. Sgt. Valdez. She was hardly surprised. He was usually the one stuck with sorting out her mistakes. Sarah was turning to answer him when Alex tightened his hold on her again, preventing her from moving.

"In a minute, Sergeant," Alex grated without taking his eyes from her, eyes that burned with a hundred raw emotions, every one making Sarah even more unsettled. "I'm sorry, Sarah. I should have known this would happen. I had a warning and didn't do anything about it."

"What would happen?" she asked, still seeing nothing but his eyes, his torment.

"What warning?" Valdez demanded beyond Alex.

"Someone came in while you were gone," Alex said to her, his voice as tortured as his eyes. "They did some damage."

Sarah felt the blood drain from her face. She knew the moment Alex's grip changed from controlling to supportive. When she turned to take in the rest of her house, he was there to protect her.

"Alex?" she said, her gaze traveling over the scope of destruction. "You do have...a wonderful sense...of understatement."

She couldn't help the catch in her voice. Tears crowded close. Shock stole her forward momentum. Devastation advanced like a cold mist that crept over the gutted cushions and slashed pictures.

Sarah tried to take in what had happened. She tried to understand that someone she trusted had done this to her. Yet it wouldn't quite gel. She couldn't do anything but mourn her small treasures, her silly little comforts that had grown so important over the years, first as she'd imagined collecting them, then when she'd actually discovered them waiting in a store or a flea market or an auction for her to find. Sarah couldn't move past the fact that her sense of stability foundered and was lost.

Then she looked up past the yawning ruin of her French doors to find her flowers. She never felt the tears.

"How long have you been gone, Miss Delaney?" Sgt. Valdez asked as gently as he knew how.

Sarah tried to pull her whirling emotions back into some kind of order. She reached out a hand to Alex, trying to regain a little of her security, and he wrapped an arm around her shoulders. She couldn't take her eyes from her flowers, dying out there in the sun, their color already dusty and faded.

"Sarah, how 'bout I get you something to drink?" Alex asked.

"Thank you," she agreed. "Tea would be nice."

But she couldn't let him go long enough to get it.

"What time is it?" she asked, finally turned to Valdez where he stood like a stiff-legged shorebird among her rubble.

"A little before eleven."

Sarah wanted to sit down, but there was nowhere to sit. No chair left unscathed, nothing. A sob escaped her and she let it.

"I think I left . . . around nine or nine-thirty. I walked." Looking over at Valdez, she sought reassurance. "You know."

"I know. You didn't see anything on your way out? Any strange cars in the neighborhood?" For a moment he dipped his eyes, escaping to his notes. It seemed to Sarah, though, that he was dodging away, uncomfortable. "Anybody you might have recognized?"

She could have taken the time to think about it, but she knew it wouldn't do any good. She never noticed things like that.

Flowers she noticed, and the crisp blue of the morning sky. The dusty browns and emerald greens of carefully tended lawns. The glaring, delicious whites of adobe against the desert morning. She might have exchanged hellos with neighbors—she usually did. She probably stopped long enough to play a little hopscotch with the Patterson girls over by the market. But she wasn't the kind of person to be distracted by something different. She had enough distractions of her own.

"No," she finally admitted on a sigh. "Nobody."

He gave a tentative nod and scribbled in his little notebook. "We're going to need to know if anything was taken."

"When she's ready," Alex said with such authority that he stole Sarah's attention. Valdez didn't think to argue.

"Nothing's gone," she said, turning back to Valdez. When he looked up with a certain amount of surprise, she offered a little shrug. "I'll check," she amended. "But I'd know by now."

"Come on into the kitchen," Alex suggested to her then, his hold purposeful. "You can sit there and we can talk."

Valdez immediately stiffened. "I think I'd like to talk to you about that warning, Mr. Thorne."

Alex nodded, his attention on Sarah. "In the kitchen."

Alex and Sarah made it there before Valdez did, because just then the lab crew arrived. Sarah caught their offhand greetings to Valdez as she walked out. The police took over her living room, and she escaped into her kitchen.

It was the same, only worse. The cabinets had been emptied, the refrigerator struck and left gaping like a wounded thing. The phone torn from the wall and the handmade little plaques and dried flowers and baskets ripped from the walls and strewn over the floor. And there was more.

Sarah stood before her wall, quiet and amazed. "They even knocked holes in my wall," she murmured.

There was a moment of uncomfortable silence before Alex answered. "No, they didn't."

Sarah turned to find him standing right behind her, a little awkward with embarrassment. "I did it."

Sarah's eyes widened and she took one more look at the three evenly spaced holes punched right through the wallboard.

"You?" she echoed in some astonishment.

Alex? Gentle, persevering, bemused Alex? Alex who had had the control to turn down her painfully abrupt advances for so long, who had been enough of a gentleman not to hurt her?

Abruptly the window opened again, as if the holes were the entry, and she heard a terrible, raw cry of frustration and grief. Heard another, years old, that sounded even worse, like the sound of a mortally wounded animal surrounded and finding no way out.

"I guess it's something I should have warned you about," he admitted as if hearing the same echoes.

Sarah shook her head and managed her first smile of the day. "You took care of Lindsay for five weeks when she couldn't take care of herself."

"And I destroyed her garage."

"And you never once touched your wife. You never even thought to hurt her."

Alex tried to get away with an offhand shrug. "I still had Dallas Cowboys I could take it out on."

Sarah wasn't sure why that should provoke sudden tears, but it did. She wasn't sure why his protestations should make her love him even more, or why the force of his fear and fury should have made her understand him better, but it did.

Not the destruction, not the betrayal or the blank wall of silence that met her attempts to see the culprit broke through her defenses. Not police in her house picking through what had once been her life or the feeling that she had somehow been violated.

Alex did it, with his gruff concern and his harsh frustration and the stark fear in his eyes. Alex, who had arrived to find her house a shambles and her missing, and had vented his impotent rage on her wall. Alex, who had no idea how wonderful he was.

Sarah crumpled into his arms, her sobs welling up. Her world dissolved into his embrace. His hands, which had bruised her with their intensity, now soothed. They stroked clumsily at her hair and patted her back. They eased her into his arms and settled her onto his lap when he sat. They provided safe haven and support and guided her to rest against him where the steady cadence of his heartbeat settled her.

Sarah never saw Valdez appear at the door or Alex's silent glare of warning. She never saw Valdez retreat. She simply gave herself up to Alex's care and emerged stronger.

Moments later, Connie blew in with the detectives, Randolph and Thaddeus following close on her heels. Ellis called while everybody was being questioned. Every one of them hovered.

Connie looked as if her own child had been kidnapped. Randolph brewed coffee and tea and chided Sarah for not calling them right away. He acted as if he should have been the one to find the destruction instead of an outsider, as if Alex had no place comforting Sarah. Thaddeus brought the computer message with him and delighted in rehashing gory details with every detective he could find, especially those willing to share their particular expertise.

"Well, Alex," Connie finally said as they set about cleaning up some of the mess, "I'm glad you called us. Even though it wasn't quite the message I'd anticipated from you this early in the morning."

Standing at the bottom of her bed, Sarah thought of what it had held only two nights ago and couldn't even think to blush. She wanted to cry again.

"Can we do this later?" she asked in a small voice. It was like burying her family.

Connie shot her a sharp look. "Tell you what," she offered, wrapping her own arm around Sarah's shoulder. "Why don't I take you to my place for a nap and we'll let all this muscle finish cleaning up?"

Sarah was unaccountably alarmed by someone else touching her things again. Anyone else, even her friends. She wanted to sift through it herself, putting to rest her memories and gathering the courage to move on. But she wanted to do it later. Now it was all still too raw.

"No," she said, turning uncertain eyes on her friend. "I want to leave it. I want some time off first . . . please?"

Connie gave a reassuring squeeze and nodded, all common sense. "You bet. We'll leave somebody here to wait for the people to come board up and change the locks. Volunteers?"

"Happy to," Thaddeus offered.

Connie nodded. "Settled. You want to get some things to take with you, hon?"

Again Sarah had to summon her courage, because she had to tell her friend that she didn't want to go with her. It would be the first time she could remember ever challenging Connie's commanding good sense. If her life hadn't just been turned on its head and scattered about like the straw man in the wake of the flying monkeys, Sarah might have quailed a little longer. But her old points of reference were missing, her intuition cloudy and unsure. As much as she loathed to say it, the only person she could trust right now, the only person with whom she felt absolutely safe, no matter how much her brain reasoned otherwise, was Alex.

And she knew it was going to break Connie's heart.

Somehow Alex knew.

"Connie, maybe Sarah should come with me," he said diffidently from where he leaned against the wall. "I think she might benefit from talking to my sister."

Sarah felt Connie stiffen. "Your sister?" she demanded. "Whatever for?"

Sarah didn't give her a chance. "His sister's a counselor," Sarah said, locking eyes with Alex and reassuring herself with his solid support. "She deals with this kind of thing all the time. I think I would like to talk to her, Alex." She didn't mention the fact that Alex's sister was still in the hospital after giving birth.

Connie, however, had other arguments in mind. Dropping her arm, she faced off with Alex. "How safe is she going to be?" she demanded. "Can you promise to protect her? After all, you were the first one in line for this kind of treatment."

"I'll protect her," Alex answered without moving, without posing or posturing. He just leaned there, hands in pockets, eyes passive and quiet, voice even. Yet no one in the room would have questioned him.

Sarah felt the contest between Connie, born to protect, seasoned to support and provide, and Alex, whose instincts were still new. The air quivered between the two of them as old guard gave way to new.

Finally, in a sudden burst of sunlight, Connie grinned. The expression was as much acquiescence as warning.

"Okay, kid. This is your big chance," she said brusquely. "I'm putting you in the game."

Alex's smile was slow and easy. "Thanks, coach," he answered. "I won't let you down."

Alex's suite was cool and quiet, living room, kitchenette and bedroom all done up in pastels and whitewashed walls. Outside, Sarah could hear the splash of the pool, the susurrous wash of a waterfall, and the periodic murmur of people wandering by the first-floor window, their conversation vacation-tempered.

The bed was a big one, firm and overflowing with pillows, and surprisingly enough when Alex steered her into the room and closed the curtains against the sun, Sarah snuggled right in.

He'd still been there later, when she'd started awake and when she'd drifted off to sleep again. He'd been in the periphery of her senses and the center of her dreams, his eyes always smiling and sure, his arms a harbor from the storms. And when she woke again to find the room hazy with late afternoon light, Sarah heard the murmur of his voice in the other room.

"You're sure," he was saying, and immediately Sarah heard the edge. There was an energy there, a decisiveness that brought her up from the pillow.

"I'm not in the mood for games, either, Ellis. You didn't see her house."

The lingering peace of sleep vanished with Alex's words. Throwing off the quilt, Sarah swung out of bed. Something else was happening, changing, ending. She could hear it in the clipped tones of Alex's voice. Dread and anticipation. She wasn't at all sure she wanted to know what was going on, but she knew she had to.

Alex looked up in surprise when she walked in. He was seated on the couch in his bare feet, his hair tousled from running his hands through it, the phone at his ear and a legal pad covered with scribbles in front of him on the table.

"Is that Ellis?" Sarah asked, swiping at her own hair to counter the effects of sleep.

Alex nodded and then listened. "He says his mama's recalling her feathers and entrails. Something about faulty equipment."

"His version of a security system," she admitted. "Ask him if you can get refunds on spells."

The mood eased for the few minutes it took Alex to get off the phone. Ellis passed along greetings and commiserations and dire warnings to housebreakers—something to do with *their* entrails. Alex chuckled and Sarah relaxed. When Alex hung up, Sarah knew she'd have to ask.

"Tea?" was how it came out instead. She knew she couldn't put it off, but she wanted to so badly.

Alex climbed to his feet. "I'll make it. You sit down."

Sarah scowled up at him. "Don't go all Randolph on me, Alex. I'm not as helpless as I act."

Alex reached out to draw her into his arms. "It's those damn eyes of yours," he protested. "They make you look like a Raggedy Ann doll that's been left behind."

Sarah scowled into the solid comfort of his chest. "I see."

His answering chuckle was deep and melodious against her ear. "You'd bring out the protective instincts in Muammar Qaddafi."

For a few minutes they stood together, quiet, insular and content. Sarah drifted on his scent and the wash of his breathing. She eased down into his strength and found comfort, even though she knew that there would be monsters waiting when she opened her eyes again. For just that moment, the monsters were held at bay.

Finally Sarah collected her courage and stepped away. "What have you and Ellis been up to?" she asked.

Alex followed her over to the kitchenette and bent to pull a beer from the small refrigerator. "Solving Sunset's problems," he said quietly.

Sarah looked up, her breath caught somewhere beneath the big ball of dread in her chest. "You've found something?"

His eyes met hers without flinching—soft, sure eyes. Honey brown and sweet, knowing what she faced and what it would cost her. Assuring her that no matter what, he would be there for her.

"I think so," he said, the beer in his hand momentarily forgotten. "What can you tell me about Datasys?"

For a moment his question didn't register. Sarah had expected an identity, a crime, evidence. She hadn't been prepared to be led carefully in a direction that wouldn't be clear to her.

"What about it?"

Alex finally remembered his beer and turned his attention briefly to popping it open, the sound as sharp as gunfire in the quiet room. "Sunset went with the company just a short while ago, didn't it?"

Sarah shrugged. "I guess. I don't keep up with the computer stuff. It—"

Alex smiled. "Gives you a headache. I know."

Sarah lifted a hand to push at her hair again, but somehow it never passed higher than her mouth. She pressed it there for a moment, as if to keep the betrayal from spilling out. "Which is why that's where the scheme is. They knew I wouldn't pay attention."

"That you *couldn't* pay attention," Alex amended, leaning forward to her a little.

"But what about the others?" she asked, still not really wanting the truth. "They should have suspected something."

"People see what they want to see. Datasys was saving them money. It was the perfect setup for Sunset, because you didn't need the backup services of most software companies. You just needed the goods."

The little teakettle began to whistle, shrill and insistent, and Sarah turned to it. "And the new computer-animation package I wanted was so damn expensive, it seemed the perfect alternative.''

"Ellis checked for me," Alex said alongside her. "There is no Datasys registered. What we think is that the software is coming in from the black market, bootlegged stuff.''

"It did seem so perfect," she whispered, hovering over her tea like a shaman preparing for a ritual. "Especially with Thaddeus there. He was as excited as a kid...you know how he is about his own capabilities.''

"Who found the company?" Alex asked.

Sarah looked up, stricken. Afraid. The ground was crumbling beneath her feet and she didn't want to look down.

"I don't know," she admitted, hanging on to the unqualified support in Alex's eyes. "I'm never in on those meetings." Briefly her gaze dropped with her admission. "I'm no good at it.''

Alex wouldn't allow her guilt. Reaching out, he lifted her chin with his fingers. "And I can't invent life jackets," he retorted. "Come on, Sarah. You couldn't have known.''

She shook her head, miserable. "I should have. I should have anticipated something.''

Alex set his untasted beer down alongside Sarah's steeping tea and pulled her back into his arms. "And I should have told you the warning was left on the computer. My crime's worse than yours.''

Sarah settled into his hold again. "Are we going to argue over who's more horrible?''

Alex nestled his cheek against her hair. "If you insist.''

She sighed, capitulating. "Thaddeus," she said.

Alex didn't move. "What about him?''

"He's the one who orders the programs. Always has. He pores over those catalogues like a kid with the Sears Christmas catalogue.''

Alex lifted his head a little. "Catalogues?" he asked. "You get catalogues from the company?''

Sarah pulled away enough to look up at him. "I think so. I don't know for sure. Thaddeus always has something he's pointing out to get. I never really look."

"I'd like to see one," he admitted, and then suddenly relented. "But that comes later. The order of the day is a little R and R."

Wishing she felt more resolved, Sarah shook her head. "We have to find out before anything else happens."

"We are," he assured her, running a finger down her nose. "Ellis is doing some more checking for me. I'll call the detectives and give them what we've got. Maybe we can track down the owner of that post office box the company uses and get some kind of name."

"I don't want to know," Sarah blurted out, ashamed and afraid.

Alex gathered her in closer. "I know," he said, brushing her hair back for her. "I wish it could be some other way."

She searched the depths of his eyes and found what she wanted. "Will you be there with me?"

He smiled. "All the way."

She nodded, as satisfied as she could be, as comforted. Still there was a knot of acid in her chest, a rot of betrayal. The gnawing trace of guilt told her she must have failed someone to have them turn on her like this.

"I'm so afraid," she admitted softly, as much to herself as Alex. "I can't feel a thing, and I don't understand why."

"What do you mean?" he asked.

Sarah lifted her head again, sought him out. "I touch their hands every day," she protested. "Ten times a day, all of them, Thaddeus and Jill and Randolph and Connie and Hector. Avarice is one thing, a cold kind of emotion. Subtle. I might understand that I couldn't detect that. But the anger that fueled the attack on my house should be a livid slash—a hot, living current that jumps out at me. And I haven't felt a thing. I'm too close to all of them," she finally admitted with a frustrated shake of her head. "I'm too afraid that one of them really is trying to hurt me."

"One of them is," Alex answered gently.

This time Sarah pulled away, turning from his honesty because she couldn't yet face it. "I know that," she said, then amended her words. "My brain knows it. The rest of me would rather keep going just the way I was."

She could hear Alex behind her, solid and supportive and patient with her denial. Knowing when to reach out and when to wait. And that was when she turned, the surprise finally reaching her.

"How did you know?" she demanded.

Alex didn't react. "Know what?"

Sarah tilted her head, amazed that she'd missed it, even through the morass of what had happened. "*You* were the one who knew something was wrong this morning," she accused. "Not me. I walked right in there without a clue. You drove over from work even though you had no reason to."

"Your line was busy," Alex protested, a sudden defense appearing in his eyes, a stiffness reaching his posture. "I thought you might have left the receiver off the hook again."

"So you came over? Connie calls the police."

He didn't quite meet her eyes. "I'd had the warning."

"To you," she insisted. "All the attacks have been against you. But you knew there was something wrong at the house."

"Sarah," he warned dryly. "Don't look for things that aren't there."

Now she giggled, delighted that he couldn't see something so plain. "But I do that all the time," she protested, then leveled a finger at him. "So do you. You knew where I'd gone the night of the shooting when nobody else had a clue. And now this."

His gaze gathered consternation. "Sarah—"

"You're psychic, Alex," she protested. "I know it."

Alex reached for his beer then and took a good-sized slug. "I knew I was going to do that," he snapped.

"What's the matter?" she asked. "Does it worry you?"

"No," he answered with a tone of voice that should have brooked no argument. "Because *it* doesn't affect me. Have your tea, Sarah. I'm going to call the police and then we'll have dinner."

"Do you know what I'm going to say?" she teased.

"Yes," he said with great forbearance. "'Thank you, Alex. What a wonderful idea.'"

Sarah just smiled. "I'll go get changed."

He didn't smile back. "I'll call the police."

His attitude shouldn't have made Sarah happier. He looked much like a bear with a particularly uncomfortable thorn in its paw. But Sarah walked away humming nonetheless. She finally understood, and that made all the difference in the world.

Chapter 13

Who would have imagined? Alex Thorne, psychic. Pulling a lightweight linen dress over her head, Sarah found herself giggling. It was so wonderful, so...surprising. She'd been certain that he had been afraid of his emotions, of letting go. He'd been afraid of letting go, all right. Alex, who religiously observed the rituals of the left-brained adult, would never accept the fact that he was even a little psychic.

Sarah imagined that over the years he'd done quite a job of controlling that annoying little talent of his. He'd turned in the exact opposite direction, focusing on numbers and equations and logic to block out the very illogical fact that he could sometimes tune into other people.

He probably wasn't as acutely aware as she was. After all, Sarah had never had reason to question her gift. Blue and John had cultivated it as her right. But Alex, growing up in middle America with a body built for football and a brain that excelled in numbers, wouldn't have known what to do with the sudden flashes of insight he'd been given.

The logical decision would have been to simply tune them out. The problem was, of course, that when he really opened himself up to someone—like his ex-wife, someone like Sarah—his control slipped and the sight returned. It taunted him again, whispering at him when he wasn't paying attention, nudging him from sleep, too indistinct to identify, too persistent to ignore. It linked him so closely to the person he loved that he could anticipate them, could taste their emotions as well as his.

He could know, without realizing it, what was going on in their minds.

Alex was afraid of falling in love, because he couldn't control that kind of invasion. He couldn't separate it from the jumble of raw emotion that love was.

Sarah heard him talking to the detectives, his voice crisp and authoritative. Slipping into her shoes, she reached for a brush to take out some of the kinks in her hair. And she thought of how furious Alex would be when she wouldn't allow him to back off again. She smiled, as giddy and afraid as she'd ever been. As torn.

Sarah really wanted to talk to Lindsay after all. As close as Alex was with his sister, Sarah bet he could read her, could anticipate her. She bet that his ordeal with his sister's grief had been worse than even he admitted, because he hadn't just imagined her pain, he'd felt it. When Lindsay had been kidnapped beneath his nose, he'd suffered her terror as if it were his own. Sarah bet he'd never really questioned that connection like he would the ones that put him at risk.

Like women he could fall in love with, women who could take his secrets and torture him with them.

That, however, was not something to deal with right now. Sarah wasn't even sure she wanted to deal with her own sight right now. She wanted a quiet meal and a little conversation. And maybe later, they could go in search of another whirlpool.

"You're blushing," Alex noted when she walked out into the living room.

Sarah blushed even harder. "You're not supposed to notice."

Climbing to his feet, Alex assessed her with a twinkle in his eye. "Hard not to," he countered, "when it makes you look like you were just kissed."

Sarah slowed to a halt, a smile hovering and the fiery betrayal refusing to recede. "I wouldn't know," she said. "I haven't been kissed today."

"You haven't, huh? That's too bad. You look like you could use it."

"I could," she admitted with a rather plaintive sigh that belied the delicious acceleration of her heart. "I've had a hard day."

She hadn't meant to let it invade here. She'd wanted sanctuary, isolation, denial. Even so, the loss of her home bled into her expression. She could tell by the reaction in Alex. His eyes softened and his shoulders slumped a little as he approached.

"We'll take care of that later," he said, knowing without admitting it, even to himself—especially to himself. "Together. But tonight we're going to pretend that you and I are the only two people in the world." Lifting a hand, he cupped her cheek, his touch warm and gentle and heartbreakingly solid.

Sarah tried to grin, leaning a little into his touch. "Except the waiters," she amended. "I don't want to do any work."

"And the cook."

"And the man with the violin who strolls among the tables playing gypsy music."

Alex shook his head. "Sarah, this is Phoenix. The nearest gypsy is in Bucharest."

Sarah's heart lifted as she met Alex's gaze with renewed life. "Mariachis then," she bargained. "Trumpets and guitars."

Alex rolled his eyes and wrapped his hand into her hair. "You are a glutton for punishment."

She must have been. She didn't protest the whole time he was kissing her. In fact, she didn't even mind. When he lifted her face to his, she went. When he bent to taste her lips, she wrapped her arms around his neck and held on tight.

The sweetness of his touch seeped through her like sunlight. The dark flavors of his mouth surrounded her. His arms swept her up and his hands held her to him. Sarah folded into him, her body melting very agreeably, her breathing stumbling right behind her heart and her feet losing touch with the ground.

And there in Alex's arms, she found her sanctuary.

"Dinner," he murmured into her throat.

Her breath escaping in something that sounded like laughter, Sarah nodded. "I think I can already hear the trumpets."

Alex chuckled back and shook his head so that his hair tickled her cheek. "I can't seem to say no to you."

"Good," Sarah gasped when his tongue found the soft shell of her ear. "Then maybe after dinner, we can go in search...ah, of a whirlpool."

Abruptly Alex's head came up, a wicked glint in his eye. "*That's* what you were blushing about," he accused, still holding her tight.

Sarah's answering smile was coy and knowing. "You must be psychic," she marveled.

That was all it took to get Alex out the door.

Sarah was being much too docile. Alex couldn't get comfortable, knowing that at any minute she'd jump back on her latest favorite subject about him and ESP. Showed you what psychics knew. She probably saw it in all her friends, the way some people saw satanic verse in all rock music. Maybe it was a little lonely being the only witch on the block, and she was looking for some company.

Not Alex Thorne, thank you. He had enough to deal with without playing with Ouija boards and floating tables. He was an accountant, not a channeler. Trances were for people like Sarah, one foot on the ground and the other in the ethereal plane. Nobody would think twice about it. In fact, they'd probably be disappointed if she didn't profess to at least some kind of eccentricity. CPAs, on the other hand, were not valued for their prescient powers. At least, not unless it had to do with changes in the tax law, and so far Alex hadn't had any inclination in that area.

Not that he had anything like that at all.

Except for Lindsay. But that was natural. She was his sister; they'd been through a lot together. Of course, he'd have a special bond with her. Anything else was out of the question.

Now Sarah sat across from him with quiet assurance in her eyes, waiting to spring...gathering momentum to accuse. As if he didn't have enough on his mind already.

As if he weren't distracted enough with the lead suddenly turning up, and the destruction of Sarah's house and the possibility of one of her friends being the culprit. And Sarah, wide-eyed and alive, her skin like warm milk, her eyes glittering like sunlight on water. Her conversation breathy and bright, as if they'd just met that day over drinks and decided to wander on in to eat.

Sarah, who needed to be protected and led like a puppy, who deserved to be secure and happy. Sarah, who needed love more than she knew and gave it without accounting. Who touched the world like one of her flowers, bright and fragile and fleeting.

Sarah, who was not Barbi. Who demanded more from him than Barbi had ever known how.

The comparison conjured an image. A raw autumn day, the sky a flat, hard gray and the wind torturing the leafless trees. End of season, almost the end of his career. It was in sight by then, his knees constantly complaining, his times slowing. The seasonal depression hit, following him home from the play-off loss that had ended their chance at another bowl.

The depression was deeper this time, gnawing, troubling. Steering him without his realizing, building in him like a head of steam, like a load that got heavier and heavier, as if somebody had been piling bricks on his chest, one by one.

A load that refused to go away, that had been growing brick by heavy brick all season long until it brought him home on that cold, lonely day. That last day...

"Alex?"

Startled, Alex looked up to realize that Sarah had just called his name.

"I'm sorry," he apologized, plagued by the memory of the old weight. "What did you say?"

Sarah smiled and Alex couldn't think what had reminded him of Barbi. "I asked if you wanted the rest of your dessert."

He looked down to see the half-eaten cake on his plate and shook his head. "You're going to eat that, too, huh?"

Sarah reached right over. "You keep eating like that," she accused, "you're going to waste away to your last two hundred pounds."

Right then she looked like a precocious little girl, all laughter and games. Alex knew that she would return to the matters that worried her, but for now she'd decided to put them away. Totally without his permission, he felt his own mood shifting in her wake, as if she were a clean breeze tugging at him.

"How do you do it?" he demanded, fingering the stem of his wineglass instead of the inside of her wrist, which was what he was thinking of fingering.

Puzzled, Sarah looked up. She had a little smear of chocolate icing at the edge of her lip. Reaching over, Alex wiped at it with a finger. Sarah smiled and tilted her head, considering.

"Do what?" she asked, her eyes already knowing.

Alex motioned to the detritus of her once-sizable meal. "Recover so quickly."

Sarah looked down at the plates and then back at Alex. Her small shrug was eloquent. "It will all return in its time," she admitted. "But for tonight I've decided to escape." A disconcerted smile tugged at the lips Alex had just touched. "I think that for right now, I'd rather fall in love."

Alex let his eyebrow convey polite skepticism. He was glad Sarah couldn't touch the sudden squeeze in his chest or hear the stumble of his heart at her words. "That easy, huh?"

"With you, it is." Unaccountably, her smile grew a little wicked. "But then, I don't have a Barbi to keep comparing you to."

Alex had no business laughing at that. For some reason he did. "Sarah," he mourned, "someday you're going to learn to be honest and forthright."

Sarah answered him evenly. "You wanted to know."

Alex didn't know where to go from there. He ached for honesty of his own, but didn't know what that was. Except, after spending the night with Sarah, Alex hadn't been able to sleep on his own. He was nagged by the most uncomfortable feeling that he'd lost his choices long before he'd taken her into his arms.

Alex had always held control. It had been as much a part of him as his mathematical brain and agility on the field, and he'd only surrendered it once. Only once. And after Barbi he'd learned to never surrender himself again. But now, as he saw the seductive life in Sarah's eyes, as he considered her rare enthusiasm and sweet sense, he was tormented by the need to lay down in her arms and give himself up to her.

It wasn't so much that he hurt, but that for too long he'd felt nothing at all. He'd closed himself off from that with his logic, with his control, and thought himself better for it. He'd suffered with Lindsay and died a little because of Barbi. It had sent him running for cover.

Now, though, warming himself in the incandescence of Sarah's spirit, he knew he didn't want the dark again.

Around them the restaurant hummed and clinked and tinkled with activity. Waiters skirted on silent feet and women smiled. The piano player had started his set out in the bar, desultory notes cascading from the high, pale ceilings.

Within the island of their table, there was silence. Not a taut silence, but a full, throaty silence of comfort, of belonging and possibility. A silence that pulsated with promise.

Without words Alex courted Sarah. He let his eyes dance with hers, his brandy like late sunlight settling into the sea of her blue. He offered a slow smile that carried the crescive exhilaration in his chest. When she smiled back, her answer complete and enticing, he reached a hand across to hers and captured her.

Her fingers were warm and small, hesitant creatures that took captivity with a flutter. Her palm was silky and receptive, curving a little against the slow stroking of his touch. Her wrist betrayed her, the pulse jumping erratically at his approach.

Alex never released her eyes, commanding them to him, consuming them. He'd never seen such a wide expanse of blue, even the sky seeming small and confined compared to her. He'd never touched a hand that tingled with such life. She was like a force, like the sunlight or the wind that shouldn't be restrained, shouldn't be controlled. She should be praised and cherished and nurtured.

"I'm not that fragile," she whispered, somehow understanding what he thought.

Her words opened something in him, some hidden place that he had locked carefully and, he'd thought, permanently. Alex felt that locked door open a crack, creaking with disuse, jealously guarded all this time against being breached.

He recognized a new warmth, a glow like a desert sunrise seep in, clear and strong and bright, and knew somehow that it wasn't all his, that it was more. It was Sarah's. But even so, it belonged to him.

His hand tightened instinctively as he fought the hint of new emotion that buffeted him. He sat perfectly still, not hearing the persistent clamor of the restaurant, not recognizing the Beethoven from the piano. It was all he could do to hold himself together before the confusing tide that threatened him.

He straightened, tried his best to withdraw. But Sarah wouldn't let go. She held his hand and smiled, and seemed as young as birth and as old as eternity as she watched him.

"I love you," she said, still holding on. Waiting, watching, understanding.

Alex tried to answer. He wasn't sure what he wanted to say. He knew she wasn't asking for an answer. She was giving it, explaining as much as she knew how. But Alex had no explanation. He had no reference to mark this new invasion, this tumble of emotions that threatened to overwhelm his own.

He was seeing into her soul as surely as if it were his own, and the sensation pulled away his balance until he felt as if he'd fall.

Pain. He felt it sneak in under the rest, a child's hurt of loss, an adult's grief of betrayal. Like low clouds, dark and tangled, sour on the mind, igniting a like pain in him that anyone should suffer such treason. Hurting when all he wanted to feel was pleasure.

"How 'bout a walk?" he asked, needing room.

Her smile was spontaneous and delighted. "There's a moon out," she agreed.

Sarah tread carefully. She and Alex strolled down along the patio terraces, listening to the rustle of the palms and the steady wash of the waterfall. The night sky arced in milky moonlight, and the breeze ruffled the water of the pool.

Alex had an arm around her shoulder and his head down, and Sarah held her breath.

She knew, but she didn't. She'd never been taught to fight what was happening, never thought to question it. She couldn't imagine the turmoil in Alex's mind as he battled between instinct and emotion. She knew only how she wanted it to come out.

"At least you're not being smug about it," he said abruptly.

Startled, Sarah looked up to see the steel in his jaw, the strain lines across his forehead. She could imagine his eyes, lost in shadow, their brown cloudy and troubled.

Instinctively she squeezed his hand. "It's too much of a responsibility," she assured him quietly, the tension eating holes in her chest.

So much hinged on these next few minutes. So much of her. Her life was teetering in precarious balance, its only reality right now the man who held her hand. She needed him to understand, knew he had the capability, but wasn't sure whether he really, in his heart, wanted to.

It wasn't a matter of courage. Courage was beating back his sister's depression with his bare hands, walking away with grace and dignity from the sport that he loved like a woman. Courage was facing the problems of Sunset day after day when his life was threatened.

This was the left brain battling the right. Common sense warring with possibility, a possibility Alex would never have consciously acknowledged. This was a weight that, once accepted, might never again be lifted, a duty and a burden. Sarah knew.

It wasn't a frivolous thing she accused him of. It wasn't something he could ignore when he wanted, something he could give back when he got tired of it. If he truly opened himself to his sight by loving her, he would have to face all its implications. He would have to face it day after day for the rest of his life, sharing Sarah's life as exquisitely as he felt his own—more, if he loved her. If he felt toward her anything like she felt for him.

He was a storm brewing, a convulsion of emotion and denial. It buffeted Sarah like a strong wind, and she ached to ease it for him. She yearned to tell him it would be all right, when she knew that it wouldn't, really. He wouldn't just have her love. He would have her pain and her frustration, her impatience and anger. When they finally found out who was cheating the company, only Alex would really know how she felt.

Alex's head jerked up. He stopped in his tracks and turned to Sarah. She saw his eyes, dark and defensive and surprised, and knew that he'd felt her sudden pain of betrayal. Without hearing the thoughts, he'd touched the emotion.

"I'm sorry," she apologized, not sure whether she really was, wanting soul mates but never wanting them to share the bad parts. "I don't know how to close off from you."

Sarah was afraid Alex would turn away again, that he would try to escape into his shell. Instead, he faced her. Sarah held her breath. Her heart stumbled, righted itself and went on. She couldn't see past the emotions that skittered across the surface of Alex's eyes like tattered clouds skirting the moon.

He took her by the arm. "You scare the hell out of me," he rasped, his hold almost as fierce as that morning.

Sarah refused to flinch before the turmoil in his eyes. "I'm really not Barbi," she whispered, aching for his eyes to clear, to see his sweet smile take hold.

He didn't smile. Instead, he crushed her to him, his head down, his arms tight, his voice tortured. "I know that," he admitted. "I know."

Sarah wrapped her own arms around him, wanting so much to offer some kind of comfort, to convey the love that swelled in her as she thought of the steel in Alex's determination, the gentleness in his hands. As she thought of the life he'd denied himself because one woman had betrayed him.

"What did she do to you?" Sarah demanded, accusing the other woman, condemning her for what she'd done to so vibrant a man.

Alex shook his head, his hold fierce, his heart thundering in Sarah's ear. "I knew," he admitted, his words harsh and abrupt. "That was it. I *knew*."

Like a cancer eating at him; uncertainty, dread, shame. The growing realization that his wife was deliberately hurting him. Worse than the mere suspicions Sarah held about her friends, more desperate, more inexorable. Sarah understood; she sagged beneath the weight he must have carried without having understood it.

"I love you, Alex," was all she knew to say to counteract it. "I love you."

He pulled away long enough to tilt her face to him. It was then, unbelievably, that Sarah saw the smile. Darker than it should be, less free, but there nonetheless. Wondering and amused and glad. "I know."

And then, slowly, deliberately, he bent to kiss her. Sarah sighed, answering with her lips, with her arms and her hands. Her body swelled in anticipation, hummed with welcome. Her frustrations and fears fled before Alex's gentle assault.

He surrounded her, his arms a haven, his mouth greedy and delicious. He'd sipped at bourbon with dinner and it lingered, smoky and sweet on his tongue. He plumbed the depths of her mouth and nibbled at her lower lip. Sarah stretched up to him, her body seeking the solid planes of his, her breasts already aching and anxious. She felt lifted and free, shot with chills and sweetened with a slow, dark heat that spilled before Alex's hands.

"Oh, Sarah," he whispered against her, his beard chafing and his hands taut, "what are you doing to me?"

Sarah couldn't withdraw. She reached up to him, her hands topping his shoulders, her cheek nestled against his. He seemed the only warmth on this cool evening when the moon silvered the night and the desert wind chilled her skin. Alex was the only life, and Sarah sought him.

"I'm falling in love with you," she murmured back, her heart now a stumbling runner. "I told you."

"You're making me do things I don't want to do," he accused, sounding more breathless than upset. "You're making me fall in love with you."

Sarah backed away enough to look up into his eyes, her own filled with as much ingenious question as she could, even though she knew exactly what he meant. "You don't want to fall in love with me?" she asked.

He scowled with the gruff exasperation that she so delighted in. "I'd rather be audited by the IRS."

Sarah chuckled, resettling herself enough to widen his eyes a little. "You'd probably have more fun," she agreed sagely.

"I'd sure as hell have more peace," Alex countered, his voice a little tighter as her breasts brushed against his chest. His one hand moved, almost as if of its own accord, searching out her breasts where they were trapped against him. Sarah felt him snake up against her, his fingers reach the soft fullness and hesitate. She moved again, an instinctive undulation that brought her right into his grasp.

He faltered. His breathing stumbled a little. His eyes narrowed. But his hand stayed, closed, captured. The night paused, suspended in anticipation. Even the distant rustle of the restaurant seemed to still. Blue eyes locked with golden and hoped. Golden challenged, the cool moonlight stirring something surprisingly hot in the depths. Alex's hand opened, then advanced, his fingers tipping Sarah's nipple in fire.

She gasped, the contact jarring her, splintering something in her that tasted suspiciously like control. His eyes held her, pored over her and brought her to a halt in his hands. The smile that grew on his features lifted her again.

"I think I'd like to go back to the room," he said simply.

Sarah managed to tilt her head in question. "The room?"

Alex nodded. "I believe it's my turn for responsibility," he countered, his sane words a sharp contrast to the rasp of urgency in his voice, "and unlike some others, I don't carry it around in my wallet."

The sun broke through and Sarah grinned. She wanted to giggle, to sing, to fly. She wanted to soar right into Alex's arms and find her freedom there, too.

"Besides," he added with deliberate meaning. "The whirlpool's well within view of the entire hotel."

She was air. She was light and sweetness and life. Alex pulled her into his arms and filled himself with her, drinking in her sighs and capturing the dance of her body. He plundered her mouth and trapped her against him with his hands, winding them in her hair and not letting go. He crushed her against him, starved for her softness, for the faint scent of morning that surrounded her.

His own body took control, drowning out the questions with his need, silencing the turmoil with the maelstrom her hands stirred. Alex ached. He groaned with hunger, strained against it, knowing that he couldn't stop any more than she could, hoping only that he could wait.

She surprised him again, this flighty creature of the twilight, this fairy child who didn't seem to live in the real world. Passion welled from within her, hot, seething hunger that stunned him with its ferocity. Alex had called her a woman of pastels, seeing and feeling the world in shades. He'd been wrong. Here in his arms, she writhed, she whimpered. Given Alex's encouragement, she stoked his fires with hands that seemed insatiable.

The moments fused into sensations. The courting of lips, the silk of hair tumbling around his arms and sweeping his cheek as they fell together onto the bed. The whisper of material as it brushed together, as it parted and fell to the floor. Murmurs, words exchanged on sighs and groans, hearts thundering in syncopation as hands sought and surprised.

Desire flared suddenly and then coalesced, thickening like molten steel. Stretching across his belly and searing his groin. Sarah's hands stirred it, deepened it. Her lips quickened it.

Alex tried to hold back, to savor and praise. He couldn't. His hands fled on, intoxicated with the velvet-soft feel of her skin. His body shuddered with her torment. He drank the salt from her passion-dampened skin and sated himself on the button-hard arousal of her nipples. And when he knew he couldn't wait, he dipped his fingers into her and found her full and weeping and hot for him.

It cost everything to turn away from her even for a moment. When he returned, her arms were open and she was smiling. Her eyes were wide, languorous, a summer's sky. Her skin glowed and her breasts taunted. And Alex, afraid and amazed and struck by the power of what Sarah offered, entered her arms. He wove his hands into her hair and pulled her mouth back to his. And then he eased into her.

She surrounded him, so soft and warm, so welcoming. She arched against him, pulling him deeper. Whimpering, tossing, she wrapped around him and began the dance.

Alex fought for control. He groaned, a growl of pain at waiting, at the torment Sarah was igniting with her lithe body. He could feel the shivers gather in her, heard the shudders, suddenly saw the surprising storm that swept her as he stoked the lightning in her. He felt the tide sweep her, inside and out, her fingers raking at him for purchase, her cries breathless and pleading. She clamped around him, pulling him home, tumbling, flying, shattering him with her surprise.

The storm reached him, broke in a fury as he plunged deeper, deeper, dancing with her, mingling his own groans with hers, crushing her softness, her fragile, sweet softness to him, wanting her impossibly close and knowing she couldn't be close enough, disappearing within the wind and then tumbling back slowly to the ground.

They were still wrapped in each other's arms, cooling in the night air, quiet with contentment, when the phone rang. Alex wanted to ignore it. He frankly never wanted to move again, to leave Sarah even that much. She still held him, and he nestled against her hair.

"Alex—"

He didn't move. "If we ignore it, it'll go away."

It didn't. The phone went right on ringing, as if having heard Alex's challenge.

Again Sarah moved, enough to lift her head. "I could probably reach it from here."

Alex sighed. Moving nothing but his arm, he found the phone.

"Hello?"

"Alex? Are you all right?"

Alex couldn't believe it. He wasn't sure whether he wanted to laugh or curse. "Trust me, Lindsay," he growled with meaning, "I'm just fine."

"I've been calling you all day, damn it. Something's been wrong, hasn't it, and you haven't told me because of the baby. Damn it, Alex—"

He shook his head and handed over the receiver. "Here," he suggested. "I think she'd like to talk to you. I'll be right back."

By the time he climbed back into bed, the two women were talking like sorority sisters. He might have known it.

"Now—" Sarah smiled a little while later when Lindsay had been pacified and the receiver replaced "—where were we?"

The phone rang again.

Alex looked at it as if it were alive, sure it was malevolent.

"Are you going to get it?" Sarah asked, barely able to keep a straight face.

"No."

But he did anyway.

"Alex, are you okay?"

Alex groaned. "Ellis, if you had any idea what a ridiculous question that was, I'd be in a neck brace."

"Congratulations, my man." He sounded like he really meant it. "I knows you is gonna do the right thing by her. Ain't dat right?"

The street-boy accent was one Ellis reserved for on-field intimidation. It sounded almost as impressive over the phone. Only a few hours earlier it would have aggravated Alex. He didn't like being pushed, even by good-intentioned friends. After what had happened between Sarah and him, though, he found himself smiling.

"That's a fact, Bubba," he retorted easily, his mind and eyes on Sarah, his decision made before he asked the question. "Now, why did you decide that I needed to be awake at this hour of the morning?"

"Because I have some new information for you."

Alex tried his best to keep the sudden tension to himself. "Uh-huh. Will it wait for the sun?"

"What? You tellin' me after all this, you don't wanna know?"

"Not right now."

Ellis took a moment to enjoy his pique. "You don't want to know."

"Ellis," Alex suggested evenly, his voice much too calm for the new storm encircling in him. "Call me in the morning."

Without another word of explanation, Alex hung up. Then he took a moment to call the desk and have them stop further calls. The two calls had gelled something in him, some suspicion that had hovered closer all evening, and Alex needed to deal with it. He needed to face it and name it. And he needed to do it alone with Sarah, without intrusion of the company or friends or family.

"So," Alex said, turning back to see Sarah watching him, her hair tumbled and her eyes bright and welcoming. "Where were we?"

"What's happening?" she asked, her eyes concerned.

Alex smiled. "I'm falling in love," he told her, slipping down to take her into his arms. "Any objections?"

Her eyes widened. "That simple?"

Alex would never lie to her. "Nope. Do you mind?"

Her smile was wanton and guileless at the same time. "Not as long as you show me what I can do to help."

Alex was afraid. He couldn't call it anything else. But he couldn't do anything but try. "Oh," he said with an answering smile. "I think I can do that."

Chapter 14

Sarah didn't sleep. Even after making love again, slowly, deliciously, eye-to-eye and graced with the music of Alex's praise, even after curling into his arms and listening to the gentle rhythm of his sleep.

The future was closing in on her. She could feel it rising in her like a tide, stifling and surging at once, terrifying and wonderful. Deep into the night when the world had slept and moonlight died, Alex had allowed himself to love. He had told Sarah about Barbi, what it had cost him to walk in one fall day and find his wife in his bed with another man. What he had lost, what he had sacrificed.

He hadn't made any promises. Sarah knew it was too soon for that. He was still having trouble trusting, accepting. Where Sarah was sure, so sure she wanted to sing and laugh and dance, she knew she had to be patient with Alex. He'd spent an awful long time tempering his passions to suddenly let them free again. He'd distrusted his instincts too long to simply change his mind.

Normally Sarah would have been patient. She could have waited as long as Alex needed and more for him to reach his decision. But this wasn't normally. This was when Alex was in danger, when somebody was out to hurt him for helping her. This was when she wasn't supposed to trust anybody around her even though that went against all her instincts. Sarah didn't know how to be patient when possibility crowded in so closely, when happiness and grief could wear the same words.

It would be soon. The certainty of that roiled in her like acid. Alex had yet to make a decision that would steer him away from the danger.

Sometimes Sarah could forget all that, losing it in the immediacy of his smile, or shoving it away when she couldn't face it. But it always returned, stealing in on her sleep or surprising her when she wasn't paying attention.

Alex was more at danger now than ever, and it was her fault.

"Are you sure you want to go over there this morning?" he asked from the other room.

Standing by the sitting room window, Sarah looked out on the bright morning. "I have to face it sooner or later."

Last night had been so wonderful, so full of promise and anticipation. This morning the rest invaded, as it always did. Dear God, but she wanted it over.

She never heard him approach. Standing right behind her, he settled his hands on her shoulders. "Later's just as good as sooner."

Sarah couldn't face him. She kept watching a little boy splash out in the pool. "I don't suppose it would do any good to ask you to leave for a while?"

"Not any more than the other thirty times you asked."

She turned then, accepting his embrace, his comfort when he was the one in peril. "It won't go away, Alex. I can't make you safe."

He dropped a kiss on her head. "I'll be fine, Sarah. I promise."

"You'd better be," she retorted without much heat against his chest. "Or your sister's going to be really mad at me."

He lifted a hand to her hair. "She likes you, y'know."

That made her hurt even more. "I like her, too." Sarah didn't want to have to call her with bad news. She didn't want to hear any kind of pain in that woman's voice. Please, God. Please.

Sarah straightened. "Can we go now?"

Alex's eyes were soft and patient. "Only if you kiss the cleaning crew."

She did, much more enthusiastically than the union demanded.

Connie and Randolph beat them to the house. Sarah was glad Thaddeus had opted to spend the day at a long-planned seminar in Las Vegas. After listening to the evidence against him the day before, she didn't really want to face him. She didn't want to believe that the same man who had revolutionized the company could be stealing from it, too.

Sarah needed to keep busy, so it was just as well the house was still a shambles. Her friends kept up a steady stream of conversation, and Alex appeared time after time when she needed him, holding her or taking her hand when the scope of the destruction became too much.

A little before eleven, Alex made a phone call from the bedroom. When he came out, he excused himself for a while and left. Sarah knew what he was doing, knew it had to do with the company and Thaddeus. She didn't ask him where he was going. She told him to be careful and kept on cleaning.

Time collected, massed, filling the empty silence of her house with dread, marching toward the morning when she'd have to face her friend and accuse him. When she'd have to know why he'd not just stolen but tried to hurt her.

Alex returned in the afternoon, weary and wilting a little. Nobody looked up from what they were doing when he came in. By that time the house appeared to be almost healed. Sarah was sitting cross-legged on her living room floor, sifting through a pile of books and knickknacks to see what was salvageable. Across from her, Connie did one last circuit with a broom, and Randolph was reassembling enough furniture to get by for the time being.

Alex brought sodas with him and passed them out. Then he leaned against the wall, sipping.

"Connie," he said in a carefully even voice, "who buys your computer programs?"

Both Connie and Randolph came to a sudden halt. Sarah went right on sorting, certain that she didn't want to hear this.

"Thaddeus," Connie answered as if Alex should have known better. "Why?"

"Was he the one who suggested you go with Datasys?"

Sarah held her breath.

Connie thought. "I guess," she admitted slowly, propping her can on the end of a table. "We were all in a meeting at the time. It was when we decided to go with the new animation software to update our computer. We knew it was going to be expensive... Randolph, do you remember?"

Randolph looked very uncomfortable. "Thaddeus," he admitted. "Why?"

Alex rubbed the condensation from the can, his eyes on his work, brows drawn. "The computer software you've been getting has been bootlegged."

Connie froze. "Oh, God."

Randolph looked over to Sarah, but she was still facing her book, her hands trembling.

"Poor Thaddeus," Connie said. "He was so excited about finding such a cheap company. He'll be crushed when he finds out somebody's scamming him."

That brought Alex's head up. "Some of those programs were bootlegged through Sunset's computers," he said.

Now the silence was complete. Sarah closed her eyes against his accusation. Her heart died a little. Her throat stung. She thought of Thaddeus, brilliant, madman Thaddeus who made evil-eye signs behind her back and turned her imagination into reality, and still couldn't believe it.

"But the catalogues," Connie protested. "I've seen them."

"Printed on your desktop publishing system," he acknowledged. "Did Thaddeus have free access to the building?"

"We all do," Sarah finally answered, her head up, her eyes glittering. "All the officers have their own keys. Any one of us wanders in and out of that office all the time."

"Even *I* have a key," Randolph admitted, instinctively gathering the wagons against the accountant.

Sarah wanted to smile. She wanted to cry. These were her friends seeking to protect each other.

"What do we do?" Connie asked, her voice stricken and small. "He isn't even in town today. He's at that seminar up in Las Vegas."

"I'll talk to him," Sarah said.

She felt Alex object before he ever said a word. She turned on him, for once the one who wouldn't be challenged. "I'll talk to him first thing tomorrow," she repeated emphatically. "Then we can call the police if we need to."

Taking a telling look around the room that still bore the marks of destruction, Connie couldn't agree. "Sarah, what if he—?"

Sarah swung on her friend. "This is Thaddeus we're talking about, Connie. He's my friend, and I owe him a chance to explain. We'll talk to him in the morning."

For a moment the tableau held, uncomfortable, uncertain. Unbelievably, it was Randolph who broke the tension.

"I've had enough slavery for one day," he announced, deliberately setting down his can and facing Sarah with his big, sad eyes. "What about a balloon ride?"

Sarah turned to Alex. "What about it?"

She saw a frown cross his face, felt the hesitation in him like a horse breaking gait. "I'm afraid I'll have to bow out, Sarah. I'm waiting to hear from Ellis again. You go, though."

Something warred between them—hesitation, denial, fear. Fear for each other, she for his life, he for her happiness. Sarah knew that Alex felt himself her tormentor, no matter that she'd asked him to do the job. His success had upended her carefully constructed universe, and Alex hurt for her because of it. And he knew it would only get worse.

And Sarah, terrified of the mists that still crawled around in her subconscious, could only think of how she'd brought Alex to danger.

But Thaddeus was out of town. Alex would be all right if she left with Randolph and Connie. He needed to talk to Ellis, and he needed to do it alone, without Randolph's accusing eyes or Sarah's pain.

Still, Sarah didn't want to leave him.

Thaddeus. Sweet, mad Thaddeus.

Alex crouched down before her, a hand to her cheek. "I know," he said softly. "But it'll all turn out okay, I promise. Remember that it wasn't to hurt you. If it had been, you would have been here when this happened. He waited, though. He's only angry at me, and I can live with that."

There was something in his eyes, Sarah thought, some knowledge that escaped her. She desperately wanted to reach in and tap it. Her world was whirling about her, its logic and order tumbled, day now night and the seasons scattered. The one thing she'd tried to build with her company, the sense of family, of worth and sharing and generosity, had been poisoned.

Sarah needed Alex's strength now, his sanity. She clung to the certainty in his eyes like a toehold on a high cliff. She soaked in the love that only the two of them could feel throb in the still air.

Finally she managed a smile. "While we're up, I'll look for a place for us to build a house," she teased. "All alone in the desert."

"Desert?" he countered with a crooked smile. "Oh, no. The Denver Chamber of Commerce is waiting to tell you how much you'd like creating near the Rockies."

"We only have so much daylight left," Connie reminded them dryly.

Sarah looked up at her friend and grinned. "What do you think, Connie? Would you like to learn to ski?"

Connie scowled, the previous few minutes still telling their toll on her features. "Right after I find another computer genius who can communicate with you. Now, come on and let Alex finish his work."

"You'll be here when I get back?" Sarah asked him.

Alex smiled and her world settled a little more. "I'll say 'hi' to Ellis for you."

His parting kiss was long and deep and rich with memories of the night before. Sarah wished she could have enjoyed it more. She just couldn't stop thinking about Thaddeus. About what would happen in the morning, and how it might affect Alex.

Alex didn't wait very long. The minute Connie's Audi rounded the corner, he turned back for the phone. But he didn't call Ellis. Not yet. He had other business to take care of, business about Thaddeus.

Thaddeus, the wizard who had broken the security codes in school and then left with only a taunt. Thaddeus, who thought Sarah was possessed and yet understood her enough to transfer her designs to computer animation.

Thaddeus, who had been brilliant enough to break into the Landyne's computer and pull out the new animation program whole, who had printed up his own manuals and catalogues.

Thaddeus, who had shown Alex how to find out when and where a computer activity had originated, and then left his own out in plain view to be found.

Alex didn't spend much time on the phone. When he got off, he headed out on a chore of his own, knowing how much time he'd have before Ellis did call back, knowing that Sarah would be upset with him. At this point he knew he had to risk it. There was a brick on his chest, and he only knew one way to prevent it getting heavier.

If he was psychic, if this was what it was like all the time, he didn't like it much.

His head said that Sarah wasn't in personal danger yet. The latest attack had been against her, but she'd been at a safe distance. Like a child destroying its doll instead of its mother. Besides, Sarah was with both Randolph and Connie. That kept her safe no matter what.

Alex went on his errand anyway, his suspicions crowding out his reason, the feeling of running out of time propelling him.

The phone was ringing when he walked back into Sarah's house. Alex checked his watch, just to make sure. Ellis was early. That was either very good news or very bad. It was all coming together now, and Alex found himself growing more unsettled than ever with the outcome.

"That you, Bubba?" he asked, receiver to his ear as he checked the fridge for anything salvageable. He was hungry.

"Alex? Is that you? Where have you been?"

Alex forgot the refrigerator. He forgot his stomach. Something was very wrong. The weight had just multiplied.

"Connie?"

"I don't know what to do. I just can't believe it, and now he's up alone with her—"

Alex straightened, ran a hand through his hair and closed his eyes. "Connie, slow down. What do you mean he's up alone with her? The three of you aren't back on the ground?''

Her voice was tight and frightened, at the edge. ''The three of us didn't go up. Only Randolph and Sarah. Oh, Alex, I didn't know. I'm sorry. It was Randolph all along, and I sent him up alone with her.''

''Randolph isn't going to hurt Sarah,'' Alex said quietly, his eyes opening again, their color suddenly cold and flat. It was all changed now, the dynamics thrown off. ''What do you mean it was him all along?''

''I was so mad,'' she gulped, as if words were air. ''I wanted to know how the hell Thaddeus had pulled that over on us. I told Randolph I'd pick the two of them up, but that I should check on something at work...and I found it. In *his* desk. In Randolph's desk when I went looking for keys. He's been working with Peter. They've been siphoning the stuff straight from Landyne all along. The two of them, when I thought Peter was dating me for my sexy body.'' The laugh wasn't pleasant. ''He was playing perimeter guard. What are we going to do?''

Again Alex checked his watch. ''When were you going to pick them up?''

''What if he knows?'' Connie demanded. ''What if he realizes I found the note from Peter? Alex, I left Sarah up *alone* with him!''

Curiously enough, Alex felt very calm. Purposeful. Connie's words gelled his suspicions, his uneasiness. He knew now what had happened and what he was going to have to do. He knew that he wouldn't let Sarah down. He just had to get to her in time.

''There's something else,'' Connie admitted in a rush. ''I kept...I kept a gun in my desk since this has all started. A .38.'' She took a breath and hurried on. ''It's gone, Alex. It was there Friday when I left. I couldn't find it today.''

''Do you want to call the police?'' he asked.

"He'll see them," she protested harshly. "Alex, anything could happen if he thinks he's caught. Look what he did to Sarah's house."

"Then we'll be there. Where were you going to meet him?"

"Where you guys landed when you went up. It's a spot he uses a lot."

"All right," Alex agreed, checking his watch again, thinking and shoving back the rising tide of impatience. He had to do this right or Sarah would be hurt. He had to keep his head. Even so, the next few minutes roiled in him like acid. "Give me a few minutes. I'll swing by the office and we'll go in your car so he doesn't suspect anything. Let's keep this real low-key, Connie, and everything will be all right."

"No police," she reiterated. "We can do this ourselves."

"Just you and me, Connie," he agreed. "Now, let's get going."

Randolph had been right. The sky was a robin-egg blue with fleecy clouds ringing the horizon like an old man's hair. Sarah tilted her head back and savored the music of the mountains below, cherishing the brief reprieve. Alex and Connie waited in Phoenix, and Thaddeus waited in Las Vegas, but for the moment she had freedom. She had sunlight and hot breezes.

Thaddeus. She still couldn't come to grips with it. Her mind skittered away from him, the truth too painful to approach. Sarah wanted so much for the culprit to be someone she didn't know, some faceless stranger who hadn't brought her meals and driven her home on rainy days. She wanted it to be someone she could have foreseen.

She wanted to at least feel resolution now that they had Thaddeus's name. But she didn't. She still felt churned up and uneasy and afraid. She wanted to get to Alex and make sure he was all right. She wanted to slip into his arms and reassure herself.

"You're a genius, Randolph," she murmured, hands clutching the wicker, head back to the sun.

"Nothing like a little aerial jaunt to escape the pressures," he offered alongside her. "Are you really thinking of moving to Denver?"

At that, Sarah opened her eyes to find his serious. "I don't know," she admitted. "What would you think about it?"

She expected concern from Randolph. What she got was a careful shrug and a glance out over the hills. "I'd like to think you wouldn't dump the lot of us for a set of big shoulders."

Sarah squinted at him, surprised. Unhappy. "You really think I'd do that?"

Again the shrug. "Love is blind, sweetie. I mean, look at Jill and Hector."

For a moment, only the creak of the basket could be heard. "What about Jill and Hector?"

Randolph shook his head. "I didn't think you knew. Jill wouldn't say where she was the other night, because she was with Hector. They've been . . . *with* each other a lot lately."

Still Sarah had trouble with his revelation. "Jill and Hector?"

Randolph nodded, eyebrows raised in evidence of his opinion. "Like I said. Love is blind."

Hector. Stringently, upwardly mobile Hector threatening his marriage with pudgy, uncertain Jill. And Jill attracted to the superficiality of Hector. Sarah couldn't believe it.

"How did you find out?"

Randolph just shrugged, and again his expression was curiously eloquent. "I seem to be a safe repository for female anguish."

Sarah looked away, out over the clean, crisp hills, to the future and the past. "I thought I knew all of you. I thought we could trust each other."

A hawk skirred the currents, sweet and sharp and free, and Sarah watched him. He soared straight up past the balloon, right into the sun. Sarah saw stripes of green and yellow and pink. She saw the pallid blue, the burning sun.

And suddenly she saw the shadow.

The shadow that wasn't there, that had fallen on her drawing and settled over her flight with Alex. The warning. The omen.

"No..."

Her hand came up, holding in fear that squeezed at her lungs and drowned out the breeze. Sarah heard the hawk screech and thought of someone falling. Someone dying.

The world tilted. A cracking echoed off into the hills and Alex's face betrayed surprise. His own hands came up, holding in his life, clutching to his chest, flying. Flying, falling, failing.

Falling. Hurt. Now.

Move, Sarah.

"Alex!"

She didn't even feel Randolph's hand on her arm at first. Her eyes were wide and staring, unable to look away from the scene her gauze had just lifted to reveal. The dust brown of the desert, the cactus spearing the sky like accusing fingers. The blood, so red, so livid against the wan colors. The gasp of Alex's pain.

"Sarah, what's wrong?"

Randolph was shaking her, gentle hands holding her up, cushioning her.

"Sarah!"

"Randolph, it's Alex," she gasped, turning, trying her best to focus. The terror had struck as sharp as glass, shattering her calm, freezing her, flaying her with haste. "We have to get to him now. Something's wrong."

"What do you mean?" he demanded. "He's at your house. Sarah, we can't get there from here."

"No," she insisted, shaking her head, grabbing hold of her friend. "He's coming to meet us. He's coming here, and we have to stop him."

"Who's going to hurt him, Sarah?"

"I don't know," she groaned, straining to see, unable to. Only feeling the blood drain from Alex even before it blossomed on him.

"Where?" Randolph asked.

Sarah pointed, certain even though they could see nothing beyond the hills. "Hurry, Randolph, please."

"All right," he agreed. "I'll try. Now, you settle down, Sarah. Take a sip of that water or something. We'll get there when we can."

"We have to hurry," she persisted, bending away, answering Randolph's suggestion. Water would be good. She felt so hot. So dry, so frightened.

Reaching for the jug of water, Sarah bumped into Randolph's shoulder bag, the one in which he kept his maps and glasses and calculator. It tipped, spilling a map and a book on ballooning. Holding the gallon jug in one hand, Sarah bent back down to right the bag.

"Don't worry about it," Randolph said, his attention on the flame above his head.

Sarah didn't hear him over the sudden, roaring burn. She tried to push the map in one-handed with no success. Dropping the jug, she reached back down.

Randolph's hand was there to stop her. "Don't," he objected.

Sarah straightened, the bag already in her hand. Randolph yanked it away, almost upending it again.

"I said don't," he said, setting the bag by his feet. "I'll take care of the maps."

But it was too late. "Randolph," Sarah said, looking up at him with sudden hesitance, "where did you get a gun?"

Chapter 15

It was all Alex could do to sit still. His chest felt like a barbecue pit. His stomach knotted and he was sweating. He wanted to move or pace or talk. On the surface, though, he maintained the calm that had soothed Connie's agitation after it had taken him almost a half hour to reach her.

He seemed to be carrying it off, because the farther out into the hills they drove, the quieter Connie grew. Connie had asked Alex to drive and then had sat in silence, her hands worrying over the purse she always carried and her attention ahead, as if it could somehow hasten their journey. She never once looked away from the road.

Alex saw, though, that her knuckles were white where they gripped the leather, and her jaw was working faster and faster, until it looked as if she were demolishing gum. Alex decided to keep the silence as long as she did.

Hurry. Hurry. Time's running out.

He heard it, as if Sarah's voice were singing in his own head. He felt the stampede of seconds, the drain of sand from the hourglass. He saw the thing she had feared loom in the distance like a gathering storm cloud.

Alex didn't know what it was, not like Sarah would have. He just felt it building in him, brick by heavy brick. He and Connie were driving to the point of resolution. Of truth. They were headed toward a confrontation that Sarah had already seen. Only Alex saw something else. He saw now that Sarah was in danger, too.

He didn't know how. This time he didn't question it. He just measured the acid that built, the weight that accumulated, and knew that he didn't have much time left to protect her.

Hurry.

"She's not going to understand at first," Connie suddenly said as if continuing a conversation. "Sarah's so trusting. She won't believe it's Randolph. She couldn't believe it was Thaddeus."

"It *wasn't* Thaddeus," Alex offered with a quick look over at her drawn features, wishing his voice didn't betray his tension.

Connie didn't even seem to hear him. "It'll take time, I know. It'll take some hard work, but she'll pull through okay. She always has."

Alex wrapped his hands more tightly around the steering wheel and glanced out over the empty sky. "Looks like we're still early."

"It has to work out all right," Connie insisted. "It just *has* to."

"She'll be fine, Connie," he assured the woman. Connie started a little, as if she'd almost forgotten he was there.

"I know she will be," she said with a tight smile. "I'll be there for her. Just like I always am."

They were about five miles shy of the landing point when Connie suddenly straightened. "Turn left up here."

Alex looked over at her and then at the unmarked turn that led back into the hills. "Where?" he asked. "We're not anywhere near the spot."

"I know a shortcut," she insisted, pointing now. "Turn there. We'll save time."

"We have plenty of time," Alex assured her. "You're asking me to turn five miles short and head north on a dirt road. I don't think it'll help."

"No," she argued, shaking her head. "We don't have time. Now, turn."

Alex really didn't expect it. Not like that anyway. He was turning to challenge her yet again, to make sure he got the directions right, when he felt a nudge at his waist. A cold nudge.

"I said turn," Connie ordered, and shoved the gun harder against him.

"Hurry, Randolph, please!"

The air was getting cooler. Far below, the hills were corrugated cardboard. Randolph turned from his propane gauge. "If I go any higher, I'll run out of fuel, Sarah."

"No, you won't," she insisted, leaning over the side to get a better look. "We're so close I can feel it. But in another few minutes we'll be too late. You said the winds will carry us faster if we're up higher."

Randolph looked down, checked his gauges and opened up the burner. The roar spilled into the basket like the belch of a dyspeptic dragon, and the balloon soared higher into the clear sky. The earth shrank away, and the distant hawks circled in silence. But Sarah saw more. She saw the glint of a vehicle and knew it. She felt the anger even this high, heating in her chest and forcing tears to her eyes. She knew the terror of frustration, when time compressed too quickly and the way was too long, when the future rushed up to meet the present and she drifted, unable to do anything to stop it.

"Connie, no," she moaned, tortured. "Don't do it."

"Pick that gun back up," Randolph commanded. "I carried it for protection, and you're going to be protected."

"She won't hurt me," Sarah protested in a strangled whisper, her eyes focused far below.

"You don't know that," Randolph retorted hotly. "She's gone too far, Sarah. None of us know what she's capable of."

But Sarah couldn't listen to that. Her best friend. Her family. Her mentor. The ground crawled by and Sarah could do no more than worry at the picture of Alex in her mind. Alex hurt, dying. Alex shot by her best friend, and Sarah impotent to stop it. She knew somehow, even without seeing what was happening, that only surprise would save Alex. Only silence until the very last moment.

"Come on, Randolph," she pleaded. "Work some magic with this thing."

Connie knew how to hold a gun. Now she had it trained on Alex with both hands, eyes as steady as her hold. Alex thought she was sweating. *He* sure as hell was.

They were standing alongside the bend on the side road, where the tan sedan had come to a rest. The hills rose close north and south, blocking them from view from the main road.

"Sarah will never forgive you if you shoot me," he said, putting his hands carefully raised, as he stepped away from the car. Praying for time.

"Sarah will never forgive *Randolph*," Connie corrected, lifting the gun enough to let him know that she wasn't going to let him get away with anything. "When Sarah goes to look for you, Randolph will come with me. And, later, the police will find you both. Randolph couldn't take the duplicity. Couldn't live with himself after what he'd done to you. It'll seem like he killed himself, too. And old Connie will be left to clean up the mess, just like always."

"Is that what you want?" Alex asked, checking for any kind of cover. The ground was sere, the chaparral scarce. A few saguaro cacti pointed skyward, but they didn't offer much to stop a bullet. He'd have as much luck rolling under the car.

"That's the way it has to be," she assured him, a curious fire now in her eyes. "I like Randolph, but we can do without him. And you, you've tried to ruin everything I've built.... Sarah will depend on me even more now, because I'll be there when you're gone ... she's always depended on me."

"How did you do it?" Stall. Keep her talking. Let her ramble on about whatever she wanted. All Alex needed was a little time, and a lot of luck.

How the hell did he keep getting into situations like this? Accountants weren't supposed to end up facing a gun, and here he was on his second visit.

"Do what?" Connie demanded, stepping closer, her elegantly cut slacks and blouse strangely at odds with her purpose.

"Set up the phony company. Did you have Peter help you?"

"Him?" She didn't seem amused, even though she laughed. "He had no idea what was going on. The security at Landyne is a laugh. I was into their computers after our third date. I was pulling off their programs in another week. The master manuals came right from the storeroom."

"Why?"

"What?" She *was* sweating. She lifted a hand away to wipe at it, evidently not as nonchalant about killing face-to-face as computer theft.

Alex made a shrugging motion, his shoulders beginning to shriek in protest, his gut churning, his patience lost. *Come on. I'm running out of time here.*

"Why did you do it? The money?"

"For Sarah," she said. "She wanted the new animation program. And you know Sarah, she just doesn't think of things like cost and budgets. She's like a little girl with her nose pressed up to the toy shop window. So, I got her her toy."

"And found out how easy the rest was."

Now Connie was amused. "Thaddeus really ended up thinking it *was* his idea. We could have ended up saving thousands if you hadn't butted in . . . if you hadn't *changed* everything!"

The gun was beginning to waver. The venom was spilling over, eerily lighting her eyes and tightening her face into a mask. It was all Alex could do to hold still. To wait.

"If it hadn't been me, it would have been somebody else," he countered quietly. "Somebody would have uncovered the fraud."

"But they wouldn't have made Sarah fall in love," she hissed, leaning forward with her outrage. "Sarah had us before. She had her *friends*. She didn't need you to come along and make her . . . make her *dissatisfied*! She didn't need anybody but us until you *seduced* her. Randolph was right."

Alex was trying to keep eye contact, to soothe. Connie was building up a head of steam, the kind that could demolish the interior of a house. The kind that could pull a trigger.

Come on.

Then he saw it. Sinking straight out of the sky like a brightly painted stone. Silent, streaking at them like a bulbous arrow right between the row of hills.

"No," he whispered involuntarily. Not yet. Not now.

Connie didn't see. She didn't hear. Alex couldn't believe it, but she didn't know that a hot-air balloon was just over her shoulder.

"Now, Denver," she was ranting, the gun dipping in rhythm to her vitriol. "Just what were we supposed to do when she went traipsing off after you? What would have become of *me*? After all I've given to her?''

Alex tried to ignore the balloon. He could feel its approach in his chest, piling up with the bricks, stifling his breathing, tripping up his heart.

''Are you listening?'' Connie shrilled. ''Answer me, damn it! What was I going to do when Sarah quit to have your babies and join the damn Junior League? What were all of us going to do?''

She lifted, sighted, wiped away the sweat.

''Connie, don't!''

Sarah's voice shattered the moment. From one second to the next, the entire fabric of tension was torn. Control burst like an overblown balloon.

Connie's cry of rage was guttural, hoarse, primal. She faced Alex, knowing Sarah's voice and realizing what it meant. Shattering, crumbling, spinning over the edge of control. The balloon was ten feet from the ground, shooting at a point to Alex's left. Sarah was already trying to climb out.

Alex saw her and involuntarily moved toward her. He fully expected Connie to come after him. She didn't. Pulling the gun with her, she whirled toward the balloon.

''No!'' she screeched. ''No, you can't!''

She pointed the gun at Sarah.

Alex didn't think. He didn't have the time to even warn Sarah or notice the sudden throb of lights over the dusty landscape. The minute he saw the gun start to move, he threw himself at Connie. He was midair, stretched out as if he were reaching for a long pass, when the gun went off. The impact spun him around. His hands reached for the thud that had taken his breath away. His legs buckled and he fell.

''Alex!''

Sarah tumbled out of the basket, even though it was still five feet in the air, and she hit the ground running. Alex had crumpled into a ball on the ground, blood staining the dirt. Sarah screamed his name and screamed it again. She didn't see the loose gun or Connie scrambling to pick it up. She didn't see the police cars pulling off the main road beyond the hills. She just saw Alex, bleeding, his life soaking into the arid land.

"No, Sarah, please," Connie begged, crawling toward the gun, scrabbling in the dirt to get beneath Alex where the weapon lay. "Leave him alone. Leave him alone."

Sarah couldn't see for the tears. "Alex," she sobbed, reaching shaking hands out to him. "Oh, God, Alex."

She pulled at him. He rolled free of the dirt, his eyes squeezed shut, his breathing a rhythmic grunt.

The gun glinted in the afternoon sun. Connie reached for it. "Let him go," she demanded, lifting it. "Let him go, now. He's wrong..."

Sarah didn't even hear her. She just saw the sudden pallor on Alex's skin, saw the blood that stained his shirt. "Please be all right, Alex," she pleaded, trying to gain the composure to help him, afraid of what she'd find. He wasn't answering her and his breathing didn't seem any easier. She didn't know whether he was dying or not. "Oh, God, please, Alex."

"Sarah, *listen* to me," Connie sobbed, pushing at her.

Sarah looked up, seeing something that she didn't recognize, a poison that had been so deep in her friend that it had been unnoticed. She sobbed, lost, frightened, angry. "Get away from me," she demanded in a voice that echoed from the hills.

Connie flinched. "It's *his* fault," she insisted, turning the gun on Alex.

Sarah didn't think. She jumped to her feet, wanting to be between the gun and Alex, fighting something she didn't understand. "You hurt me," she accused, deathly cold and flushed. Raging when she never had before. "You hurt people I love. How could you?" Stepping forward, one step at a time, one step away from where Alex lay helpless behind her.

"For you," Connie objected, the gun still pointed squarely at Sarah's chest, bobbing with Connie's anxiety, unstable as she. "Don't you understand? You never deal with the real world. How the hell can you understand what I have to do to protect you? What I've *always* done?"

"Connie, how could you?" Sarah demanded, the only thing she seemed able to say.

Connie lifted the gun even higher. "You don't know. You still don't know." She gripped it with her other hand, lined it up to Sarah's face.

Sarah froze.

She heard the roar behind her. Connie flinched, faltered. Sarah thought to charge. She never got the chance. Crouched and howling with fury, Alex barreled into Connie like a defensive tackle.

The gun skittered away into the rocks. Connie flew back and landed in a crumpled heap. Alex faltered to a halt, doubled over and gasping.

"Son of a—" wrapping his arms around his chest, he dragged in a breath "—bitch. I think my ribs are broken." With that, his strength gave out and he ended up on his knees.

Sarah knelt by him, trying her best to pull everything together. "Alex? You're not dead?"

Still facing the dirt, Alex managed a grin. "No, Sarah. I'm not. But the Phoenix police are going to be mad about their equipment."

Sarah couldn't stop the tears. They spilled over, stained the dirt alongside the blood that still oozed from between Alex's fingers. She tried to stop her hands shaking long enough to check Alex's wound. She tried her best to be controlled and helpful. All she could end up doing was shiver and sniffle.

"What equipment? What happened? Oh, Alex, are you all right?"

"You sure do know how to put on a show, boy. You think next time you could give the police better directions so we can save you in time?"

Sarah looked up, stunned, to see Ellis towering over them. Alex was still rocking back and forth, his arms around his chest. Behind them, Randolph was battling the balloon into submission with the help of a couple of police. Several more had arrived to retrieve Connie and the gun.

"I'll . . . remember that," Alex answered his friend.

"I bet you even ruined that fancy tape recorder they taped to all your chest hair, huh?"

In explanation, Alex pulled up his shirt. There, taped to his sternum, was a small square plastic-and-metal box: a small, square, badly dented box. Slashing along from it toward Alex's right side, a long, deep gash bled steadily.

"Impressive." Ellis admired it, then bent to help Alex up.

Sarah couldn't move. "You knew?" she asked, her voice very small, the tears dissolving into little sobs.

Ellis flashed her a smile. "He ain't my accountant 'cause I like his suits, little girl."

Sarah was watching Alex though, where he stood with Ellis's help. "You knew?"

Alex shook his head for her. Then, holding out a hand, he smiled. "I had this . . . feeling," he admitted.

Sarah's eyes widened. She climbed to her feet without using Alex's hand and faced him again. "You did, huh?"

He settled one arm around his chest and took her hand with the other. "Sgt. Valdez doesn't believe in funny little feelings, did you know that?"

Stunned, quiet, Sarah nodded. "I know."

Alex nodded back, squeezed her hand. "It's sure a good thing I do."

Sarah couldn't take her eyes from him. "You do?"

Alex's eyes warmed, brightened, opened like a sunburst. Sarah felt their kick all the way to her toes, filling her, lifting her, settling her, surrounding her when she needed it. "I do. I thought you and I could talk about sharing some ... feelings."

"Right after you explain everything to the man," Ellis objected with a suspicious smile.

"He has to go to the hospital," Sgt. Valdez said in his best authoritarian manner as he strode forward.

Alex never looked away from Sarah. "Meet me there later?" he asked. "I think we have some negotiations to settle."

Sarah smiled, feeling the burden begin to lift for the first time. Filling herself with the relief in his eyes and his heart. Sustaining herself on the love that emanated from him like heat from the sun.

"As soon as I get Connie settled," she answered.

"Are you kiddin'?" Ellis demanded instinctively.

"She's her friend," Alex reminded him. "Sarah has to make sure she's all right."

Sarah smiled for Alex in silence. *I love you*.

He smiled back. *I love you*.

Sarah knew then that both her premonitions had come true. There was a lot she had to deal with. Connie's actions lay like ashes on her tongue, weighed like grief in her. She would have to understand that and get by it. But she had Alex to help her. Alex to help share the burden. And Alex to share the future with, as well.

As premonitions went, she figured she'd still come out ahead.

Alex was right. Sarah had to admit that she loved the Rockies. Where Phoenix was spare and almost stark, the mountains outside Denver were green and deep and rich. Fragile wildflowers nodded in the field, and blue spruce shadowed the hill behind the Mitchell house. A stream chattered in the shadows at the back of the property, and bare gray rock shouldered into the sky.

It was Labor Day, and the Mitchells were having a barbecue.

"You really got him to admit it?" Lindsay Mitchell was asking.

Her attention equally divided between the baby in her lap and the sight of Alex lounging in a nearby chair talking football with his brother-in-law, Sarah smiled. So this was a family. This was how Alex had been raised, how he celebrated his life and marked his seasons. She had to admit she liked it. She liked it a lot.

"The psychic ability's been there all along, from what he's said," she told Lindsay. "Alex just didn't understand it. All I did was give it a name."

Lindsay's chuckle was delighted and mischievous. "I bet he bucked like a mule at the idea."

Sarah couldn't help an answering chuckle of her own. "He considers it the ultimate insult to suggest that a CPA is psychic. I've been instructed not to 'bandy about' the information."

Lindsay's laughter was full throated and delighted.

"That sounds like trouble," Jason announced from where he was sharing Alex's beer.

Alex snorted. "They're talking hippie stuff. Ignore 'em."

Sarah kept her smile. Her gaze was on Alex's namesake, a bright-eyed little thing with a ferocious grip and a lusty set of lungs. The owner, so far, of a train set, football, baseball, glove and Snarkalump, all compliments of his godfather.

Sarah remembered the babies back on the commune—chubby, placid things passed from hand to hand and slung on hips when work was done. She never remembered experiencing such delight when one fixed its astonished smile on her.

"Sarah," Alex warned without turning from his conversation. "You're getting a little too interested."

Sarah looked up. "Have you ever thought about it?"

She didn't notice Jason and Lindsay follow the half conversation with no little interest.

"Not till we decide where we're going to live, I won't."

Sarah smiled, satisfied. It was easy access to Alex's pride, his melting adoration of his nephew and namesake, his surprise at his new paternal feelings. It wouldn't be long before the need for his own child met hers.

"You still haven't decided?" Lindsay asked, her expression betraying perfect understanding of what Sarah and Alex had alluded to.

Her finger caught firmly in little Alex's grip, Sarah shook her head. "The company's voting on it this week. They liked the Denver proposal, but they are all pretty settled in Phoenix."

"Have you replaced Connie yet?"

Sarah nodded, still unable to talk about her friend without the pain. "We voted on that last week," she admitted, trying her best to smile. "Randolph has taken over the duties. He's a natural, you know. Besides, he knows more about what's going on in the company than even Connie did. And Ellis is staying in town for a while to clear things up."

Sarah felt Lindsay's hand on her arm and understood the other woman's empathy. She heard the question before it was asked.

"Connie's . . . uh, still not doing very well. We asked that she be able to stay near us in Phoenix so we could all be there for her. Especially since her parents don't care . . . still, they said yes."

Sarah never heard Alex approach. The baby fluttered in her lap, his arms waving and his mouth working up to a wail of impatience. The firs sang with a breeze, and birds chattered. Sarah's sight was inside though. Deep in where the hurt and betrayal and guilt still lived.

"Whose fault is it?" Alex asked gently to remind her, his hand on her shoulder, his strength surrounding her.

"No one's," she answered as she always did, not quite believing it yet, but hoping she would soon. Lifting a hand, she placed it over Alex's, holding him to her, securing herself with him.

"So, tell me," Lindsay spoke as she stood to scoop up her son before he got a chance to make good his threat, "if the company votes to stay in Phoenix, what happens to you two?"

Sarah looked at Alex, waiting for the little frown to appear. It did, right between his brows, betraying the lengthy negotiations that had taken place on that very subject.

"We're considering several options," he admitted. "The only thing we've agreed on so far is the marriage part."

Lindsay grinned. "Have you guessed Sarah's surprise yet?"

Now Alex was really scowling. Plopping down into the chair Lindsay had just vacated, he actually harrumphed. "You mean about the wedding plans? No. It probably involves standing buck naked in a stream somewhere and chanting mantras or something."

Sarah laughed, the joy bubbling up as it always did near Alex. She squeezed his hand and held on tight. "There are better things to do naked in a stream," she assured him. "I was thinking more along the lines of a visit to Portland."

Alex frowned again, puzzled. "Portland? Why?"

Sarah shrugged, savoring her little surprise, anticipating his reaction. "I thought we'd be married in the same church as your parents. We could have all your family there."

Alex's eyes widened. He went very still. "And all the Sunset people," he answered, a smile breaking over him like sunrise. "You're sure?"

Sarah nodded, losing Lindsay and the baby and the rustle of the early evening meadow for the golden sun in Alex's eyes. "I'm beginning to like this tradition stuff. Do you mind? I see us getting matched rocking chairs and a front porch."

"And Thanksgivings at the house...wherever that's going to be."

"And a boy for you and a girl for me."

He smiled for her, a private smile that betrayed all that was kept between them, and it filled Sarah like sweet dawn.

"You still see that, do you?"

Sarah tilted her head. "Sure. Didn't I tell you? And a white picket fence."

"Do you also see what I'm thinking right now?" he asked, his eyes suddenly languorous and intimate. Neither of them saw Lindsay ease away. Neither heard Jason join her or the screen door close.

Sarah's eyes were only on Alex's. "Something to do with that stream, I think."

"Wrong," he disagreed, his fingers testing the sudden throb at her wrist. "The other part."

She saw the hunger rise in him, sparking in the honeyed depths of his eyes. She felt the energy leap from his fingers.

"The mantra?" she asked anyway, loving to tease him.

He didn't even smile. "You only get one more guess."

Sarah wanted to squirm with the sudden heat. "Oh," she whispered with a slow nod. "I see. Is this going to happen soon?"

Alex's smile was enough to make Sarah sigh. "Almost immediately, I'd think."

Just as he said it, Sarah saw it. Late sun dappling them in light, a breeze whispering across flushed skin. Murmurs and sighs that danced amid the rustle of leaves. And something more. Something that made her smile.

"You know," Alex amended, his voice husky. "It is hot out. Maybe that stream wouldn't be such a bad idea after all."

Some premonitions ended up being more fun than others. As Sarah let Alex pull her to her feet, she had the feeling that this would be one of the best.

* * * * *

Double your reading pleasure this fall with two Award of Excellence titles written by two of your favorite authors.

Available in September

DUNCAN'S BRIDE
by Linda Howard
Silhouette Intimate Moments #349

Mail-order bride Madelyn Patterson was nothing like what Reese Duncan expected—and everything he needed.

Available in October

THE COWBOY'S LADY
by Debbie Macomber
Silhouette Special Edition #626

The Montana cowboy wanted a little lady at his beck and call—the "lady" in question saw things differently....

These titles have been selected to receive a special laurel—the Award of Excellence. Look for the distinctive emblem on the cover. It lets you know there's something truly wonderful inside!

Take 4 bestselling love stories FREE

Plus get a FREE surprise gift!

PASSPORT TO ROMANCE
SWEEPSTAKES RULES

1. **HOW TO ENTER:** To enter, you must be the age of majority and complete the official entry form, or print your name, address, telephone number and age on a plain piece of paper and mail to: Passport to Romance, P.O. Box 9056, Buffalo, NY 14269-9056. No mechanically reproduced entries accepted.

2. All entries must be received by the CONTEST CLOSING DATE, DECEMBER 31, 1990 TO BE ELIGIBLE.

3. **THE PRIZES:** There will be ten (10) Grand Prizes awarded, each consisting of a choice of a trip for two people from the following list:
   i)   London, England (approximate retail value $5,050 U.S.)
   ii) England, Wales and Scotland (approximate retail value $6,400 U.S.)
   iii) Carribean Cruise (approximate retail value $7,300 U.S.)
   iv) Hawaii (approximate retail value $9,550 U.S.)
   v)   Greek Island Cruise in the Mediterranean (approximate retail value $12,250 U.S.)
   vi) France (approximate retail value $7,300 U.S.)

4. Any winner may choose to receive any trip or a cash alternative prize of $5,000.00 U.S. in lieu of the trip.

5. **GENERAL RULES:** Odds of winning depend on number of entries received.

6. A random draw will be made by Nielsen Promotion Services, an independent judging organization, on January 29, 1991, in Buffalo, NY, at 11:30 a.m. from all eligible entries received on or before the Contest Closing Date.

7. Any Canadian entrants who are selected must correctly answer a time-limited, mathematical skill-testing question in order to win.

8. Full contest rules may be obtained by sending a stamped, self-addressed envelope to: "Passport to Romance Rules Request", P.O. Box 9998, Saint John, New Brunswick, Canada E2L 4N4.

9. Quebec residents may submit any litigation respecting the conduct and awarding of a prize in this contest to the Régie des loteries et courses du Québec.

10. Payment of taxes other than air and hotel taxes is the sole responsibility of the winner.

11. Void where prohibited by law.

COUPON BOOKLET OFFER TERMS

To receive your Free travel-savings coupon booklets, complete the mail-in Offer Certificate on the preceeding page, including the necessary number of proofs-of-purchase, and mail to: Passport to Romance, P.O. Box 9057, Buffalo, NY 14269-9057 The coupon booklets include savings on travel-related products such as car rentals, hotels, cruises, flowers and restaurants. Some restrictions apply. The offer is available in the United States and Canada. Requests must be postmarked by January 25, 1991. Only proofs-of-purchase from specially marked "Passport to Romance" Harlequin® or Silhouette® books will be accepted. The offer certificate must accompany your request and may not be reproduced in any manner. Offer void where prohibited or restricted by law. LIMIT FOUR COUPON BOOKLETS PER NAME, FAMILY, GROUP, ORGANIZATION OR ADDRESS. Please allow up to 8 weeks after receipt of order for shipment. Enter quickly as quantities are limited. Unfulfilled mail-in offer requests will receive free Harlequin® or Silhouette® books (not previously available in retail stores), in quantities equal to the number of proofs-of-purchase required for Levels One to Four, as applicable.

OFFICIAL SWEEPSTAKES
ENTRY FORM

Complete and return this Entry Form immediately—the more Entry Forms you submit, the better
your chances of winning!
- Entry Forms must be received by **December 31, 1990**
- A random draw will take place on **January 29, 1991**
- Trip must be taken by **December 31, 1991**

3-SIM-1-SW

YES, I want to win a PASSPORT TO ROMANCE vacation for two! I understand the prize includes
round-trip air fare, accommodation and a daily spending allowance.

Name_____

Address_____

City_____ State_____ Zip_____

Telephone Number_____ Age_____

Return entries to: **PASSPORT TO ROMANCE**, P.O. Box 9056, Buffalo, NY 14269-9056

© 1990 Harlequin Enterprises Limited

COUPON BOOKLET/OFFER CERTIFICATE

Item	LEVEL ONE Booklet 1	LEVEL TWO Booklet 1 & 2	LEVEL THREE Booklet 1, 2 & 3	LEVEL FOUR Booklet 1, 2, 3 & 4
Booklet 1 = $100+	$100+	$100+	$100+	$100+
Booklet 2 = $200+		$200+	$200+	$200+
Booklet 3 = $300+			$300+	$300+
Booklet 4 = $400+				$400+
Approximate Total Value of Savings	$100+	$300+	$600+	$1,000+
# of Proofs of Purchase Required	4	6	12	18
Check One	___	___	___	___

Name_____

Address_____

City_____ State_____ Zip_____

Return Offer Certificates to: **PASSPORT TO ROMANCE**, P.O. Box 9057, Buffalo, NY 14269-9057

Requests must be postmarked by **January 25, 1991**

- ✂ - - -

ONE PROOF OF PURCHASE

3-SIM-1

To collect your free coupon booklet you must include the necessary number of proofs-of-purchase
with a properly completed Offer Certificate

© 1990 Harlequin Enterprises Limited

See previous page for details